Contents

**This book is to be returned on or before
the last date stamped below.**

RENEWALS   *Please quote:* date of return, your ticket number
and computer label number for each item.

Capricorn and Cancer

Also by Geoffrey Household

Novels
ROGUE MALE
WATCHER IN THE SHADOWS
ARABESQUE
THE THIRD HOUR
FELLOW PASSENGER
THE HIGH PLACE
A ROUGH SHOOT
A TIME TO KILL
THING TO LOVE
OLURA
THE COURTESY OF DEATH
DANCE OF THE DWARFS
DOOM'S CARAVAN
THE THREE SENTINELS
THE LIVES AND TIMES OF BERNARDO BROWN
RED ANGER
HOSTAGE: LONDON
THE LAST TWO WEEKS OF GEORGES RIVAC
THE SENDING

Autobiography
AGAINST THE WIND

Short stories
THE SALVATION OF PISCO GABAR
TALES OF ADVENTURES
THE BRIDES OF SOLOMON
SABRES ON THE SAND

NOVELLA
THE CATS TO COME

For Children
THE SPANISH CAVE
XENOPHON'S ADVENTURE
PRISONER OF THE INDIES
ESCAPE INTO DAYLIGHT

Capricorn and Cancer

Geoffrey Household

Michael Joseph • London

First published in Great Britain by Michael Joseph Ltd
44 Bedford Square, London WC1

© This collection by Geoffrey Household 1981

ISBN 0 7181 2003 5

Printed and bound in Great Britain by
Redwood Burn Ltd., Trowbridge and Esher.

Capricorn

1

The Salvation of Pisco Gabar

THE *Santa Juana* glided towards the Equator with the overpowering coast of Peru five miles to starboard. The setting sun rested neatly on the tangent of the horizon as if an almighty sextant were about to shoot it. To the east the vast yellow foothills of the Andes turned green and purple where the level rays dug into scattered deposits of copper and gold. From his deck-chair on the after verandah Manuel Gabar watched the metallic immensities of the coast. His pleasure was calm and reflective, for he was used to having beauty spread for him on enormous canvasses.

His origin was unknown and of no great interest to himself or to his friends. His passport declared him Ecuadorian; but that he knew was untrue, since he himself had bought the document from a friendly official in Guayaquil. His native language was Spanish. His name was one of his earliest recollections, and he was sure it was his; but it gave no definite clue to his ancestry. Nor did his appearance. He was a shortish, powerful man with slightly bandy legs and a snub nose. High cheek-bones and wide mouth were evidence of some Indian blood on the mother's side. Grey eyes, thick dark hair on head, hands and chest suggested a Central European immigrant as father. A charity school had picked him off the streets of Buénos Aires, taught him to read and given him to the sea. The sea taught him self-reliance and socialism and cast him up again in South America. Since then he had been a good citizen of the five Andean republics, courteous to all men, breaking only such laws as were meant to be broken, and employing his rough energy and his capital (when he had

any) in developing odds and ends of trade that nobody else
had thought of.

Gabar had an enquiring mind and was well able to
divert himself by elementary speculations on man, his surroundings and the reasons for both. At the moment it was
geology that interested him. He wondered whether the
Andes were still pushing westwards into the Pacific. They
gave so definite an impression of an advancing wave
topped by all the mineral debris of a continent. He also
wondered if schools of mining could teach one to spot an
exploitable quantity of precious metal by its appearance
under the horizontal rays of the setting sun. He had an
exaggerated respect for secular schools of all sorts, never
realising that they could but analyse and express the
accumulated experience of such adventurers in life as
himself.

His reverie was broken by a pleasant but too determined
voice.

'If the señor permits, I will join him for a moment.'

Gabar looked round. The setting sun was blotted out by
a tall pyramid of black cassock. Dismayed by the silence of
the priest's approach and the blackness of him at close
quarters, he followed the pyramid to its apex and met the
commanding eyes of Don Jesús.

Manuel Gabar welcomed companionship; he was
entirely without prejudice against human beings of any
colour or class, of any degree of virtue or criminality. But
he could not abide priests. To him they were enemies of the
intellect, money-grubbers, hypocrites, and buffoons in the
fancy dress of piety. Being naturally courteous, he was even
more resentful of the intrusion than a ruder man would
have been. But he said nothing. There was nothing to say.
It was obvious that Don Jesús intended to sit down with or
without his permission. He was a magnificent blue-jowled
Basque in the flower of middle age. He joined in the deck
games and would certainly become a bishop.

'The señor will pardon my interruption,' said Don Jesús, 'but am I right in supposing that he lands tomorrow morning at Mollendo?'

'You are.'

'I have a great favour to ask you, if you would be so kind.'

'At your complete service,' replied Gabar with conventional politeness, adding, with detestation of himself and the title, 'reverend padre'.

After all, he argued, what did it matter? One said friend to cut-throats, chief to naked savages, *caballero* to gringo oil-drillers — why not reverend to a priest?

'My friend, Don José-Maria, also lands at Mollendo,' the priest said. 'He is an old man and before this journey he had never left the plateau. Might I ask you to see him through customs and as far as Arequipa by the train?'

'Yes, but —'

'You yourself, I suppose, are going to Arequipa?'

'I am,' said Gabar.

He would have dearly loved to say he was not. But all the trains from Mollendo passed through Arequipa. It was also certain that he and this José-Maria would leave Mollendo together by the first train after the arrival of the *Santa Juana*. Nobody ever left Mollendo by any but the first train.

'In that case you and he will be travelling companions. I commend him to your courtesy.'

'Very well,' said Gabar. 'Very well. I shall be delighted. But I am not a wet-nurse, you understand. I won't take any responsibility for him. You had better know that I am not fond of the Church.'

'You will like Don José-Maria. He is only a child. So pious, so simple, an angel among Indians! He understands them very well — too well, perhaps. But there! He is left to himself and we cannot blame him if he takes his own line.'

'I blame nobody,' said Gabar. 'We are animals. Will you have a pisco?'

For the first time in his life he had invited a priest to have a drink. It was not because he liked Don Jesús. He detested him. But it was Gabar's fixed habit to drink while talking. His friends had nicknamed him Pisco Gabar — not that he drank more than was reasonable, but he considered the delectable Peruvian grape spirit a necessary prelude to conversation. Even in the Montaña, the network of valleys that ran down from the Andes to become the Amazon, where he travelled with only such essentials as could be carried on his back, he was never without a tepid half-litre of pisco to celebrate the improbable meeting of another white man.

Don Jesús was flattered when laymen invited him to have a drink. He seldom refused, but never took more than one. Gabar ordered two pisco-sours. They drank them while Don Jesús talked with worldly and accomplished ease. Gabar answered him chiefly with scowls. He was slightly, and inconsistently, shocked by the priest. At last he made an effort at politeness.

'Have you come from Europe, reverend padre?'

'No, no, my dear sir! From Buenos Aires, from the Eucharistic Congress. A stupendous spectacle! A hundred thousand of the faithful of all nations attending open-air mass! A supreme affirmation of the faith of America!'

'The opium of the people,' grumbled Pisco Gabar.

'Pardon?'

'I said religion was the opium of the people,' repeated Gabar with a determined piety as of a martyr before his judge.

'I have heard,' said Don Jesús unruffled, 'that opium is very comforting. Are you a communist, señor?'

'I think for myself and I do not believe all I am told. I am a human being, a worker!'

Pisco Gabar was eager for battle, and rapidly assembling his anti-religious munitions, which included Marx, Payne, Ingersoll, some Mexican manifestos and the invincible materialism of his own spirit. Don Jesús had no difficulty in perceiving his intention, and avoided engagement. He would willingly have tackled a heretic, but with an atheist there was no common ground for discussion.

'A worker?' asked Don Jesús. 'A miner, I believe?'

'I am against the whole rotten system,' began Gabar excitedly. 'Now take the Mexican Church, for example—'

'Gold!' Don Jesús interrupted dreamily. 'Gold! A fascinating subject! You should ask Don José-Maria about gold. Of course his parish is a little difficult to reach.'

'Where gold is, it is always difficult to reach,' said Gabar. 'But it can be done.'

'The spirit of the *conquistadores*! You should have been born four hundred years ago!'

'In my way I follow their tradition,' said Gabar, flattered. 'In my way!'

It was true. For several years Pisco Gabar had been engaged in a trade of his own invention as profitable and uncomfortable as any in Latin America. The streams of the Montaña were full of alluvial gold. They paid to wash but did not pay to work intensively, the cost of transporting machinery being prohibitive. Some of the valleys were earthly paradises, but only a mule could reach them. Others were drenched in summer by the steady purposeful rains of the Amazon, and in winter by the steady purposeful rains of the Pacific. Even the English went mad after 365 continual days and nights of rain. The Indians worked intermittently at panning the inaccessible streams, but the gold dust had small value to them. A day spent in hunting or cultivation was more productive. Sometimes a trusted fellow-tribesman would set off with the communal bag of gold to Cuzco or the nearest mine, and return, if he were neither robbed nor tempted to drink, with such goods as he could carry on his back. It was hardly worth while carrying the gold to a market.

Pisco Gabar hit on the idea of carrying a market to the

gold. He established small depots of cotton and leather goods, nails, tools, beads and whatever was light to carry and considered by primitive minds to be either useful or decorative. At these depots he loaded his back and that of a mule and vanished into the tumbled forests. Weeks later he appeared at the edge of civilisation alone and on foot, having given his goods, his animal, and sometimes his coat and shirt in exchange for the ounces of gold dust at his belt. The profit, Gabar explained to Don Jesús, was considerable, but so was the benefit to the Indians. He was, he admitted, a parasite, although a useful one. He compared his function in the Montaña to that of a waste-paper merchant (a profession he had also followed) in a town. He called as regularly as he could, took away an unwanted commodity and gave unexpected value in return.

At seven the following morning the *Santa Juana* lay two miles off Mollendo. A string of barges, loaded with copper and alpaca, undulated towards her over the long Pacific swell. The tender heaved up and down alongside, her gunwale at one moment below the foot of the gangway and, at the next, ten steps up. The brown boatmen fended her off skilfully while with lazy patience they watched Don José-Maria saying his farewells. Gabar, already seated in the tender, began to look at his watch. He was not in a hurry, nor indeed did he ever allow hurry to afflict him, but he objected to being kept waiting by a priest.

José-Maria insisted on saying good-bye to all the passengers who were up, and was only with difficulty restrained from waiting to say good-bye to those who were still in their bunks. He was seven-eighths pure Indian, yellow and fat and given to simple ecstasies. Since Buenos Aires he had lived in a pious daze. The Congress and the journeying by rail and water had opened the gates of the world to him. He who had never been off the highlands of Peru in his life had dwelt in a modern city, had heard the Holy Father speak over the radio, had realised the true meaning of distance and seas and lands beyond them, had found to his amazement that there were actually Christians who spoke neither Spanish nor Quechua; it was difficult to understand how they could say their prayers. He believed that death would be something like his voyage to Buenos Aires; a stupendous experience shattering all preconceived ideas and startling him with the truth of angels, as had the truth of automobiles.

In his sadness at the end of this adventure he lost count and bade farewell to captain, officers and passengers over and over again. This done, he lingered at the gangway making a third interminable speech of thanks to Don Jesús. Gabar cut it short by pressing the button of the tender's siren. The sudden and commanding growl brought Don José-Maria hastily down the gangway.

The boatman, settling his straw hat firmly on his head, extended his hand and told the priest to jump. José-Maria bent his knees, prepared, but hesitated. The boat sank far below him. He regarded the rise and fall of the swell in benevolent surprise. With his almond eyes and yellow beaming countenance he resembled a rotund Chinese statuette. The boat rose again and he grasped the outstretched wrist, but still he did not jump. Nor did he let go. The tender sank from under the boatman, who squirmed and kicked in mid-air like a hooked fish. Don José-Maria, having hung on at first from terror and now hanging on lest the boatman should drop, tried to get both hands to the job and overbalanced.

Gabar hurled himself forward to break their fall. José-Maria landed safely, cushioned on him and the unfortunate boatman. While they extricated themselves indignantly, he remained in an unwieldy black ball, his eyes shut and his lips moving in prayer. As no one was hurt, the tender chugged off towards Mollendo.

'I have more luck than I merit,' murmured José-Maria. 'I am always in peril by land and sea, yet mercifully delivered.'

'You try your pet saint too far,' said Gabar coldly.

'Impossible—especially when he works through such kindly instruments as yourself, Don Manuel. I am very grateful to you.'

'No reason to be! I'd have done the same for anyone,' Gabar answered ungraciously. 'Are you all right?'

'Yes, yes, Don Manuel! A little bruised, a little shaken, but I only need a glass of spirits.'

'I can offer you some pisco.'

'Thank you. Thank you. You are very kind.'

Gabar drew out a half-litre of pisco, conveniently placed among his pyjamas at the top of his bag, and offered it to José-Maria. The priest put it to his lips and drank three-quarters of the contents.

'Thank you. You are very kind,' he repeated. 'I was in great need. Don Jesús did not wish me to drink on board. He is a stern man. Very stern.'

'He certainly gets his own way,' said Gabar resentfully.

'So clear! So knowledgeable in this world! He told me there were four things I was not to do. Let me see! Four things! I was not to drink—that was one. And second—he said I was not to let you leave me till we got to Arequipa.'

'The hell he did!'

'And there were two more. I was not to forget—let me see! My glasses? No, I have them. My trunk? No, it was not that. It contains all I possess, Don Manuel, for I thought I might be years on the road. And then there is a present in it for one much greater than I. No, I could never forget my trunk. Let me see! What was it I must not forget? . . . Ah, my passport!'

Don José-Maria began to search through his pockets. He looked at Gabar with the simplicity of a child.

'I have forgotten it,' he said.

Gabar with unconcealed disgust told the boatman to put back to the ship. He silently consigned Don Jesús to the deepest pit of hell and Don José-Maria to a lunatic asylum,

16

with the added hope that each of them would meet his destiny before there was time for him to deliver the old fool at Arequipa.

'I will go and get it,' said José-Maria, jumping up energetically as soon as they lay alongside the *Santa Juana*.

Gabar hastily got between the priest and the gangway. He did not dread the difficulty of re-embarking the old gentleman so much as the lengthy good-byes which he was certain to say all over again. He hailed Don Jesús, asking him to search José-Maria's cabin for the passport.

'It would be so much better if I went myself,' suggested José-Maria appealingly.

In a few minutes Don Jesús returned with the passport. He handed it to a steward, waved good-bye curtly and turned away with a certain air of annoyance as the man brought it down to the tender.

'He is angry with me,' José-Maria sighed.

'It doesn't matter if he is.'

'Oh, not about the passport. No! But he must have seen the empty bottles.'

'The empty bottles?'

'Yes, Don Manuel. You see, I felt seasick, and as Don Jesús did not like me to drink and as I needed a little cheer for my stomach's sake . . .'

Pisco Gabar began to choke with laughter. José-Maria's besetting sin was obvious. Hypocrites! What hypocrites! He did his best to feel indignant but was overcome by amusement. He began to like José-Maria, chiefly because the old man had annoyed Don Jesús. And then it was really impossible to dislike anyone so simple.

'What was the fourth thing Don Jesús told you to remember?' he asked.

'I forget,' answered José-Maria humbly. '*Ay!* It is hard to remember so many things. I am no traveller, Don Manuel. Once a week I go from Huanca del Niño to Chiquibamba

17

—twenty kilometres, Don Manuel—and that is all the travelling I have done since I left the seminary at Cuzco.'

'Huanca del Niño? I have seen a track that leads there. It starts from the valley of the Inambari.'

'Our only road, Don Manuel. A devil of a road! But it matters little since it is seldom trodden.'

'Isn't there a fort or temple up at Huanca?'

'There are great walls and within them was once a temple. But it is now a church, Don Manuel—my church.'

Gabar, whose memory was criss-crossed by the lines of obscure pathways, knew the lower end of the track that wound up to Huanca del Niño from the valley of the Inambari. His Indian friends had told him that it was one of the ancient roads from the Montaña to the altiplano and that up on the bare hillsides, where vegetable growth was slow to cover, it was still paved. This he doubted. Huanca he knew only by name as one of the towering bluffs thrown out by the Andes towards the Amazon, and by a solitary glimpse of it from ten thousand feet below. On the distant skyline had been a straight line of somewhat paler yellow than the yellow flanks of the mountain, which suggested that the summit was crowned by prehistoric masonry.

The tender drew alongside the jetty and Don José-Maria hastily followed his black tin trunk ashore and into the customs shed. Gabar went in search of the inspector, for he never paid customs duties on his own west coast. He would have indignantly denied that he bribed, but he took great satisfaction in being on friendly—genuinely friendly—terms with all those in authority. He especially liked to give christening presents to their children. As he seldom entered any port more than once in nine months, he was sure to find that the inspector's señora was either expecting or recovering.

The inspector, with tears in his eyes and gestures of arms and shoulders which violently suggested the upward movement of a corkscrew, was explaining to Gabar the latest obstetrical problem when a customs officer saluted and interrupted them.

'There's a priest,' he said. 'A mad priest! He put a curse on me in Quechua. Not of course that I believe in such nonsense, being an educated man and a servant of the republic. Still, it is an insult to the uniform and one is not comfortable—'

'One is not,' said Gabar, instantly making a friend for life. 'And so I will remove the curse.'

He pronounced an impressive blessing in the Indian language.

'You all know that I am no friend of the Church,' he explained. 'It does not fit into our system. But this old fool is in my charge.'

'In that case, friend Pisco, it is different,' said the inspector cordially.

They found José-Maria sitting broodily on his tin trunk and glaring, so far as it was possible for his eyes to glare, at an interested crowd of idlers.

'He shall not touch it, Don Manuel! He asked me to open it and I opened it, but he shall not put his hands inside. It is sacrilege. I cannot allow it!'

'You see, señor Pisco, he is mad! I said so!' exclaimed the customs officer triumphantly. 'My hands are clean—look at them! And I am always ready to use discretion. I would never embarrass a traveller by exposing to the public what he would rather they did not see!'

'I am sure of it,' said Gabar solemnly. 'But the reverend padre is very obstinate, and we do not want discussions.'

The inspector, for the sake of the onlookers, sternly ordered José-Maria's trunk to be carried to his office, and from there sent it through the gates with Pisco's baggage, which naturally was not examined. On the way to the station the priest overwhelmed Pisco with thanks, which he waved aside with the remark that had he known Don

José-Maria did not wish to expose the contents of his trunk it could have been arranged without so much fuss.

'What have you got there?' he asked. 'More empty bottles?'

'Don Manuel,' replied José-Maria, 'if I had not received so many favours from you, I should not forgive that question. I am a sinner, but not so wretched that I would pack the signs of my folly next to a sacred garment.'

Gabar was so surprised by this answer that he apologised. The old man had suddenly and unexpectedly put on the full authority of the Church. José-Maria retreated into a dignified silence, while Gabar let himself go in mental abuse of priests in general and this particular nuisance that had been inflicted on him. It occurred to him, however, that he only really liked José-Maria when he *was* a nuisance. His theory was promptly proved right at the station, for there the priest discovered that he had forgotten the fourth essential which Don Jesús had told him not to forget. It was his return ticket. As José-Maria had only a few centavos in his pocket, Gabar paid his fare to Arequipa. Don José-Maria, who had no idea of how to get money from Arequipa to Mollendo and had had gloomy indefinite visions of sleeping on the streets and growing his own maize on the rubbish heaps, was correspondingly grateful.

Gabar's gold-peddling had not yet been discussed. José-Maria had heard of it from Don Jesús and wished to invite the trader to bring a stock of goods to Huanca del Niño. He hesitated to do so because he did not consider a few ounces of gold worth weeks of travelling, and, feeling very dependent on Gabar's kindliness, did not wish to abuse it. Pisco, on his part, had given little thought to Don Jesús' advice to ask José-Maria about gold, believing it on later reflection to be a jesuitical lie.

Now that the train was climbing fussily up into the desert foothills and no further difficulties immediately threatened, José-Maria asked Gabar what route he would take on his next journey.

'To Cuzco and north,' answered Gabar, 'unless anything offers at this end of the country.'

José-Maria was silent for a minute or two while he considered whether or not he should accept, without further polite preliminaries, this invitation to talk.

'It's very hot in the train,' Gabar said, taking down from the rack a fresh bottle of pisco which he had bought on the way to the station and handing it to José-Maria. The priest said a short grace and applied his lips to the bottle. He decided that he might take courage.

'How much gold would you expect, Don Manuel, to make it worth your while, if you were to take a long, a very difficult journey to a very distant *pueblo*?'

'As much as a man can carry and still carry his food,' Gabar replied.

'Not more?'

'*Hombre!* I've seldom got so much!'

'I think if you came to Huanca and Chiquibamba,' said José-Maria timidly, 'we could trade you all you could carry. That is—if you stayed a little while.'

Gabar took a pull at the bottle.

'Where do your people get their gold?' he asked. 'Have you found an Inca treasure or do you pan streams?'

'Neither one nor the other, Don Manuel. There is a bank of pebbles, and when we have enough water in the stream we wash them down a trough and a little gold remains behind at the bottom.'

'Good God! But with pumps and hoses you could get millions out of those gravel beds!'

'It may be so, Don Manuel. I know nothing of that. But there is hardly enough water for ourselves, and none for the troughs except in the two months of rain.'

'In that case it looks like my usual business,' said Gabar calmly—he was used to having his dreams of instant wealth swiftly shattered. 'How do I get to Huanca? Isn't there a road from the altiplano without going down to the Inambari?'

'*Ay!* If only there were! There was such a road in colonial days. But many years ago, before my time, perhaps two hundred years ago, the western side of the hill was washed away. And now a man must go down from Cuzco to the Montaña and up again to Huanca. But you will travel with me, Don Manuel, and a guide will show us the way.'

'Another pisco?' suggested Gabar, avoiding the invitation.

'Thank you, Don Manuel. It is indeed hot in the train.'

'I know the way to the foot of your mountain,' Gabar said. 'But what happens then?'

'You follow the track up, always up, till you come to a steep gully which cuts a line of cliffs. Here one must turn right or left along the foot of the cliffs. The right path leads to Huanca and the left to Chiquibamba. There is a patch of bog below the fork.'

'What would you like me to bring your people?'

'Some tools and rough steel for working, Don Manuel, and a few pretty things for the women. I like to see them look well at mass. And some images. St Joseph, I advise.'

'I will not encourage superstition,' declared Gabar firmly. 'No saints!'

'What a pity you do not believe! It is a shame that so good a man should be a heathen! But do not be angry with me if I ask you to bring some little St Josephs. Quite little ones, Don Manuel. The Child and his Blessed Mother can never feel neglected by us, but my parishioners have so little to put them in mind of poor St Joseph. And they will pay you well, Don Manuel. Gold for little St Josephs that only cost you a sol apiece at Cuzco!'

'It's against my principles,' said Gabar. 'I can't be bought. And I will not be a party to perpetuating the present system!'

'I do not understand,' said Don José-Maria unhappily. 'How is it possible that you can hate what is so simple and good? I will pray for you, Don Manuel.'

'If it gives you any pleasure,' remarked Gabar shrugging his shoulders, 'you can add the other hundred million workers who don't believe fairy tales.'

At Arequipa Gabar handed over Don José-Maria to a bevy of local churchmen who were at the station to meet him. The priest intended to stay there for a week or two while he made arrangements for a guide and transport to take him home. Gabar, although he had developed a toleration for José-Maria, had no intention of being his companion on a journey which would certainly last ten days and possibly more. When he saw the old man again, he pleaded urgent business in the north and roundly declared that if he were to go to Huanca at all it must be immediately. He made a selection of the goods he had in store at Arequipa and took them by rail to Cuzco where he bought two llamas and a mule. Within a week he was on his way to the upper Inambari.

It needed a fine eye for country to cross half a dozen of the great herring-bones of ravines and ridges lying with their heads up against the main range and their tails in the Brazilian forest. Pisco Gabar travelled partly by instinct and partly by enquiry from occasional Indians. A compass was useless, since most of the time he was travelling in the only direction allowed by the ribs of the herring, which was never at any given moment the direction in which he wanted to go. Movement for man and animals was appallingly hard. A day's march was a scramble up from a gorge, a laborious working in zigzags through semi-tropical forest, where the mincing steps and high-carried heads of the llamas well expressed their distaste for such vulgar luxuriance; rough trampling over the scrub above the tree-line; and a rush over the barren hilltop in order to get out of the wind and down into shelter for the night's camp—

twenty miles across-country from the previous camp, but not more than three by the straight line of an imaginary tunnel.

There were, however, few serious discomforts, for that part of the Montaña was a paradise of trees, flowers and running water. Even the insects were more spectacular than bloodthirsty. Pisco was accustomed to the utter loneliness of the Montaña, and loved it. His religious emotions — he himself would never have called them such — were satisfied by the worship of Nature. He delighted to muse by his camp-fire on the curious habits of orchids, pumas, caverns and storms, and to find explanations; but he was unaware that his own appreciation of them also demanded an explanation.

On the evening of the eighth day he camped on the upper Inambari at the foot of the track which led to Huanca del Niño. He was up before dawn, and two hours later on top of the ridge that bordered the river. A close-set group of conical mountains faced him, their peaks rising to an average height of 16,000 feet. This was the eastern rampart of the main range. The high points which appeared to be peaks were not really such, but bluffs rising comparatively little from the altiplano beyond. On one of them he saw again the straight yellowish-white line of a pre-Inca wall, flattening the top of the escarpment and marking the site of Huanca del Niño.

The track dived off the ridge into a last valley and then began to climb the irregular ravine that separated the height of Huanca from its neighbour, which was, he supposed, Chiquibamba. The llamas quickened their pace towards the undecorated horizon of their desires.

Pisco, plodding ahead of his animals, was fascinated by the track. What the Indians had told him about it was true. It had a purposefulness lacking in the familiar paths of the Montaña. The latter scuttered from cover to cover like the savages who had made them. They had been widened and deepened by *arrieros* and their pack animals, but they preserved their inconsequential lines. The track which he now followed was narrow and rough, but it struck out boldly along the contour lines and had a certain air of triumph in surmounting rather than circumventing the minor obstacles in its path. Pisco was aware of pride in it. It was not the absurd self-satisfaction of an American arrogating to himself, merely by virtue of living on the same continent, the achievements of a people without the remotest relationship to him in blood or culture, but a pride of closer parentage. Pisco was unconscious of his Indian blood when he was dealing with white civilisation or forest savages, yet he felt a community of thought and interest, which did not at all fit his habitual conception of himself, with the builders of this road.

The trees had given place to low scrub when he came to the little patch of bog which José-Maria had described. He was right up against the main escarpment. The ravine rose sharply ahead of him in a tumble of rocks. A natural platform which the hand of man had certainly aided by levelling and facing overhung the bog, and two paths led off it, at right angles to the track up which he had come. The right-hand path, leading to Huanca, looked a hair-raising piece of mountaineering. It followed the foot of the cliff while the slope beneath it grew steeper and steeper until the path was a mere ledge on a sheer face of rock. Pisco decided to tackle it in the morning and camped on the platform.

With the rising sun throwing its angle into stronger relief, the path clung more firmly to the mountainside. It was definitely, though primitively, engineered, paved here and there with massive stones and cut a little back into the cliffs where the natural slopes and ledges were not wide enough for easy passage. After leading him up for some two thousand feet, the track turned on to the northern shoulder of the mountain. At the bend was a niche in the rock marked, so that no traveller should miss it, with a black cross. A three-foot cow's horn hung from a hook within the niche. Pisco Gabar had seen a similar horn in the Argentine Andes and knew its use. It invited the passer-by to give warning of his approach, since the path was about to become so narrow that two mules could not pass abreast. He put it to his lips and blew a doleful blast that might have proceeded from the cow itself. Then he waited twenty minutes in case an *arriero* should be already on the path, meanwhile tightening the girths of his three animals.

Gabar found the track spectacular rather than alarming, for he had as good a head for heights as his own llamas. It was about three feet wide with a slope on the inner side which, while not quite perpendicular, was quite unclimbable, and a sheer drop on the outer side. The path, varying little in width, clung to the edge of this precipice for a full mile. Then it opened out, passed another horn for the use of descending travellers and wound up a windswept slope of scanty turf and gravel which continued as far as the wall of Huanca del Niño.

There were no pure whites in Huanca, though half the population of the *pueblo* had a little white blood. They preferred to speak Quechua, but, if Spanish were required, they spoke it with a perfect accent, an archaic diction and a very limited vocabulary. Gabar was welcomed with grave, unquestioning hospitality, and then, when he said he had come by invitation of Don José-Maria, with frank curiosity and good-fellowship. There was a drink-shop which called itself an inn and was used as one when an occasional trader or *arriero* visited Huanca. Gabar was given the room of honour which had been prepared for the diocesan inspector a year earlier with furniture lent by the whole *pueblo*. Since they were not a little proud of the room and it was easier to leave the furniture where it was than to take it back, the place had remained a permanent exhibition of their treasures. It would have been pretty clean had not the chickens adopted two Talavera chamber-pots as nesting-places.

Every evening the patio of the inn became a shop where all the inhabitants congregated whether or not they had gold to sell. Business was accompanied by leisurely drinking and interminable stories. There was plenty of gold. Tiny quantities of dust were even used as an internal currency, as small change to adjust the equitable exchange of commodities. After a week Gabar had traded goods worth about £40 in Arequipa, including one of his llamas, for over a pound and a half of gold dust — which meant that he had more than trebled his outlay. Finding that he had then exhausted the market, he decided to try his luck at Chiquibamba. He left Huanca in the early afternoon, intending to camp for the night at the natural platform above the bog.

Pisco Gabar swung down the path in an excellent humour. Huanca del Niño could make him a nice little fortune, especially if he visited it after the rainy season when the inhabitants would work their gravel bank intensively and hold the proceeds for his coming. At the same time he was treated by the *pueblo* as a benefactor and even as an easy mark for keen traders, for he haggled no more than was necessary to gain their respect. He had not a care in the world. All of three senses were thoroughly satisfied. The smell of the animals, of leather and mountain air tickled his nostrils. His belly regurgitated a pleasing flavour of rice, roast kid and alcohol. His fingers toyed with the wash-leather bags in his belt, squeezing the soft, heavy dust. The mule and the llama tripped confidently after him. At this moment, rounding a bend in the path, he came face to face with Don José-Maria.

'*Padre de mi alma!* How are you?'

José-Maria looked at him with mingled fear and pleasure.

'Don Manuel! I am glad to see you! That goes without

saying. But what are we going to do? How was I to know you were on the way down?'

Gabar awoke to a sense of his surroundings.

'*Condenado* that I am! I forgot to blow the horn!'

He strung together some blazing jewels of oaths which ended before completing their rhythmical pattern, partly from respect for Don José-Maria and partly because Gabar had suddenly looked down past his left knee and become aware of the emptiness beyond.

'And you, padre! You did not blow the horn either!'

'I blew it, my son. But it was not very loud. I have been so long in the lowlands that my breath does not come as easily as it did. Yet you would have heard had you waited and listened.'

'The fault is mine,' admitted Gabar. 'And now, how are we going to pass?'

They stood facing one another like a metope carved on the face of the rock. The two men formed the high and central point of the design. Behind José-Maria were a mule, carrying his tin trunk, and a donkey for riding; behind Gabar, his pack-mule and the remaining llama.

'We cannot pass,' answered José-Maria simply.

'Let us sit down,' Gabar said. 'There is nothing impossible.'

The two sat down on the path with their backs against the rock and their heels overhanging two hundred feet of sheer cliff. Ten thousand feet below, the Montaña spread out its tumble of hills mapped into orderliness by the occasional gleaming threads of water. In the far distance the green of the forest faded away into the blue of tropical haze. It was utterly silent except for the tinkle of bridles and bits and the occasional snatches of wind that sung and stabbed like giant insects.

'A cigarette?' suggested Gabar.

'Thank you, my son.'

'And a pisco, perhaps?'

'With pleasure. I have not eaten nor drunk since morning.'

Gabar stood up to fetch a bottle from the mule's pack. The full realisation of their position came to him when he found that he could not get at the straps. The inner pack was jammed against the rock, and the mule refused to be forced any closer to the edge. The outer pack could be reached by pushing the mule's head to the rock and standing alongside its neck. But it was by no means a healthy position. One's life depended on the uncertain patience of the mule.

'It seems we must go thirsty, padre,' said Gabar unconcernedly.

He pulled his heavy poncho over his head and wrapped himself in its folds before sitting down again. He looked perfectly prepared to spend the night where he was, and thus in the master position for any bargaining there might be. Both knew that the only solution was for one of them to sacrifice his mule. But neither was yet ready to admit it. There was no hurry.

'How is it you are alone, padre?' asked Gabar.

'I hired my guide only as far as the Inambari, Don Manuel. He was a Montaña man and did not wish to climb to the altiplano.'

'And the animals are yours?'

'They belong to the Church, Don Manuel, and were lent to me in Cuzco. I have become very fond of them. This one'—he reached up and stroked the mule's muzzle—'is almost a Christian.'

'This one,' said Gabar, waving a hand at his mule, 'has a soul like mine. He eats when there is food and fasts when there is none.'

Don José-Maria also drew on his poncho and made no reply. For half an hour they sat side by side without a word. Finally the priest said reproachfully:

'You did not blow the horn, Don Manuel.'

'I did not blow the horn,' Gabar agreed, stating it as a matter of fact, without a shade of guilt or regret in his voice. 'Shall I roll you another cigarette?'

'Thank you, Don Manuel. You are very courteous.'

José-Maria preserved silence till he had smoked it. Then he murmured:

'It is a shame you are not a Christian.'

'Why?'

'Because—' José-Maria hesitated, feeling that he had been forced on to dangerous ground, 'because you would give way to a priest.'

'Equally I might cut his throat,' said Gabar, 'and give him a little push and a little push to each of his animals. There are plenty of Christians who would do so.'

'But you would not,' answered José-Maria calmly.

'You are right. Instead of that I shall offer to buy your mule.'

'It is not mine to sell. It belongs to the Church.'

'Then give the money to the Church.'

'I have no authority, Don Manuel. And I love this mule like a son. You must give way to me, for you did not blow the horn. Kill your own mule.'

'I will not. I should lose half my goods with him. You saw for yourself that I could not get the pack off. Sell me your mule and name your price.'

'No, my son. God will decide between us.'

The pack animals pawed and fussed impatiently. The sun had passed westwards over the brow of the mountain and it was turning cold. Gabar got up and endeavoured to force his mule back along the path, though he knew it was a hopeless task. The mule backed three yards willingly, two resentfully, put down a hindleg in space, reared, and refused to budge. Gabar sat down again, and rolled some more cigarettes.

'Reverend padre,' he said, 'when I was at school the

priests taught me that Christians should sacrifice themselves.'

Don José-Maria groaned.

'So I have said to myself for two hours past. But I find
that I am not a saint.'

'I will pay well for your mule,' Gabar repeated. 'To you
or to the Church, as you wish.'

'Well, perhaps I will let you buy him. But, Don Manuel,
all I possess is in that trunk. All I have ever possessed. You
must get it off first.'

'I doubt if I can.'

'Then—nothing!'

'I will see,' said Gabar.

He edged past José-Maria and seized the mule by the
bridle. He had to brace one leg firmly against the rock in
order to send mule and trunk over the precipice, and the
movement was enough to show José-Maria his intention.
The priest with astonishing swiftness snatched his other leg
from under him, leaving him hanging to the mule's neck
for support.

'Do not fear! I have you fast, Don Manuel,' he said
quickly. 'But you must not throw my trunk over!'

'Let me go!' yelled Gabar. 'I swear I will not!'

'It is well,' said the priest, allowing him to recover his
balance. 'And now stand aside and let me unrope the
trunk!'

'You can't, priest of the devil!' exclaimed Gabar. 'It's
suicide.'

'At least I will try,' José-Maria answered. 'I am in my own
country now, Don Manuel. I shall do what I like!'

He stood on the foot of ground between the mule's neck
and empty air, holding the bridle with his right hand
and casting off the lashings with his left. The trunk
slipped downwards and outwards, supported only by the
prominence of José-Maria's stomach. Gabar caught his

bridle hand and hung on.

'Everything is lost,' said José-Maria mildly, resigning himself to the inevitable. 'If I move it will fall. *Bueno!* Then we will be content to save what is not mine. Hold me fast, Don Manuel!'

Gabar, amazed at his obstinacy, tautened his grip on the priest's right hand. With his left, José-Maria felt for the catch, opened the trunk and extracted a flat cardboard box marked with the name of a Buenos Aires department store. As soon as he stepped back, the trunk slid off the mule's back, hit the edge of the path with one corner and vanished into space. José-Maria sadly leaned over the cliff to watch the funeral of all his transportable possessions. Long before the trunk reached the distant tree-line there was left no part of it large enough to follow with the eyes.

'After all you are a saint, padre,' said Gabar consolingly.

'I do not want flattery, my son — especially from you who would not know a saint if he stood before you in the very robes of heaven. We will now speak of the price of my mule. How much is it worth in Cuzco?'

Gabar opened the animal's mouth and felt its forelegs.

'It's a very poor mule,' he said. 'For ten libras one could buy two such in Cuzco. But I will give you eight.'

'It will cost you sixteen,' said José-Maria.

Gabar from sheer habit had offered rather more than half the real value of the mule. José-Maria knew this, and Gabar, aware that he knew, suddenly felt ashamed of himself.

'I will pay you sixteen,' he said apologetically. 'Will you have it in goods or gold?'

'Neither. You will pay it to the Archdeacon of Cuzco when you next go there.'

'How do you know I will pay?'

'You are honest.'

'Many thanks! Then it's a deal?'

'Not yet. I have sold you the mule at a fair price, but now

I want the price of my trunk. It held things I have treasured since childhood, Don Manuelo'

'You will say, padre.'

'To-morrow is the fiesta of our Child, the Niño of Huanca. You will attend the mass, and you will help to carry the image. He is a very ancient Niño and he will be more beautiful to-morrow than he has ever been. This' — Don José-Maria held up the cardboard box as if it were the Host—'is for him.'

'Nothing more?'

'Nothing more.'

Gabar considered the condition. He did not like it. He was enraged by the superstitions of the average *pueblo*, and nauseated at the thought of his own pious assistance at the midsummer festival of Christmas Day.

'I offer you another sixteen libras,' he said.

'I am not interested, Don Manuel.'

'I won't accept,' exclaimed Gabar furiously.

'Then we will stay here.'

'But I don't believe in your miserable Niño! I should be out of place. It would be an indecency!'

Don José-Maria said nothing.

'It's a joke!' shouted Gabar. 'Think of me carrying an image!'

José-Maria still said nothing. He drew his poncho round him, carefully keeping between Gabar and the mule.

'Very well!' said Gabar, beaten. 'Then I accept! I go to mass and I carry the image. But that is all.'

'That is all I ask of you, my son.'

José-Maria turned on his heel, inserted his bulk between the mule's neck and the rock, and heaved forwards. The beast reared up and then set forth on its last and swiftest journey to the Inambari. The priest unconcernedly walked through the space it had occupied and patted the shivering donkey. He persuaded it, not without difficulty, to turn round, and the little procession marched downwards towards the widening of the path. Gabar, his mule and the donkey were shaken and ill at ease. Don José-Maria and the llama, since they had lived their lives in closer touch with the law of gravity, were less disturbed by its pitiless violence. At the niche where hung the lower horn there was room to turn. They re-formed the caravan and retraced their steps.

José-Maria had a triumphal entry into Huanca del Niño. As soon as his people saw him toiling up the last slope, the town, perched on its isolated promontory, awoke like a colony of seagulls. Strident voices of women called to their children. The church bell clanged with the irregular speed of a fire alarm. Men shouted their welcome. The feet of excited animals clattered on hard stone. The inhabitants crowded round their priest, kissing his hand and asking innumerable questions. Gabar's unexpected return was accepted without comment. Except for a swift and kindly greeting here and there, he was ignored. Stabling his two animals at the inn, he climbed to the top of the wall and sat down to watch the hubbub in the plaza at his feet.

The wall was an integral part of the town rather than a fortification. The outer face, crowning and continuing the escarpment, was well preserved. The irregular polygons of the cyclopean masonry fitted one another as precisely as the cells of a honeycomb. Since he contemptuously dismissed all legends, Pisco Gabar did not believe the Indian tradition that the builders had known how to liquefy stones and pour them together, but he had no alternative explanation to offer. On the inner side the masonry merged into the existing town, forming the foundations for houses and lanes. The plaza itself was a stone terrace within the prehistoric building. One side of the square was occupied by the sixteenth-century church. The colonial architects had evidently added nothing but a tower, a roof and some upper courses of masonry to a temple already in existence. The church lamps were lit as he watched, and the dusky plaza began to wink with candles and torches.

34

José-Maria was being escorted to his church. It was clear that the priest was the temporal and spiritual ruler of his people with an absolutism that his Indian ancestors, however powerful, might have envied.

The spontaneous show of affection for the priest and pride in him filled Pisco with disgust. If only these Peruvian Indians could see what had been accomplished by their cousins in Mexico! If only they would unite against priests and landlords, and organise a state which should preserve the best of the ancient culture and reject the alien influence of the Church! Pisco Gabar identified himself with the Indians and mestizos, since they were the true proletariat; and his reverence for their great civilisations, first felt on the way up from the Inambari, had increased during his stay at Huanca.

He saw José-Maria cross the plaza between ranks of frankly worshipping men. Pisco swore aloud. One could have understood it had they been women; but that these men, faced day and night with the barren realities of their cruel plateau, should believe in infantile superstitions — *santisima virgen!* In what was this folly any better than the old religions? José-Maria might have been a feather-crowned priest of the sun, going to the same temple from the same house with the same adoring crowds believing in the same fairy tales! Pisco Gabar got up angrily from his perch, aware that somewhere in his line of thought there was a contradiction. It made him uneasy, for his wonted thoughts on religion were simple enough to be crystal clear.

He returned to the inn. It was completely deserted. His room was exactly as he had left it that morning, except that the hens had returned to their favourite nesting-place. He boiled three new-laid eggs on his spirit lamp, ate them, and lay down on the unmade bed. He was awakened about three hours later by José-Maria and a party of his parishioners.

'Where were you, Don Manuel? We looked for you. My

friends want to thank you for all you did for me. I told them how you saved me in the boat and how you would not let me be left behind at Mollendo. Get up and join us! You must eat and drink before midnight. To-morrow, remember, you have to fast till after mass!'

Gabar was touched by the welcome extended to him by Don José-Maria and his boon companions. It had seemed to him that he had been cordially received before, but there was now an extra warmth in their hospitality which made him feel as if he himself were a son of the *pueblo*. He had expected a lessening of his popularity owing to the inconvenience he had caused their beloved priest on the road. But this episode had run widely and humorously from mouth to mouth until Gabar appeared in it as a comic hero rather than the villain.

'Would you all believe,' roared José-Maria, 'that this man, this friend, is a heathen?'

'Let us take him to see the Niño!' exclaimed one of the men. 'Then he must believe. Our Niño is so pretty—so divine a child!'

'It is good,' said José-Maria. 'Let us drink a last *copa* and we will all go to see the Niño.'

Gabar's protests were overruled. They treated him as a curiosity, as a fellow whose education had been oddly neglected, and they were all sure that the fault could be quickly remedied. He joined good-humouredly in the procession to the church.

As far as the door it was a carousal which then instantly changed into a pilgrimage. The men entered silently and reverently and knelt before the famous Niño.

The head of the image was a splendid piece of portrait pottery, brought up from the coast by the Incas or their conquerors. It was the head of a gentle child, the sensitive lips caught at the beginning of a laugh. Two emeralds had been set deep in the painted eyes, giving a curious effect of unworldly life and changing expression with the moving lights. The fine hawk nose and high cheek-bones were hardly formed, but promised the later beauty of a true Child of the Sun. It was robust and living portraiture — the face of a child compelling obedience because so happy and so sure that its innocent desires would be granted.

The body was hidden under a stiffly embroidered surplice of linen. Round its neck and pinned to its smock were the offerings of the faithful: a pearl necklace, some silver spurs, ear-rings of all sorts and many little crudely moulded shapes of pure gold. In this it was no different from the average image in any poor Peruvian church. But the head was an astonishing and accidental conception of an Indian Christ.

'Isn't he pretty?' asked José-Maria proudly.

'He is very original,' Gabar admitted.

This remark was taken as high praise, for had not Don Manuel travelled all over the world and seen many much more splendid images? The men nodded their heads wisely, implying that they had known all along that their Niño would compel this heathen's admiration.

'Since we are here,' said José-Maria. 'I will show you what I have brought him for tomorrow's fiesta.'

He disappeared into the sacristy and came back with the cardboard box which he had saved from his falling trunk.

'When I was in Buenos Aires,' he explained, 'I saw so many rich. There must be more rich people there than in all the rest of the world. And so well dressed! I would never have believed it! So I thought I would buy a new garment for our Niño. I went to a shop — such a shop, as big as a town and with all the goods in it brought from Europe, they say! There was a shopman — most courteous, altogether a *caballero* — who asked me what I wanted. I told him there was a child in my *pueblo* whom I loved, and I wished to buy for him a very rich, very simple dress. I asked him to give me what the Buenos Aires children would wear on a Sunday, the wealthiest, noblest children! This' — he reverently opened the box — 'is what he sold me.'

It was a white sailor suit: blouse, trousers, blue collar, black scarf and a jaunty little cap with 'H.M.S. Triumph' embroidered in gold across the ribbon.

Don José-Maria's parishioners gasped with delight. It was so white, so little, so beautiful. And was that really what rich children wore? *Vaya! Vaya!* How proud they would be of the Niño! Gabar hastily sat down behind a pillar, exploding with laughter. Incredible José-Maria! Amazing superstition! He looked at the image and his laughter changed to indignation. It was such an exquisite head. It ought to be in the Lima Museum. And they were going to put a carnival hat on it and double their prayers! The men, chattering excitedly, began to disperse. Gabar composed his face, slipped away unnoticed and made his way back to the inn.

The following morning the lanes of Huanca del Niño were packed. Many of the inhabitants of Chiquibamba had come in for the day, and there were some solemn semi-Christian Indians from the Montaña. Pisco Gabar attended mass in accordance with his promise and, when it was over, took his place in the procession with the three other bearers who were to carry the Niño. The image was mounted on a solid stage carried by four poles projecting from the corners. The beauty of the face was actually set off by the cap across the terracotta forehead. The Niño looked like a small boy laughing in joy at his new suit. The crowd was charmed by this realism. The image had not and had never had any legs — a fact that had escaped notice under the surplice — but José-Maria had got over the difficulty by stuffing the white sailor trousers with straw. Nobody but Gabar seemed to see anything odd in that. If God had no legs it was obviously their duty to supply them.

The procession left the churchyard and started slowly round the plaza. It was led by riders, shouting, letting off firearms and mounted insecurely on the only mules the two *pueblos* possessed. Then followed Don José-Maria and his acolytes; then the Niño on the shoulders of the four bearers; then the faithful carrying candles in their hands — some of them with a candle between each pair of fingers, thereby obliging friends and relatives who had vowed to bear a candle in the procession but had been prevented from attending.

Pisco soon realised that Don José-Maria had not only wished him to perform a religious penance, but had deliberately chosen him as a porter because of his strength and steadiness. The public thronged around the image, praying, kneeling, dancing, offering drink to the thirsty bearers. His three colleagues were soon none too steady on their feet and yielding to the small excitable sea of human beings which washed against them. He found himself in command of the party and entirely responsible, by quick anticipation of their erratic movements, for keeping the Niño in a fairly perpendicular position.

Every few minutes the procession stopped at a house or corner, a patch of cultivation or a water channel which José-Maria blessed in Latin, afterwards freely and fervently translating the blessing into Quechua. He used the correct words of power and thus delivered his hearers from any temptation they might have to employ occasional pagan rites of their own. Pisco's shoulder, though protected by a leather pad, ached abominably from the continual raising up and setting down of the image. He was still fasting and very thirsty. He began to accept some of the cups of maize spirit proffered to him on all sides.

Up to the wall went the procession, with José-Maria almost dancing ahead. The crowd chanted whatever came into their heads, and sudden tenor voices threw their impromptu poems into the thin mountain air. Pisco cursed his companions, adjuring them for their pride in the Niño to stop trying to dance. He was completely absorbed by his job, a little affected by the prevailing hysteria, and gathering an obscure and obstinate affection for the Niño, which any man is bound to feel for an object that he is struggling to save from destruction.

At last the procession returned to the church. The faithful dispersed to their houses and to food. The other three bearers and a few of his favourite parishioners went into the sacristy with José-Maria. Pisco was momentarily left alone in the church. He sat down on the altar steps and rubbed his shoulder.

'You,' he said to the Niño, 'should be very grateful to me.'

The exquisite little face laughed at him. The sailor cap was awry, and the Niño looked as if he had been enjoying the fun.

'You ought to be ashamed of that suit,' said Pisco solemnly. 'You are of the people. You have nothing to do with the present system. You understand us.'

The Niño continued to smile. His face was nobly unconscious of the suit. He seemed to Pisco to be returning a diviner pity for his human one. Pisco felt very weary and very much alone.

'You,' he said, 'have nothing to do with the Church. They put things into your mouth that you never thought. I've seen the same thing myself. The priests and politicians and philosophers make us all say what we don't really think.'

The tears came up into his eyes. On a sudden impulse he rolled over on to his knees before the image, and whispered:

'O Son of God, help us to make the earth as you would have it be.'

2

Heart in the Mouth

THE death of General Covadillas? Yes, of course there was something that didn't come out in the papers. He died of a fit of laughter. When five of his political opponents escaped from gaol and forced a pilot to fly them out of the country with a gun at the back of his neck and then shot him by mistake just as he had taken off, Covadillas was so amused that he had a stroke. That was the only fact which wasn't public knowledge.

Assassination? Now look here, old man — I know who you are and all that, but I earn my living in this country and I don't want to be expelled for offending the national dignity. If they like to say the general was murdered, it has nothing to do with us. The general was a cattleman, and he didn't approve of the oil interests. And there's the motive, and who am I to contradict the voice of the people? When North, South or Central Americans decide that a myth is worth believing, you just have to let them believe it.

Good Lord, no! *I* don't believe it! I know most of the oil executives out here, and in fact they rather admired the general. As dictators go, he was a gentleman. A trifle ruthless, of course. But most of his competitors turned up at his funeral and dropped tears. One of thankfulness to one of sorrow, and that's as much as any of us can expect.

The funeral was a wonderful show. There was the old boy laid out on ice in the Cathedral — oldest Christian building on the American continent, they say — with eight tall lancers, all plumes and pennons, round the bier, like weeping willows providing shade for a horticultural exhibit.

I'm the resident correspondent for a group of British

41

newspapers. It's hard to get anything at all printed about this happy country, but just to please my friends here I have to try. I was wandering round the cathedral after visiting hours, hoping to get a touch of atmosphere, when in came a newspaperman from New York insisting that he must take a few shots for the world.

It was the word *world* that flattered them — though it may have been the name of his paper. We feel a bit out of the world down here and, instead of thanking God for it, we take it as a reproach. So they propped Covadillas up for his photo and shovelled away some flowers and moved the candles. The dean told the lancers to look sorrowful, and preached them such an impromptu sermon on the nation's loss that they wept buckets. Then the reporter flashed his shots and strolled out — whipping off his hat again when he suddenly remembered where he was — and the old boy was eased back to a more comfortable position on the ice. It takes an American to understand Americans.

Well, I couldn't compete with that. A quarter inch of space was the utmost my papers would give to Covadillas' funeral. It wasn't news. After all, nobody can plant a statesman as magnificently as we can ourselves — as we'll know very well if we are ever buried in Westminster Abbey and have any bit of us left that isn't too bewildered to be impressed.

So I decided that my only chance of persuading the Republic that the London dailies knew it existed was to describe the quiet country ceremony. Editors would at least be interested. It's a queer thing about the English — like the general, they all want to be planted in two different places, and one of them is usually in the country.

Covadillas, you'll remember, had asked that, whatever the politicians did with his body, his heart should be buried on the estancia at Manzanares where he was born. He had no illusions about all the pomposities of Church and

42

State. That was why the people who loved him really did love him.

Manzanares is eight hours from the capital on a line that goes wandering up over the savanna to nowhere in particular. It has one train a day; and that I took, the morning before the ceremony, in order to avoid the crowd on the funeral special which was travelling up that night with a load of big-wigs and personal friends, and leaving again in the afternoon.

Now that I've got as far as this, I'd better tell you the rest. After all, you're sailing to-morrow. My dear fellow, the evidence for assassination was overwhelming! It's a revolting story. Ha! Ha! Ha! Just plain revolting!

When I got to Manzanares, I found that there was no village at all. There was a patch of dust on the plain, where stood the station, two iron huts and the *fonda*, and no landmark but the railway which cut the visible world into two exact semi-circles. It was obvious that no one could lose his heart to a station, so I made some enquiries. The estancia and its chapel turned out to be over that featureless horizon, and seven miles away. There must have been other estancias over other bits of horizon, for dirt tracks radiated away from the station into the purple haze of the evening.

The *fonda* was the usual drink-shop plus general store plus hotel. It was owned by the stationmaster, an old Hungarian immigrant called Timoteo who had been there for the last thirty years and made himself pretty comfortable. He had sunk an artesian well, and installed some very classy pale-green sanitary ware — which must have been left on his hands when one of the local cattlemen went bust. In spite of the blowing dust and corrugated iron and the feeling of being all alone at the centre of an invisible world, the *fonda* was an oasis of civilization. I gladly took a room for the night.

Timoteo was over-pleased to see me. There was no doubt

that he was harassed and in need of help, like those chaps in ghost stories who have been all alone till the stranger pulls the door-bell. At the time I put down his manner to alarmed anticipation of the next day. The guests were to have a light breakfast on the train and start straight away for the estancia, but Timoteo was sure to be overwhelmed by politicians demanding drinks in a pious whisper.

Well, I had a bath and an excellent meal, cooked and served by the mestiza staff, and shared by Timoteo's tomcat: a great, friendly, short-haired beast who stood much higher on his fore legs than his hind, and looked like an amiable hyena. In a joint of that sort you'd have expected nothing but canned goods, but there were fresh fruit and vegetables and meat in plenty—good evidence that somewhere across the savanna was rich country which Covadillas could well have chosen as a resting-place for his spare parts.

There was no one in the drink-shop. It was between pay-days. So Timoteo and I took our glasses and settled down on the terrace. It was a night of black velvet, and there wasn't a sound in the soft heat but the muffled thump of the electric power plant.

Timoteo felt he should apologize for making his home at the centre of an empty circle. I asked who lived in the two iron huts. His staff. Two men in each hut. A stationmaster, he explained with patient dignity, could not be expected to load and unload trucks. I protested that such a thought had never occurred to me, that my question was mere idle curiosity, that I had noticed there was no sign of life in the huts — no light, no guitar, no woman complaining of the universe. Oh, he said, they had all gone off to collect the cars and buses from the neighbourhood and see that they got to the station in good time. It was obvious that Timoteo, as a former subject of the Austro-Hungarian Empire, still considered he should set an example to the weaker Latin brother. A stationmaster was a public servant; there could be no hitch allowed in his arrangements.

After a while the thump of the power plant seemed to me to have developed a disturbing echo. I was about to suggest that we go and see if the big-end had broken, when the thump became a gallop—a real gallop, though still very distant. Timoteo listened and cheered up at once. He put his glass under his chair and took out a comb and swept the drooping grey hairs out of his mouth until his moustache looked decently stationmasterish.

Four cavalrymen charged up into the light of the doorway, covered with dust and sweat and all in full-dress uniform, as if they'd just finished an old-fashioned battle. There were a captain, a sergeant and two troopers, themselves and their horses bristling with firearms. So much lethal modernity was incongruous with all that pale blue and gold.

Timoteo trotted happily down the steps to meet them, and got a reception that startled him. The captain jumped off his horse and grabbed him by the shoulder.

'Are you mad?' he yelled. 'Is it all right? I hold you responsible. You are responsible towards the State.'

The captain feared he was going to be blamed for something, and was taking the initiative in shifting the blame on to Timoteo. Anyone who knows these people like I do could see that.

'Of course it's all right,' Timoteo answered solidly. 'You come a little late, captain.'

'Late? By God, we knew nothing till a telegram two hours ago! How long have you had it?'

'Since the day before yesterday,' said Timoteo. 'They sent it straight from the hospital.'

The captain delivered a really eloquent speech on surgeons and hospitals and the Ministry of Internal Affairs. He finished with a classic peroration on the virtues of General Covadillas—which gave me plenty of time to work out what had happened.

The hospital, told to send Covadillas' heart to Man-zanares, had simply and sensibly sent it there. Meanwhile the Ministers had been so intent on preparations for the cathedral ceremony and on keeping their successors out of the treasury till the accounts had been cooked, that they forgot all about the heart; and when some wretched little clerk, probably with a salary of forty bob a week, remembered the blessed thing and went round to the hospital to enquire, he found it had been sent off by the daily train to Manzanares like any other parcel. No guards of honour. No fuss and bother. I repeat, it seemed to me remarkably sensible. But governments never like to do any-thing the obvious way.

I said so to the captain when Timoteo introduced me — as representative of all the chief papers of Europe — and the captain seemed to think my point of view fresh and delightful. 'Governments never like to do anything the obvious way,' he kept on declaring and slapping his breeches. He changed over to the most complete geniality. That's one reason why I love this country so much. They dramatize whatever they think they ought to feel; and then if you puncture the grand attitude — of course with the politest lace ruffles and the most delicate touch of the point — their Spanish horse sense gets the better of them and they roar with laughter. I don't want my anatomy dis-tributed. They can plant the lot right here where it has enjoyed itself, and good luck to it!

There we were, surrounded by nothingness and with a secret of our own. It was an excuse for a party. The captain, once he had cooled down, was a delightful chap, and turned out to be a great-nephew of Covadillas. He was full of yarns about the old boy, and they rang true. The general's character was simply incrusted with stories — generally of his unusual punishments. That accounted for his power. Not his cruelty, I mean, but his perverted sense of humour. Be an original, and you can do anything with the Spanish-American!

The captain was patting Timoteo's shoulder and telling him what a fine public official he was, and Timoteo liked it, and kept filling up their glasses. After thirty years in the country he still hadn't got rid of his Central European conviction that a stationmaster is a long way below a cavalry officer. Then they decided all of a sudden that the world would be improved by imported lager, and went out to the refrigerator to collect bottles. The sergeant, the troopers and I stuck to wine.

When the two came rolling back with their lager, their conversation was fragmentary. The captain asked if that was the way they had sent it up; and Timoteo replied that it was, and he had thought it best, the weather being warm, to keep it in the refrigerator. The captain said he didn't think the surgeons had been complimentary to his great-uncle in using a plain wooden box, and Timoteo said a wooden box was all we got, anyway, and no absorbent packing in it at that.

This aroused my curiosity, and when I went out to attend to the needs of nature I had a look at Timoteo's refrigerator. The happy pair had left the door open. As I say, we were having quite a party. There was the wooden box, all right, just as it came from the hospital — except that Timoteo had wisely forced up the lid so that the cold could circulate round the contents. But what surprised me was that there were no contents.

On my return I told Timoteo I had shut the refrigerator door — just in case he had left it open for any particular reason — and asked him where was the object of his lonely vigil. I had a feeling that the captain might have taken it out in order to hold it in one hand for appropriate gestures while he made a speech to the empty kitchen.

'*Hombre!* In the box,' Timoteo replied.

'It isn't,' I said.

The five men were on their feet in an instant, and all jammed in the doorway. Then they tumbled over their spurs into the kitchen and stared over each other's shoulders into the refrigerator and swore that the heart *must* be in the box. But it wasn't.

The captain called his sergeant to attention, and asked him why he had been sitting at drink when he should have been guarding the most precious possession of the nation. The sergeant saluted and turned to the troopers and insisted that they should repeat their orders—which, in loud military voices, they did. Timoteo, yielding to the Latin atmosphere, prophesied for us that he would no longer be stationmaster at Manzanares, but begging his bread and lifting loads among negroes in intolerable swamps. He was still developing the intolerable swamps, when he suddenly shut up and went pale yellow.

He dropped on all fours, looking under the stove and the dressers, and calling:

'Tsiu! Tsiu! Tsiu!'

We stared at each other. I could feel the cold sweat outside and the wine inside trickling down, as it were, to my feet, and leaving me sober as—as a man in a nightmare.

We swooped on the yard outside the kitchen window, and Timoteo snapped on the lights. The yard was empty; but in that tenth of a second before we realized its emptiness we were overtaken by infinity, by a vision of cause and complicated effect that could endure, I tell you, timelessly. We saw Timoteo's tom-cat vanish, quick as the movement of the switch itself, from light into darkness with a shadow in his mouth.

He had all the Americas before him, and night on his side. On the other hand, fine cat though he was, he couldn't go very far with such a burden to carry.

You'll understand that it was absolutely essential that Tsiu should not be allowed to settle down for a moment. We fanned out and advanced across the plain. We had four torches between us. They were good enough within friendly walls, but in a blank outdoors their beams were just pool after pool of dust and stones and waving grass. They merely limited our fantastic world.

Timoteo managed to contact reality. His torch picked up a long tail, held straight and gripping the ground. Tsiu had crouched down and was about to get to business. Timoteo cautiously approached, offering a piece of prime liver that he had grabbed from the refrigerator as we dashed out. Tsiu was interested. There was no doubt that he was interested. We stood still, waiting for our daily life to return.

Tsiu let his master come near enough to reach out a hand. Then he skipped out of the circle of light with a little kittenish wriggle and dance, and the nation's most precious possession still in his mouth, saying as plainly as grace and muscle could put it: *what I have stolen, I have stolen.*

The captain called us together to give a few swift orders, in a hoarse voice which kept choking on the word desecration. It was his duty to speak, and by speech he was able to relieve himself and us. He detailed the two troopers and the sergeant to keep Tsiu on the move, while the rest of us went back to the *fonda* for weapons. Action restored us to sanity. I could even feel sorry for Tsiu, but he should not have taken upon himself the mischievousness of the immortals.

The captain chose two rifles for the troopers and one for himself. He murmured savagely that the only army equipment his sergeant could understand was a typewriter. He was whispering to himself all the time. Myself, I borrowed a .45 automatic — in an experienced fist there's no more accurate weapon at close quarters — and Timoteo stuffed his pockets with fresh fish.

When we returned to the distant flicker of the torches, we found that the soldiery had successfully prevented Tsiu from breaking off the engagement. I think he didn't want to. This was a new and entertaining game, so he kept bobbing about just at the extreme range of vision.

At last the captain got him in the full, fair light of the sergeant's torch, and let him have it. Tsiu sacrificed one of his nine lives then and there, and the bullet kicked up a spurt of dust exactly where he had been standing when the captain squeezed the trigger. He streaked for the Southern Cross with nothing in his mouth, and we all ran forward to recover our trust. The beams of the torches were wavering, of course, all over the sky and then over segments of savanna that were quite indistinguishable one from the other, and we arrived at six different positions.

The captain—as is, after all, the right of captains—insisted that his position was correct; so we joined him and began to search. The sergeant, who should have pin-pointed the right spot, had brandished his torch in excitement, and then directed it heaven knows where. Timoteo was the only one of us who had any sense. As soon as he saw that some of the party were wandering off, eyes on the ground, quarter of a mile of nothingness from the proper area, he sat down where he was, right or wrong, and told us whenever we got impossibly far away from him.

We went over that ground for two frantic hours. I must have picked up and put down at least fifty stones, and when the battery began to run low I tried to pick up one of my own footprints. The only landmark was a little ditch or hollow that we all agreed was very near the right spot; but when the sergeant found a similar hollow two hundred yards away, and Timoteo was sitting right between the two, we were no longer sure which was the original.

Outside our own circle Tsiu was roaming about in one of his own. Every now and then, plaintively, as much as to say that he would like to call it all off and go home, he sung out:

'Morow!'

And his master would answer invitingly:

'Tsiu! Tsiu! Tsiu!'

At last Timoteo suggested that Tsiu was in the mood — if we all lay down and stayed quiet — to come back and find the Possession for us.

Patience was a lot to ask of desperate men, for we had little time. Dawn was not far away, and the special train from the capital would arrive soon after the sun. The captain, exhausted, lay down by my side. He asked me what I proposed to do in case we should not recover anything presentable. I replied that I was going to hire at any price one of the cars that would be waiting for the guests, and drive straight for the nearest frontier. I meant it, too. Americans have a lamentable habit of blaming the first available foreigner for anything that goes wrong.

His voice moaned in the darkness:

'What can you be thinking of us?'

I said heartily that it might have happened anywhere, and then, more cautiously, that there was a certain element of comedy of which only our late and revered leader could be trusted to appreciate the full flavour — though possibly he would appreciate it more if the object of our search had belonged to someone else.

'That is unjust!' answered the captain severely, and stopped for thought.

'Unjust!' he exclaimed. 'My great-uncle was very much a man! My great-uncle, if he could but see us from purgatory' — the captain began to make peculiar noises into a tuft of grass, and I feared I should never reach that frontier — 'if he could see us at grips upon the empty savanna with a cat, if he could read the agony in our hearts, my great-uncle would . . . he would . . . O *Amigo mio*, in all hell there never would have been heard such a shout of laughter!'

And the captain imitated it upon earth. Well, well, they all have a lot of Indian blood.

After that we lay still for about half an hour. The

captain moved off somewhere along the line, and I was alone, with one of the two hollows to my immediate front. We formed more or less of a semi-circle, Timoteo being out on the left wing. The sky hadn't noticeably got any lighter, but I realized that at last I could distinguish, ten yards away, one piece of blackness from another piece of blackness.

Tsiu, too, lay still, wondering what we were up to. Occasionally he asked *Morow?* to let us know he was still about and ready to join the party if invited for any really practical purpose. Timoteo would answer *Tsiu! Tsiu! Tsiu!* but he didn't use his fish—for we wanted Tsiu, I remind you, to show us what he had done with the most precious possession of the nation. On the other hand he could not be allowed to pick it up. Any determined move of his was certain to draw fire.

BANG! BANG! BANG!

'My God, look out!' yelled Timoteo. 'I am over here. Me, Timoteo!'

BANG!

I felt sure that the last shot was the captain's. There was a certain drill-book deliberation about it. It was an exhibition of the right way to shoot cats in darkness. I don't know how near the bullet went to Tsiu, but it continued through the grass about one foot from my ear. I took refuge in the ditch, calling *Tsiu, Tsiu!* very loudly to show that I was on the move.

After a bit something told me—as the big-game hunters say—that I was being stalked. The two troopers were in no mood for trifling. They didn't care whether they killed or were killed. If the essential part were not in fit condition for the family ceremony, the captain and the sergeant would pass the blame downwards through the usual channels, and the troopers, I expect, were praying that half the party, including themselves, would be safe in hospital. So before they started to shoot imaginary cats in my hollow I chucked my hat up the bank and over as far as I could. Sure enough the results were startling.

As soon as I heard them reloading with fresh clips, I cleared out to the left wing, well behind the present battle front. When I had settled down, I saw Tsiu's head peering out from behind a tuft of grass. I was very careful. I had had enough of irresponsible firing. I rested my elbows fairly on the ground, and clasped my right wrist in my left hand. I could just see the foresight of the automatic, and I took my time.

BANG!

Old Timoteo jumped up cursing. I had shot the heel off his boot at seven yards.

Then we all heard the cat purring and growling behind us. As we turned round, the names addressed to him and his mother showed that we had taken up a pretty straight line. Unconscious self-preservation, I suppose.

'Don't shoot!' Timoteo appealed. 'I'll get him! I'll get him!'

And he crawled forward, murmuring *Tsiu, Tsiu, Tsiu!*

It was a gallant deed. He was fond of that cat. Up to now he had accepted insistent necessity, but at last there was a chance of recovering the stolen goods without slaughtering the thief.

Tsiu still didn't understand that this was a serious crisis. He laughed. At least that's the only way I can explain a soft, merry sound like *eeyo, eeyo.* Then he jumped into the air with the nation's most precious possession in his mouth.

Timoteo had the sense to fall flat. The army were all round and all over the target. I got a clear shot and heard the bullet strike—though I'm never admitting that officially, mind you. Up to then Tsiu hadn't realized that these noisy flying things were intended to hit him. People didn't shoot when he stole; they said *Tsiu, Tsiu.* You never saw such a surprised cat in your life. He bolted in the general direction of the railway. I wouldn't put it past him to think of boarding the first familiar train that came along.

We picked up what Tsiu had left us. It was in fairly good condition, except that it had a bullet-hole through the middle. It also needed a wash.

There was much to do before that special train arrived, and the light was already grey as we hurried back to the *fonda*. The mestiza cook and her maids were weeping and praying in the yard. The captain shoved the Possession under his tunic, and passionately explained to them that for the greater glory of the nation's army, so dear to the heart of their late and revered leader, he had employed, while others rested, the idle hours of the night in giving his men some battle practice. You couldn't have failed to believe him. Stern duty and military science shone through every word.

Timoteo again became the solid functionary. He told the captain to leave all arrangements to him, and surreptitiously took over the essential object. Then he provided the cavalry with rooms, clothes brushes, petrol, hot water and polishes, and he and I retired to my bedroom. He was solemnity itself, just as if he'd been trained as an undertaker.

Manzanares station was beginning to fill with limousines, and the drivers were flicking the dust of the rough tracks off the coachwork and examining their springs. Timoteo summoned two of his underlings, and called to them from the window to cut the flowers off every plant in the garden and every creeper in the patio, and to pile the lot in the dining-room. Meanwhile, with only forty minutes to go, we were working desperately on the Possession. Tsiu had left some dainty marks along the outer edges, but they might have been caused by anything, and a little crushed ice did wonders. The bullet-hole, however, was a nightmare problem. We couldn't sew it up in case the stitches were noticed. So at last we tried carpentry. We took the hospital's box to pieces, made it two inches narrower and put it together again, so that it fitted tightly round the contents. The lips of that unfortunate wound disappeared in the crush.

Timoteo propped up two legs of a table in the dining-room, covered it with a beautiful lace cloth and tacked on a batten to prevent the box slipping down the slope. While I dealt with the ice and the flowers, he stuck up candles and all the religious emblems that he could find in the servants' bedrooms. We heard the train in the distance, and he just had time to leap into his best uniform and lumber over to the station like a dignified butler a bit late with the drinks.

I stayed on guard, for the military were still before their mirrors. It was as well that I did, for who should drop in (through the window) but our old friend Tsiu? He was none the worse for his night's adventure, and explained to me, with a great show of affection, that he was hungry. I shoved him though the service hatch and locked it.

The cortège of generals, family friends, politicians and dear old boys from the Jockey Club was already at the *fonda's* front door, when the cavalry, damning and blasting away, dashed into the dining-room. They had taken the big black cloaks off their saddles, and put them on. You could see just enough pale blue and gold underneath, but not too much. The captain drew his sword, took a swipe at the nearest trooper with it, and then, as the dining room was thrown open, fell into an attitude of profound mourning.

I skipped out by the door into the kitchen, and watched through the glass panel. The old boys were immensely impressed by the reverence and foresight of Timoteo and the glorious army.

'*Que espectáculo dignísimo! Que hermoso! Que noble!*' they exclaimed, and all began to file past.

The guard of honour stood motionless. They were putting on a very good show indeed for scratch troops from provincial barracks, and they knew it. I felt that great-uncle, if he had stopped laughing, would approve.

The Jockey Club had provided a handsome little chest of gold and mahogany. When the time came for the transfer, Timoteo, who was respectfully hovering in the foreground and was accepted without question (since, as you've gathered, official organization had been rather overlooked) as master of ceremonies, took the initiative, and tried to pop the hospital box, all complete, into the chest.

They weren't having any. There was an aged cousin who had been detailed for that job. He leaned his ebony stick against the table, the starch of his linen creaking and scraping at every movement, and fluttered his hands. At the last moment he didn't like the actual touch, and beckoned to Timoteo to act as his proxy.

Timoteo used the most firm and solemn care, but as soon as he laid the heart in its permanent home, it expanded a little. The captain, watching out of his downcast eyes, jumped in front of the table and saluted, and his chaps presented arms. It was an inspiration. All those cloaks, swirling in bull-ring *veronicas*, distracted attention just long enough for Timoteo to slap the lid on—but I'd seen the antique cousin adjusting his glasses as if he couldn't believe his eyes; and the reporter from the *Noticias de la Tarde*, who was out at the side of the room and hadn't got the captain between him and the table, started a little drawing in his notebook to refresh his memory. There may have been others who saw. I don't think there were. But those two were the biggest gossips in the capital.

Timoteo and the captain both received minor decorations from the President of the Republic: For Devotion to the National Honour. They aren't likely to mention the refrigerator door. And as for me, who am I that I should deny the assassination of Covadillas? Especially since I'm almost certain the bullet through his heart was mine.

3

Letter to a Sister

DEAREST CONCHITA,

You will have had my telegram that I am in Lima. I could not have stayed another day on that ship. I *had* to leave it.

Do not let Mama be worried. As we all told her, it is perfectly correct in these days for an unmarried woman to travel alone. No one showed me the slightest disrespect.

I am quite well, and I am not in love — at least not in the usual sense. I am remaining here for a few days before I continue my journey up the coast to join Papa in Panama. I have of course sent a telegram to him, too. What has happened is nearly unbelievable.

You remember the untidy foreigner who came on board singing at Valparaiso when you were saying good-bye to me, and saluted us all with such exaggerated politeness that we thought he must be drunk. He and I turned out to be the only passengers. He was travelling on the *Naarden* only as far as Peru, so I had no reason to discourage him. Besides, there was no one else to talk to.

The German captain and his officers were appallingly formal. I would not like to marry a German; it would be difficult to call him by his Christian name. And the officers would stare at my face, which I hate. I can always tell what people are like by the way they look at me. Those who are truly kind forget all about my disfigurement after the first few minutes. I do not mean that they try to forget. They really do. Are you surprised at my mentioning what we never speak of?

The tall foreigner was an Englishman, and of tradition! Our grandfathers always said they were mad, but people of

57

our generation have found them most dull and respectable. Now I know what our grandfathers meant.

His name was unpronounceable. It was written Harborough-Jones. He said that he was once a major in the Horse Guards of the Queen of England, but that he found it ridiculous to use the title of rank while travelling in jams and jellies.

Jams and jellies! You would expect them to be sold by a fat Greek from Argentina, not a major in an aristocratic regiment! I could not tell what he really was, and it would have been useless to press him for an answer. He amused himself by making the wildest fantasies sound like truth. Even when sober, his imagination was out of control.

He spoke Spanish with a queer, clipped accent and tremendous gusto. I think our language and our Latin-American civilisation intoxicated him as much as the glass which was too frequently in his hand. He told me that when he spoke English he was quite a different person and of the utmost propriety.

'I have no sympathy for Major Francis Harborough-Jones,' he said. 'The man I like is Don Francisco Jones y Harborough.'

You will see that he had the mixture of nobility and craziness which we all adore. He behaved to me at once as if I were a daughter from whom he had long been absent. Mama will think that an impertinence. But I liked it. I am so shy with strangers. With him I could be gay as I only dare to be at home. He made me feel completely irresponsible, as if nothing in life mattered but to enjoy it. I forgot my loneliness and that doctors could not help me without leaving a scar as hideous as what they removed. If he had been twenty years younger I should have fallen desperately in love.

On the last evening before the ship reached Lima, where Don Francisco was to disembark, we were sitting together as usual on deck. I will give you his own words as exactly as I can remember them, and you must fancy that you are listening to a play. My own deep voice you can imagine; his was always loud and kind and laughing. Think of Papa telling us stories in bed, and how there was nothing we could believe but his affection.

'I should like to give a party tomorrow in the ship's lounge,' he said, 'if I can get the permission of the other passenger and the purser.'

I replied that of course he had my permission, and asked if the party was for his customers.

'Buy, buy my jams and jellies!' he called like a street vendor. 'Very cheap, my jams and jellies!'

'But calm, Don Francisco!' I begged him.

'Yes, my daughter. I shall not leave out the customers. But I want the President of the Republic if he will come. The generals and the admirals and all the Children of the Sun! What joy, what joy is Spanish America!'

'Would it not be better to give the party on shore?'

'Dearest—' he used such words most improperly, but as he was a foreigner I forgave him, '—dearest, it would indeed! But the fact is that in Peru I cannot give a party because I am not allowed to pay for anything.'

That must, I thought, be due to some misunderstanding. The Peruvians are no more hospitable than the rest of us. We all entertain a foreign visitor as well and as long as we can; but eventually—at any rate in commercial circles —he is allowed to pay.

I asked him if he would let me suggest some delicate way of returning hospitality. He insisted that it was utterly impossible. And off he went again upon his love for our Americas, as eloquently as any politician upon Independence Day. The long glass at his side was frequently refilled by the steward, who had orders to watch it and take it away when it was empty. He called that being refuelled in the air.

I refused to have my curiosity deflected.

'But why, Don Francisco,' I persisted, 'are you not allowed to pay for anything in Peru?'

'Because, little one,' he answered superbly, 'I am descended from the conqueror Pizarro and the daughter of the Inca Atahualppa.'

'So at last I know why you wear a bath towel instead of trousers,' I replied, pretending to believe him and throwing back the ball.

Such was his usual dress in the morning — a bath towel and an old tweed coat. The first time he appeared in my presence like that I intended to show myself a little cold, but a moment later I was giggling childishly at the look the captain gave him.

We went to dinner — he at the officers' table, and I, by preference, alone. When I had finished, I waited on deck for him. It was his habit to sit on for half an hour over his wine, amusing himself if none of the officers remained to amuse him. That was, he said, an English ceremony.

As it was our last evening and still he did not come, I went down to my cabin for a book, but he was not in the saloon. On my return, as I passed the ship's office, I saw the purser standing in the doorway and pounding his fist into his hand with one of those clumsy gestures of northerners who do not know by nature how to gesticulate. Don Francisco, who was opposite him in the passage, must have been much angrier than he appeared; but he only smiled down at the purser and swayed a little at the knees.

The purser was shouting in English. He was a man without manners, as I think the Nazis must have been — nothing but a white uniform buttoned too tightly over bad temper. He had twice been rude to me. You will not believe it, but he made me declare that my disfigurement was not infectious. He resented the presence of a single woman among males.

There is no dignity in the English language when men

are excited. The Purser was swallowing hard, and croaking:

'Jam, jam, ja-a-am! Jam, jam, ja-a-am! Here you will not sell your ja-a-am! No and no! I forbid you to give your party. The *Naarden* is a German ship, not a grocery shop!'

Naturally I passed them as quickly as I could, and did not watch until I was sure they could not see me. Don Francisco was being very mischievous. Evidently he had given up all hope of obtaining his request. He had no interest at all in calming the purser. He smiled and weaved his tall body over him like a snake above a fat frog. He patted him on the shoulder and warned him that he should be careful, that after a heavy dinner in the tropics a man of his build might easily have a stroke. And when the purser began to insult the English in general, he waved him back into the office with the gesture of one who shoos away a fly.

I was sitting in the darkness of the boat deck when Don Francisco joined me. After we had talked a little while, he said to me that curiosity killed the cat. The proverbs of his people are coarser than our own.

I answered with dignity that if it had been I who wished to talk to the purser, I should not have approached him at that hour. Everyone knew that he liked to shut himself up in his office after his over-solid evening meal. He even had a notice of *Verboten* on his door.

Don Francisco admitted humbly that I was perfectly right, and that indeed the purser, unlike the majority of men, was less approachable after dinner than before. For that reason he himself had been particularly tactful, he said, and had knocked his forehead three times upon the purser's counter and kissed the ground.

And then, at last permitting himself some slight loss of self-control, he began to curse the purser for an unbelieving, unimaginative Kraut—which means, I think, a cabbage. And after swearing like a gaucho, though most delicately changing the words, he translated some English oaths. At any rate they were quite unlike our own and far less reasonable. It is permissible to guess at the parentage of someone who has insulted you, but you cannot anticipate the fate of his soul.

'And what astonishes me,' he declared, 'is that I damn the man so thoroughly and he is none the worse.'

'Thank God for his mercies!' I answered.

He lay back in his chair and laughed.

'Well, it is true one would have to be careful. To phrase a curse which is meant so that it can be distinguished from a curse which is not — I do not know how my ancestors managed it.'

'Pizarro? Or his Inca princess?' I asked — for you know how I adore the ridiculous, and I wanted him to recover his temper and entertain me.

'Neither,' he replied. 'From them I am descended on my mother's side. On my father's side we were always witches. Life is like that. To the rich comes more money. Upon the improbable it pours improbabilities. In my club there is a man who has the hereditary right to undress the bishop of his diocese and wash him in the River Thames. In winter he trains elephants. Why not? To him it is all perfectly natural.'

One's breath is taken away by such flights of fancy. All I could find to say was that the bishop must be glad his friend had another occupation in winter.

Don Francisco answered that the bishop could be washed on demand, whatever the weather, and that I must not put any faith in the common illusion that the English were influenced by common sense. They always preferred the fantastic to the practical.

'My daughter,' he said, 'in England everything that has ever existed still exists. That is the kind of people we are. There was once a chief witch in Hereford. Therefore there is still a chief witch in Hereford. And I, who have the honour to be at your feet, am he.'

'So it is due to your charms that we buy the Hereford cattle?'

'Not forgetting the jams and jellies.'

'And we part tomorrow and you have never shown me yourself flying upon a broomstick.'

'For that,' he said, 'one needs a familiar spirit—if it has ever been done, which I doubt.'

'Dear Don Francisco, is there any spirit which is unfamiliar to you?'

He kissed my hand. It always delighted him when I enjoyed this sort of tennis with words, though I myself would wonder afterwards if I had not been too bitter.

'Have you never heard that the soul must be fed as well as the body?' he asked. 'And, believe me, the sustenance it prefers is alcohol in moderation. Far better that than to take oneself too seriously and always be whispering *Down, Fido!* to something which would be happier in hell!'

'And without Fido?' I laughed. 'Nothing to show me? Nothing at all?'

'I am not in practice,' he replied. 'I am a traditional figure-head—a mere administrator. Old women's tricks are all I know. Like curing—perhaps—of warts.'

Little sister, I did not answer anything. I do not think I even looked at him.

'That is all it is, you know,' he said. 'A giant wart which lives on you because it has no other home. I could take it away, if you believed.'

I recovered myself at once, and told him that it was not a subject which my most intimate friends were permitted to discuss with me.

He was quite unconcerned by my rebuke. He stood over me, grinning as if he had just thought of still greater riches of impertinence.

'All the same, I want it,' he said. 'Do you give it to me?'

I answered passionately that I gave it to him with my

whole heart. I do not quite know what I meant. But I was so sincere I could have struck him.

I am ashamed to tell you what happened. I can only say that I was fascinated by him and quite helpless; and the indignity was so swift. He spat on his finger and touched my disfigurement. Then he spat to the four points of the compass and did something with his hands in the darkness which I could not distinguish.

'And now, my daughter, it is good-bye,' he said. 'You are outraged by me, and would not speak to me in the morning even if we had time to talk. I shall leave the ship early with the customs launch, and as the purser will not let me give my party I shall not return.'

I could not trust myself to speak. I stared at him as one stares at a lover who has forgotten decency.

'Remember it is not what friends say at parting which matters,' he told me, 'but what they think about each other afterwards. Half I have done for you; the other half depends on your belief.'

Conchita, I awoke in the morning utterly disgusted with myself. There might be some excuse for him, but *I* had not been drinking. What I had spoken of, and what I had allowed — all humiliated me.

I looked out of the porthole of my cabin. Two miles away were the low houses and docks and sands of Callao, the port of Lima. The customs launch was just leaving the *Naarden*, and Don Francisco was in it as he said he would be. It was the first time I had ever seen him well dressed. Immaculate, with a flower in his buttonhole.

When I came on deck, the ship was alongside the quay. I was most courteously saluted by a captain of police who addressed me by my name. He astonished me by saying that in case I wished to land and visit Lima a room in the best hotel had been reserved for me. He also presented to me the compliments of Don Francisco Jones y Harborough, who regretted that he was unavoidably prevented from escorting me since he had been commanded to accompany the Vice-President of the Republic on a visit to Cuzco.

Was I never to escape from his lunacy? I thanked the captain and remarked, controlling my voice as best I could, that it was not my custom to interrupt my travels at the request of foreigners.

'But Don Francisco does not count as a foreigner!' he exclaimed. 'He is a descendant of Francisco Pizarro and Atahualppa's daughter. There are only two of them left, and the other is old and in Spain and will die childless.'

Who could have guessed that he was telling the truth? I went back to my cabin, with all my emotions shattered. The mirror faced me. As you know, I have trained myself not to notice a mirror any more than you, Conchita, the pavement under your feet. But the man's bad taste had made me conscious of that loathsome mark. And then, hating him and in tears, I suddenly realised that never would he have forgotten his courtesy and tenderness unless he believed in himself. What I believed I could not be sure.

That night, little sister, while the ship remained in harbour, I slept sweetly. I went to breakfast early. But no, I did not go to breakfast at all! I went no further than the door of the saloon. The purser was eating alone, and fingering a black mark on his cheek. I rushed back to my cabin, telling myself that I was a romantic fool. But the lower fragment of my growth had gone, and the skin was red like that of a healthy scar.

I packed, and I fled to the room in Lima which Don Francisco had so thoughtfully reserved for me. I remembered his words: that it lived on me because it had no other home. I could not go on to Panama. How could I ever have met the purser's eyes during a whole week—the week that has just passed—while hour by hour I was returning so eagerly to my mirror?

4

Six Legs Are Welcome

IT'S no good waving at them. Take this one, for example! She'll get bored with crawling up my arm in a moment, and fly off. For twenty-seven days in the month there's just the usual mixture of insects, and on the twenty-eighth, for no reason at all, one species gets completely out of hand and fills up all the available air.

No, I don't know what these are called—apart from their Indian name. Odd-looking creatures, aren't they? Six legs. Red and black Asdic. And about an inch and a half of torpedo tube in the stern. That's only a flying ant in your gin. Just pick it out! There you are—neither of you one penny the worse!

We'll go inside in another half hour when the mosquitoes come on duty. But you needn't pay any attention at all to these fellows. They're just satisfying their curiosity with only one day to do it in, perhaps.

Well, yes, there are limits. I quite agree. I don't hold with those Buddhist chaps who won't squash a cockroach in case it turns out to be their defunct mother-in-law. I've no fellow feeling for any of the little pests. But if it hadn't been for them I should be half-way through a life sentence now instead of farming this wonderful place. A man can never quite forget a bit of luck like that. It's bound to influence him. Let me get you another glass! That one's drowned herself. Weak heart, probably.

Live and let live—that's all I say. This bit of Paraguay belongs to them quite as much as to me. I'd better tell you the story. I haven't listened to myself speaking my own language for more than a year. And it will stop you imagining that something is crawling down the back of your neck when all you need, like the rest of us, is a haircut.

I was a mechanic in Argentina then, repairing tractors and managing the power plant and refrigeration on a big *estancia* up in the north-east corner of Corrientes. That's a strip of real white man's country — in between the marshes of the Paraná and the forests of Misiones. I liked the life and the people. Took to it from the start, like so many other Englishmen.

The nearest town was Posadas, where the train ferry crosses the Paraná from Paraguay to Argentina. I used to go there three or four times a year to keep an eye on the discharge of any of our machinery from the river steamers, and arrange for its transport up-country. You could drive a truck from Posadas to the *estancia* — just — but it was more comfortable to ride.

Posadas was not much of a town. A lot of dim lights, but no bright ones except the railway coaches and the *Estrella de la Banda*. The *Estrella* was a far better joint than you would have expected to find in a little river port, not at all the usual *pulpería* with a couple of half-witted girls in a dusty corner and drunks sleeping it off outside the door. Posadas had a small floating population of travellers between Paraguay and Argentina — some of them men of distinction or money, or even both — and Don Luis, who owned the *Estrella*, found it worth his while to feed them decently and provide entertainment. There were plenty of first-class passengers who made a point of staying the night, whenever they had to cross the Paraná, just in order to visit Don Luis's joint.

He was a big buck of an Italian — padded shoulders, local politics and all — but he was born in the *pampa* and he flattered himself that he was an Argentine of the Argentines. Anyone who addressed him as Luigi instead of Luis was safer the other side of the river. I knew him well enough to dislike him thoroughly. He didn't suspect it. You can go on detesting a man for years in Spanish so long as you have good manners. That's quite impossible in English.

There was a north wind blowing on that last visit of mine to Posadas. Just like today. It always brings the damp heat and the insects. And thirst. The boat from Buenos Aires had not arrived; so, instead of the drinks with the captain which I had been looking forward to, I went into the *Estrella de la Banda*. You could trust Luis's whisky. I'll say that for him.

It was early, and the place had not got going. Luis had a new girl.

'That's a little beauty!' I said to him.

She was not my sort, he told me. She was meant for travelling senators and so forth.

'She's only a *mestiza*,' I said. 'What's so special about her?'

He whispered to me what was special about her. I didn't believe him. But one of those senators off the international train might possibly want to believe him.

I sat down beside her. She wasn't more than seventeen, and she was wearing a frock of innocent respectability just like any young girl at her first party—except that it was black. She had the wide, gentle face of the Indian, with eyes far apart and hair growing low on the forehead; but her mouth and her nose and all the rest of her were Spanish of the loveliest. I couldn't get much out of her but *si, señor* and *no, señor*. Very haughty indeed. Full of conventional little parlour tricks. She wouldn't touch anything but lemonade. The line would have gone over very well in Buenos Aires, but I thought she was overdoing it for Posadas where we all liked a bit of slap-and-tickle with, say, the third round of drinks.

I spent an hour with her and then cleared out. I told Don Luis he was right—that she wasn't at all the sort for a hard-working man.

All the same I could not get her out of my mind. Her face

was so selfless and serious, too comfortable for a place like the *Estrella de la Banda*. Not that there aren't some perfect beauties about in cabarets, as well as in shops and offices. But her type was different. I've often thought about it since, and I can't put it better than this. You did not feel she was bothering about being loved. She wanted to love. Her name was Rosalinda Torres. But I couldn't guess much from that. Rosalinda sounded professional. On the other hand they do like, out here in the backwoods, to give their daughters high-sounding names.

There was no steamer next day, so I had nothing to do but hang around in the heat and slap at all the life coming down on the north wind, just like you chaps who travel for pleasure. By the evening my curiosity was greater than ever. I call it curiosity. But I thought I would be quite ready to take it to another table if young Rosalinda showed no interest in it.

She was sitting with the Captain of the Port, whom I did not like to interrupt for the sake of favours to come. However, he wasn't a wealthy man—in spite of all the help we shippers used to give him for the sake of his dear wife and children— and he soon got the same impression as I had the previous night. Meanwhile, I was surprised to find myself a bit short with the other girls who wanted to share my whisky.

I had the sense to play up to Rosalinda's act. So, instead of beckoning or sending the waiter for her, I went over hat in hand. She gave me a reasonably courteous little nod, and indicated that I might sit down. We got on a little better until I told her that I was English. That closed her up tight. I gathered that foreigners were right out of her experience—as terrifying as a jaguar until you are sure it isn't hungry.

But I kept on treating her as if she had just been let out of the convent school for a day with uncle. I must have convinced her in the end that I, at any rate, wasn't hungry. Suddenly she burst out:

'I do not understand this place!'

'What's wrong with it?' I asked. 'It's as good a place as there is till you get down to the Plata.'

'It's not this way that a girl gets married,' she answered.

One doesn't like to be fooled. I've knocked around the cabarets of two continents, and I expect you have, too. You never know what tricks those girls will be up to. I told myself firmly that I was not rich enough to be a senator, and was too old to be sentimental.

'When did *you* leave the convent?' I asked, not making the irony too obvious.

'In May,' she said.

It was a plain fact that she was stating.

'And your parents?'

Then it all came out — as far as she herself was capable of understanding what had happened to her. She had never come to grips with everyday life at all, you see. The forest, her parents, her simple education — those were all her past.

She was Paraguayan. Her parents, both of them, were of mixed Spanish and Indian blood. Humble folk, but true Americans and proud of it. They had managed to make a good living — and a little cash over — out of a remote holding up the river. No near neighbours but the forest Indians. As a matter of fact, their original farm was a part of this one. And it was a lot harder for them to reach by paddling than for you in your motor launch.

When Rosalinda came home from the convent at Asunción, she found that the land was going back to scrub, that the few peons had left, and that both her parents had been dead for over a month. Her brother, Hilario, was away in the Chaco, where the post was not nearly so reliable as word of mouth passed from settlement to settlement.

So there she was. Relations, none, Money, none. Food, what there was on the place. And then some fool, wanting

70

to get her a free passage — but as likely as not he had no money either — put her on Don Luis's launch as a first step towards returning her to civilisation. Luis was on his way down the Paraná from Brazil, and he had some woman with him — I never found out who it was — that he passed off as his wife. Both of them, Rosalinda insisted, were angels to her. And when Luis suggested that, if she stopped off at Posadas, he would find her a husband, she believed him.

Can you imagine such simplicity? He would find her a husband, just like that. Well, after the war I gave up the sea — and me with my Chief's ticket and a good job — because a Brazilian told me that he only needed a young partner, with lots of energy and a knowledge of machinery, to develop his diamond mine. What's the difference?

Don Luis cannot have expected that she would tell me so much. Or perhaps he didn't mind. Argentines never quite understand the Paraguayans, who are nearly all of mixed blood whatever class they belong to. He may have been looking at the girl the wrong way up.

Put it this way! He had picked up a destitute Indian girl with a little white blood; if he placed her well, it would be considered — by his friends and customers — a lot kinder than letting her starve in the forest.

But call her an ordinary Paraguayan girl, decently educated by poor parents who chose to live at the back of beyond, and the thing was an outrage on humanity!

I did not know what to say to her. I could not tell her on so short an acquaintance to jump on a horse and come to me if the going got really rough. She was far too lost to understand whom she could trust. And, anyway, it was a delicate subject to approach. I felt she was so blooming innocent that she might not know what she was in for. Of course she knew. Any woman would. But it had taken her a long time to put her uneasiness into definite thoughts

71

which she could talk over with herself.

What I was really afraid of was her submissiveness. She was so used to doing what her parents told her and then what the nuns told her that she went and did what Don Luis told her. She had not grown up at all. If she stayed at the *Estrella de la Banda* for long, Indian resignation was going to overcome Spanish pride. That, no doubt, was what Luis reckoned.

'Do you want to go back to the convent?' I asked her.

'Not much,' she said, giving me her first smile.

'What can you do to earn a living?'

'Cook,' she answered, 'and sew and look after a house.'

Well, that was that! Like so many old-fashioned girls, she could spend the rest of her life as somebody's servant if she hadn't any money, or as somebody's wife if she had.

'Where are you living?'

'In a little house which Don Luis has lent me. There is a woman to look after me.'

A real professional he was! The only mistake he made was to exhibit her in the *Estrella*. If he hadn't, she would never have seen that there was anything wrong at all. I doubted if I could even get any help from the parish priest. He wasn't a man of the world, and would hesitate to believe the libellous accusations of a red-hot heretic when Don Luis subscribed heavily to the Church, and had provided the little waif with chaperon and all. As for the police, they would take the same point of view for less charitable reasons.

I had no intelligent suggestion to make — except that she should stick to lemonade — so I just sat with her till the place closed down, limiting my whisky to one every half hour and playing baby games with pencil and paper. Don Luis did not object. From time to time he would give me a grin and shake his head at me across the room. There was none of his high-class custom about.

The next afternoon the steamer arrived. By the time I

had collected the electric pump I was waiting for and stowed it safely on a truck and had a meal, it was late and the *Estrella* was full. Besides the regulars there were a young Argentine off the train — very much the moneyed *señorito* — and a mixed bunch of passengers from the boat.

Don Luis had already fixed up Rosalinda with the likely young Argentine. She didn't know the conventions of the place, and she left her escort with a polite little bow and came straight over to my table. He stared murder, half rose and thought better of it. I was a much bigger man, wearing my working clothes with the flies buzzing round the sweat stains. He couldn't quite guess what he was up against. Mark you, I've said the *Estrella* was a high-class joint, and so it was compared to the other places of so-called amusement along the Paraná; but to well-dressed young gentlemen, fresh from Buenos Aires, we probably looked a lot of customers who would stand no nonsense.

I was getting along splendidly with Rosalinda. Bless her heart, she had forgotten her troubles enough to be flirtatious! Just a matter of eyes, of course. Nothing that she wouldn't have done in her own home with proud mother looking on benevolently. And then she suddenly jumped up and cried:

'Hilario!'

We were sitting at a little table at the unfashionable end of the *Estrella*, near the angle of the bar and wall. Hilario's eyes must have been burning into us while he first watched from the entrance, and then walked the length of the room. It was the end of a long, desperate journey to his sister, during every hour of which he had imagined himself arriving too late. He did not kiss her or throw his arms round her. He was the kind of stern brother you read about in the Old Testament. I was his first objective. He said to me:

'Outside!'

Rosalinda evidently thought this was the proper way for

a brother to behave. She made no attempt to touch him until she had loosed off some quick explanations in Guarani. They had been brought up together in the loneliness of the forest, those two, and words were hardly necessary to them at all. A half sentence, an exclamation, a tone of voice could tell far more essentials than the usual forms of speech which you and I go through. Hilario begged me to forgive him, and, if I could not see my way to forget an unjust insult, to wait for him a little while until he had obliged the gentleman responsible for his agitation.

He was only about eighteen and looked extraordinarily like his sister—the same gentle, tender face with the features a little sharper and the mouth a little thinner. He was wearing the old-fashioned hat and poncho which you might see in Posadas on a *fiesta*. On working days, however, we wore coats and trousers like anyone else, with a few individualities in the way of boots and belts. Hilario and his manners belonged to the Latin-America of the last century.

'Which is this Don Luis of whom I have heard?' he asked me.

He felt it indelicate even to mention the name to his sister.

Luis had just come in from the kitchen—about the only place where his personal influence never did anything but good—and was standing near the other end of the bar, staring at the new arrival. He must have guessed who Hilario was—the resemblance to Rosalinda was so marked —but probably reckoned that a half-Indian boy, with a face made for women and the guitar, was not likely to give him much trouble.

They met in the upper half of the dance floor, and Hilario called him exactly what he was. Luis's knife was out before the second syllable. I don't know whether you have ever seen our up-country fighting. *Srrr! Click! Ssssh!* And it's all over. One moment Luis was as fast as a hornet's

74

sting, and the next moment he was lying on the floor with his works coiling out around him and the flies beginning to come in from the kitchen. He had courage. He did not complain. That sort of thing was an occupational risk, I suppose.

Hilario's face was still soft and courteous. He might have been apologising to the company for some outrageous favour which he had felt bound to extend to Don Luis. He had cut upwards and his hand had followed the knife. The blood was running down from his fist to the blade and dripping on the floor. You could hear it. That flash of red and silver under the hard white light hypnotised everyone into silence for a second or two. Rosalinda was already behind her brother—though I don't quite know how she had got there. It was the only safe place in the whole world for her. She knew that instinctively.

No one—except Rosalinda—had moved yet, but Hilario had not a hope of reaching the front door. He backed towards the kitchen entrance alongside the bar. Out to his right flank the barman reached for a gun. We didn't normally use such things in Posadas. It was the bar revolver— kept under the counter for emergencies alongside the lemons and the dishwater. I don't believe in getting mixed up in foreign rows like a drunken fireman. Still, what was I to do? Hilario was the only chap who could produce a satisfactory solution for Rosalinda.

The barman was half turned away from me, and the soda-water siphon took him over the right ear. It was far too forcible a way of expressing my sympathies with a murderer's sister, but I had nothing else handy. Disastrous! I tell you, I knew while that siphon was still in the air that the only future for me in Argentina was a long gaol sentence.

That broke the spell. A woman screeched. The room rose at us. The customers might have shrugged their shoulders and attended to their business, such as it was, if this affair had merely been a difference of opinion between two of them about an *Estrella* girl. But Don Luis was a prominent citizen, and he had been so very thoroughly killed.

If I'd had half a chance I would have slipped through the kitchen door and bolted. But Hilario and Rosalinda were blocking it. I caught a glimpse of the cook—he was a Syrian and a sensible man—sailing out through the window, and then I found myself cast for the part of Horatius on the Bridge while Hilario shoved Rosalinda out at the back and told her to run.

I wasn't alone long enough for any heroism. I remember smashing a bottle on somebody, and getting in a right hook which hurt me quite as much as the other fellow. Then a chair broke on my head. I suppose the leg was rotten. Fortunately for me, Don Luis had never succeeded in keeping termites out of the furniture. I went down and, for an instant, out. The next thing I knew was Hilario dragging me out of the kitchen into the open.

That appalling knife of his seemed a bit wetter round the point, and he had managed to slam and lock the door behind us. The pursuit—this was all a matter of seconds—had not yet had time to disengage and run round the block to the back of the *Estrella*. There were only some shanties and a lane between us and the river bank; as soon as we were clear of them and had collected Rosalinda I was running rather than staggering.

After paddling himself across the Paraná, Hilario had left his canoe about two miles down stream. He hadn't stopped to think. Indeed he had not thought at all during his journey on foot and horse and rail and river right across the length of Paraguay; he was just a moving blaze of anger. Posadas police hardly entered into his calculations at all. They preferred to spend their nights in decent gentlemanly idleness—but once their attention had been drawn to any undesirable character trying to escape from Argentina to Paraguay, stopping him was a routine job.

They knew the river bank so thoroughly that they could count on picking us up and returning to their bottles before wives or waiters had time to clear away.

The night was dark; but one can see by starlight in these parts and spot a moving figure at twenty-five yards so long as it does move. There was no cover at all along the flood plain of the Paraná. Worse still, there were creeks and patches of marsh so that we could never race off into the Americas at large or even get very far from the tracks. To my mind our chance of reaching Hilario's canoe was nil.

We just bolted along the river bank until we were stopped by a creek. We had to follow it up to its head, and that lost us our lead. Once round the creek, we had a choice of three tracks westwards—one north of a marsh and one south, and a third which ran down to the sands. We heard horses already cantering out from Posadas, and there was no time at all for hesitation.

We took the middle track north of the marsh. The going was good, and Rosalinda didn't hold us back. She was not even shocked by all this savagery. Murder didn't count when it was right. Just another example of her extraordinary innocence. She had kicked off her shoes and was running as free as a little twelve-year-old. Her education had not lasted long enough to soften the soles of her feet.

But it was the shoes which gave us away. The police troopers spotted them, lying bang in the middle of the right track. They did not have to split up and do a bit of scouting. They came on behind us like a charge of cavalry.

There was a small patch of open plain by the side of the track, and we dropped flat on it. When the pursuit—six of them—had thundered past, I began to have hopes of getting clear. The obvious move was to return to the head of the creek and try one of the other two routes. We had just reached the junction when back came the police. They must have reached some point—a customs post, I think —beyond which we could not have passed. Three of them were riding south of the marsh, and three north—at the same time quartering the narrow strip of plain where we had lain down and covering the third track to the sands.

In the direction of Posadas were more lights, carried by such of the sporting citizenry as were attracted by the chance of a free shot at human game. No hope for us there, either—so we cut down into the angle between the creek and the Paraná where our first dash from the town had landed us.

The whole of the hunt gradually converged upon our corner. I thought this was an unfortunate accident until a launch drifted down from Posadas and began to search the water's edge with its light to prevent us swimming away. The police knew exactly where we were. Long experience and elimination of all the possibilities.

'Why do they not bring nets?' Hilario whispered bitterly. He was hurt at being treated as something only fit for the taxidermist. After all, he knew that he was a harmless and honourable boy on all occasions when convention did not call for murder.

The advancing line, with one flank on the Paraná and the other on the creek, became shorter as it approached us. There was not a hope of breaking through. To judge by the lights, the gap between man and man was about forty yards and rapidly lessening. It was then that I began to see stars, and ascribed them to the crack I had received over the skull. It's not what a man really feels which finishes him, but what he thinks he feels. Just because there was a sickening, patternless mess of lights in front of my eyes, I was ready to pass out. I told Rosalinda and Hilario to slip through the line if they saw the remotest chance, and leave me.

They were whispering excitedly in Guarani, and seemed unreasonably hopeful.

'But why? Why give up now?' Rosalinda asked me.

There was a sob of disappointment in her voice, just as if

I had refused her something which she had set her heart on, when all the rest of her world agreed.

I tried to pull myself together, and noticed that some of the lights, instead of dancing in front of my eyes, were stationary in Rosalinda's hair.

Then I understood. There had been a hatch of fireflies on the river flats. The muggy weather and the hot north wind had brought on the one day in twenty-eight that I was telling you about. They might have been ants or flies or these savage-looking fellows which you seem to have forgotten about for the moment; but they happened to be beetles — fireflies.

Beautiful? I don't know whether it was or not. It was mad. I tell you that there wasn't a cubic foot of air — literally— without a firefly in it. You couldn't see. No wonder I thought I was fainting! It was like — well, I've often tried to describe it to myself. Imagine yourself infinitely small and suspended in a cylinder of gas! Imagine the hot molecules rushing about and cannoning into each other. No, it wasn't beautiful.

The three troopers on the left of the line had been following the bank of the creek. They were now so close that we didn't dare whisper. Not that they would have heard us. They were cursing and damning and waving their hats about. Quite useless, but it's a human instinct to try and clear a space in front of the eyes. Their horses were nervous and giving any amount of trouble. I doubt if they were in the least bothered by the fireflies; they had caught the exasperation of their riders, as horses always do.

Hilario started to squirm forward foot by foot, and Rosalinda and I followed. You couldn't tell where the police troopers were going, fighting their horses in that damned silly way instead of showing confidence. One of the poor beasts was just about to tread on me when it saw me. It shied, and its rider's language was worse than ever. He did not look at the ground. He was trying to pierce the intolerable flickering on a level with his eyes.

It was perfectly safe to stand up and run as soon as we were past them. At the head of the creek we took the track down to the sands, and reached Hilario's canoe by swimming and wading.

Of course I can never go back to Argentina, but who cares? Three thousand acres I farm here. When Hilario showed me this place and its own private river with a flow of 300,000 gallons a minute and an even drop of twenty feet in half a mile, I saw what could be done in the way of power plant and refrigeration. It wouldn't suit everyone. But we often have visitors like yourself. And they are very welcome whether they have two legs or six. Hilario himself always preferred mining to farming. He has done very well at it.

Rosalinda? Well, they get a bit full in the figure, you know. But does that matter when the only face you ever want to look at is on top of it? Our boys made her go out fishing this afternoon. They'll be back any moment. Certainly before the mosquitoes start. Well, yes, if you look at it that way, I suppose they have started. But don't go slapping at them! Round here nobody has ever died of fever since her poor mother and father.

5

The Brides of Solomon

IN spite of heat, insects and isolation, Don Felipe had made himself comfortable. He had two more years to serve in the Peruvian forest, administrating the head waters of the Madre de Dios, and every reason to believe that he would finish them with some remnants of health and a reputation as a reasonable man. He preferred his cool office to the jungle. That, too, was reasonable. It was the first duty of a government servant to be easily and courteously accessible.

He was intimidated — though he did not for a moment show it — by the determined Diocesan Visitor who had so smoothly come up from the river. Father Hilario held himself most unnecessarily upright in the curves of his basket chair. He seemed to set an awkward standard not only for administrators of Indian territory but for the flowers and creepers which rioted over the patio and were so obviously and carelessly growing when compared with the rigid black figure of the Diocesan Visitor.

'It is true then that this Englishman has two hundred wives?' Father Hilario asked.

'If one believed all one heard,' answered Don Felipe with a prudent wave of the hand by which he hoped to dismiss the subject, 'there would be no end to investigations.'

'You have not confirmed the rumour yourself?'

'I cannot afford to be absent from my post so long, padre. And for what? There is no objection to a serious anthropologist living among the Indians.'

'Provided he confines himself to the interests of science,' Father Hilario said. 'But this Englishman is conducting a mission.'

'I do not remember that he had any interest at all in religion.'

'It is nine years since you saw him.'

Don Felipe looked surprised. Time ran away while one occupied oneself at leisurely government pace. But it was indeed all of nine years since Solomon Carver had called on him with — after a full measure of formal courtesies — the bald statement that he intended to go into the forest and study a primitive tribe. Don Felipe told him that he would not be allowed to do any such thing, that the days were long past when you could paddle up the rivers and establish, if you lived, a mission or a private army or your own little slave state. Peruvian policy was all against irresponsible interference with the Indians.

'Here as elsewhere,' Don Felipe had explained to Carver, 'he who desires to serve must be appointed to do so.'

'I am.'

'But by whom?'

'Myself,' Carver said.

Don Felipe pointed out that he had been thinking of some official body like a botanical or geographical society.

'If you mean,' replied Carver, 'that I must be vouched for by any committee which will take the trouble to print a few letter-heads and obtain some half-witted minor royalty for a patron, then I will see that it is done.'

Being a son of parents so poor that his career could only be made in territory where no one else would serve, Don Felipe was bewildered by the arrogance of an ancient university. He perceived, however, that his decayed bungalow, commanding nothing but a landing-stage, a handful of demoralised military and a collection of thatched roofs hardly distinguishable from the surrounding forest, was being invited into partnership against the whole easily impressionable world.

'It will take me a month,' said Solomon Carver.

It took him two. When the plane from Lima set him

down once more on the river, his credentials were in perfect order and described him as an anthropologist.

The Diocesan Visitor, disapprovingly silent while Don Felipe repeated this conversation, replied at once that Carver indeed had influential friends. The suave enquiries of the Church had found out everything about the man. Before the war, a lecturer on anthropology and comparative religion. A serious and too self-sufficient colonel at the end of the war. And then, in his early forties, he had considered it his duty to reject civilisation, earnestly proclaiming that there was no other hope for the future of humanity but intensified study of its beginnings. That in itself, Father Hilario insisted, was a doctrine which might lead to all kinds of aberrations.

Don Felipe did not agree, but had no wish to argue with Authority. From the government point of view it was far more important that he should be able to reply to consuls and relatives that Carver was safe and well, and that no unseemly expedition was required to look for him.

News of the man had filtered down from Indian to Indian, and Indian to trader, and trader to Don Felipe's office. He had wandered about among the tribes who understood a little Spanish, learning their languages and how to keep alive. He penetrated further and further into the vaporous gorges where the Amazon forests became the Andes, and settled down at last with the dying, melancholy Icuari. Apparently he had found what he wanted, or they had.

His polygamy was a fact. Down the years the number of wives credited to Carver had grown from forty to two hundred. Don Felipe had once or twice considered whether it might not be his business to remonstrate with him; but it was never urgent business. The Icuari were not — by the standards of the Amazon — particularly difficult to reach; they were just of no interest. They had neither mines nor trade nor cultivated clearings nor a navigable river. Water cataracted into their country or shot out of high caves like jets from giant hosepipes.

'He has gone native,' said Don Felipe. 'That is regrettable, but of no importance.'

Father Hilario stabbed with two restless fingers at the report which lay on the administrator's desk, as if laying anathema upon it. It was the report which had brought him up the river. It came from Bolivia; it was detailed and official; and it stated that Carver was not an anthropologist at all but some sort of protestant missionary in disguise.

'And that is of very great importance,' he pronounced. 'When Anglo-Saxons give themselves to their peculiar religions, they become enraged as mad dogs.'

'You have no idea of what it means, father,' Don Felipe protested in a voice of official caution. 'Twelve days by launch, eight by canoe, weeks when we shall be wading rather than walking, and without food for the porters.'

'When did you last undertake the regulation tour of your district?'

'*Bueno! Bueno!* But when I am away there is no one to attend to the correspondence.'

'Your secretary, perhaps—'

Don Felipe made a last, hopeless attempt to avert the inevitable.

'Look, father—is it likely, this story of wives? Doubtless it rises only from the unfortunate name with which his godparents presented him. Down here it is hard enough for a man of taste to find one tolerable woman, let alone two hundred.'

The Diocesan Visitor showed the teeth of the Church as well as his own in a formal smile.

'But if the doctrines of this man of taste—whatever they may be—were to spread to Christian Indians, you realise that my bishop would be bound to protest to Lima.'

Don Felipe surrendered. He gave orders that his camp equipment be packed and that the white-and-gold uniform by which he was accustomed to impress the more accessible native chiefs be left behind. He knew as much about travel in the forest as any trader's headman; that was why he had used all possible tact to avoid it.

The river journey turned out to be more tolerable than he expected. In thirteen days — four by launch and nine by canoe — the party reached the end of the navigable waterways and the last of the Indians who had any regular dealings with the white man. Father Hilario, having got his way, was an excellent companion. He was quick to adjust his approach to any objective. Severity towards officialdom. Considerate and amusing manners in camp.

He also had patience — and that, as soon as they set foot on comparatively dry land, was an indispensable quality. Carver and his Icuari could only be reached by choosing the right valley to follow. The ridges ran more or less parallel to the Cordillera, and each was a range of mountains in its own right. Sheer cliff and impassable forest barred all crossing from one valley to the next.

Neither map nor instinct was the least help. A guide who knew the gorges was essential. The first deliberately wasted time. Don Felipe, who was mild as the Indians themselves, dismissed him with courtesy after four desperate days in the bed of a torrent. The second insisted that they had taken the wrong tributary of the Madre de Dios, and that they must return down river and try again. Don Felipe stood by his own notes. True, he had compiled them in his flowery patio, but the facts of geography were more easily seen from a basket chair than the bottom of a gorge; he knew that his route was not so mistaken as all that.

The third guide, obtained when food was already beginning to run short, had traded with the Icuari and had no doubt whatever of the path. He insisted that a white man had persuaded the tribe to leave the dripping forest and take to high ground. Their country could be reached in three days' march.

Don Felipe understood that confidence had been established and that this at last was the truth. He decided to send his men downstream to the launch and to food, and to go on alone with Father Hilario.

'Ask him about the two hundred wives,' ordered the Visitor, who did not speak the language of the river sources.

The Indian, not being sure of any numbers over ten, replied to Don Felipe's question:

'The cacique has as many as there are stars, and all dressed in white.'

Feeling a natural sympathy for anyone who merely desired to be left in peace, Don Felipe was reluctant to stir up trouble before he had to. He translated tactfully:

'He says that when we get nearer to the stars, we shall see women dressed in white.'

'You see!' exclaimed Father Hilario. 'The fellow is teaching some sort of Mohammedan paradise!'

'Very likely.'

'And false doctrines travel as far and as fast as the true. This Salomón must leave the country at once.'

In the next two days they approached the stars a deal nearer than suited Don Felipe, who believed in letting a mule do his climbing, or Father Hilario, who usually carried his bishop's authority by canoe. The guide's route, hardly ever perceptible as a path, would have nothing to do with water and rose seven thousand feet to the top of a ridge.

Forty miles to the west, across canyon after canyon unexplorable by anything but vegetation, they could see the mists recoiling from the sheer cliffs and gravelled slopes of the Cordillera Oriental. Don Felipe looked longingly at the edge of the high Peru which was his true homeland. To reach that glimpse of bare skyline would mean, he reckoned, a journey of over six weeks, down the rivers to the frontier of Brazil and Bolivia and then up again.

'And now?' he asked the guide, dreading lest the appalling gorge beneath them should have to be crossed, and the ridge beyond it climbed.

'Not far. We sleep here.'

Slow questioning revealed that they were within three hours of the nearest Icuari village; but the guide was unwilling to appear at dusk without warning—though he agreed that the tribe was very peaceful and had no fire-arms, not even the white man. He spoke of them, now that he was on the edge of their country, with almost religious respect.

Don Felipe was surprised at his tone. The Icuari, so far as he knew, were still in a state of transition from food-gathering to agriculture—hardly better, in fact, than a dejected band of apes which had retreated westwards from war and the rivers to die, alone, in the uninhabitable country of the spray.

The two Peruvians and their guide slept in the shelter of an overhanging cliff where camp-fires had been numerous enough to burn the moss from the rock. In the morning their path entered a cleared and beaten track. The ridge broadened and then dipped to a saddle. Looking down on it, they could see huts and cultivated clearings among the trees. A white-robed woman crossed from shadow to shadow.

'It is true!' exclaimed Father Hilario, eager with indignation.

Don Felipe, who had expected nothing more than the hardly visible, timid shelters of savages, was far more impressed by the signs of a purposeful community than by the flicker of white. There was even an alignment of huts; you could almost call it a street. He guardedly expressed his surprise, and was conscious of a humble pleasure that there below them was a situation which could not be bullied into shape by any Diocesan Visitor.

Having no other evidence of his rank and importance,

he assumed an official bearing and preceded Father Hilario into the village. There was a reserved welcome. It was clear that the Icuari expected them and had no fear. The men were the usual bobbed-haired, stocky, copper creatures of the forest, but they carried no arms and their manners were self-assured rather than chattering.

Most of the women were heavy, apathetic and busy with objectless activities; but among them moved a kind of Wellsian *élite*, all very young and dressed in sack-like tunics of white cotton confined at the waist by brilliantly-dyed cords. They looked competent — the last quality one would expect, Father Hilario thought, in idle and corrupted women. Yet there could be no doubt who they were. The devil, too could sing a psalm when he wished. And why were all the visible children — plenty of them — between the ages of two and four?

Out of the trees, upon the edge of which the children were playing, came a European woman, severely dressed and freshly laundered. She greeted the party in blunt but fairly efficient Spanish, and invited them to accompany her to the upper village.

Invited? It was an order from the matron. Don Felipe explained that he and his companion were by no means the casual and predatory travellers they looked, but the administrator of the district and the representative of the bishop.

'We know that already, Don Felipe,' she answered, 'and we are all very glad you have come.'

'How did you get here, sister?' he asked, knowing that she had never passed through his territory.

'From Bolivia.'

'On foot?'

'On foot. It takes weeks, but it is not really difficult since Señor Carver made the track. A wonderful man! He has worked alone for so long.'

'Alone except for you?' Father Hilario asked.

A slight lift of her heavy eyebrows suggested that she did not consider his remark in the best of taste.

'Except for my cousin and myself,' she answered. 'Naturally there are two of us.'

'You are missionaries?'

'No, father. We only serve.'

'But Christians?'

'Of course.'

As a priest, Father Hilario knew simplicity when he saw it. As a man of the world, he also recognised its dangers. It was quite possible for this thin, straight woman in, he supposed, her middle forties to belong to some curious sect which practised polygamy. He remembered the strange, selfless aberrations of the Middle Ages, the calm bestialities of the seventeenth century and the odd privacies of modern prophets. He was careful to phrase his next question so that its meaning was not too definite.

'These women in white—are they the wives?'

'Oh, you have heard of them! How unexpected!'

She gave a professional laugh which, under the circumstances, sounded shameless.

'We have heard that Señor Carver has two hundred.'

'That would be too many even for him, father. At the moment he has eighty-nine.'

The Diocesan Visitor stared into the tired, greyish face. Her reserved eyes might have belonged to a nun, and he was startled to find that he could not meet them.

'Who—who looks after this—er—family?' he asked uneasily.

'My cousin does. I care for the children.'

'But is there not a—a chief wife, shall we say?'

'No, father. We sell them when they are fifteen.'

It was incredible. Heaven alone knew what mad heresy was at work among these defenceless Indians! The woman talked as if it were Christian and reasonable to have eighty-nine wives and sell them after . . . after . . . oh, ghastly thought.

Even Don Felipe, though not without a shade of envy, was shocked. He decided to test the matter immediately, and beckoned to a smiling girl whose clumsy Indian figure was all turned to softness by her cotton sack.

'Are you a wife of the white man?' he asked.

'No. I was.'

'You have a husband?'

'I am her husband,' said a young man at her side.

He leaned upon his digging stick, and regarded both his wife and Don Felipe with proud satisfaction.

'You like her?' enquired the administrator.

'Yes! White man's wives are the best! Many children! White man's wives—'

Don Felipe listened gravely to a flow of praise which would have been markedly indelicate in civilised society. The unnecessary details made it quite clear that girls who did not wear the white tunic were still sunk in the old tribal apathy, but that those who did wear it were enchanted by the attentions of husband and children.

He permitted himself to remember that his own private life in his river settlement was extremely unsatisfactory. If only one could get Father Hilario out of the way, a conversation with Don Salomón might be profitable. Yet he felt instinctively that Carver's transactions would be, in some way, far too individual to supply home comforts to lonely and deserving administrators.

'Señor Carver will be glad that you can talk to the Icuari,' said the sister.

'You understand the language, too?'

'Naturally. I think Señor Carver would wish you to come with me now,' she added.

'Magnificent! What patience! What devotion!' exclaimed Don Felipe to cover his embarrassment.

The track, gravelled like a garden path where the slope was steep and the mud slippery, led them up the other side of the saddle and on to a considerable plateau. Its extent could only be guessed, for the climate was still warm enough and damp enough for the taste of the Icuari and for trees; but here and there the forest had been cut and the bogs primitively drained, leaving glades of desolate beauty.

As they entered the upper settlement, Carver, accompanied by a respectful retinue of men and women and the prancing gaieties of tiny children, came out to meet them. He had aged twenty years in nine, but was still recognisable: still a square, shortish man with a face like a hammered chunk of coarse-grained granite upon which some friend of the sculptor had drawn a burnt-cork moustache.

If he had been attired in a string instead of a shirt and trousers, his build, Don Felipe realised, would have been exactly that of the Indians. No doubt the appearance of common humanity had helped his success. He was neither too slim nor too tall to be unfamiliar.

'I must offer you my excuses. This friend—' Carver laid his hand on the shoulder of the guide—'should have brought you straight to us instead of coming first to ask for permission. I have never forgotten, Don Felipe, that it was you who allowed me to live here.'

An odd reason for gratitude, you would think—to be allowed to die slowly of heat and mildew. But one grew to be content with little. What was Don Felipe himself but an underweight bag of bones and bacteria in a yellow skin?

He responded generously, quite conscious of his Spanish pleasure that there could be courtliness between two men at the world's end, and one of them dressed in rags.

'My distinguished friend! How should I not allow it? A man such as you wishing to study our country and its people! And now I have the honour to introduce to you

Father Hilario, the representative of the Bishop of the Diocese.'

'It is indeed an honour,' said Carver, with a scrupulous bow.

'You are not, I believe, of the Church?' Father Hilario asked.

'Father, I fear the differences between one form of Christianity and another are—if I may say so without lack of respect—quite over the head of an anthropologist.'

'But what, Don Salomón, do you teach?'

'I came here to learn, not to teach,' Carver answered. 'But I must admit my hand has been forced. We will speak of it later. You must be very hungry.'

Father Hilario was—and the business of satisfying a stomach which had been three-quarters empty for a week enabled him to control his indignation.

Under a leaf shelter Carver and his two guests squatted on stools before pots of food which was dully unpalatable by any civilised standard, but far more nourishing than that of the forest tribes. The plateau grew corn and four different kinds of potato. From the lower slopes the Icuari had bananas and a little coarse rice. Don Salomón apologised for the absence of meat. They killed occasional birds and deer, but it was impossible to keep meat for more than a day or two in their climate. He might, he said, have experimented with cattle if the clearings had not been just within the range of the vampire bat.

'But they do not look like a dying tribe now, would you say?' he asked proudly.

Sister Janet was passing the eating-floor, trying— perhaps for the sake of Father Hilario—to look stern while being pulled apart by four-year-olds. In the middle distance Sheila, surrounded by half a dozen of the white-robed, was superintending a sinister cauldron in which bones were being boiled for the manufacture of soap. The two cousins had a tendency to grow black hair—Janet

between her eyebrows, Sheila upon her upper lip. Other-
wise they had little in common, for Sheila, defying the
climate, was bouncing and plump — a fit person, thought
Father Hilario still scandalised in spite of a surfeit of
potatoes, to seduce . . . to recruit . . . intolerable.

'How did you obtain these unfortunate English women,
Don Salomón?' he asked.

'I knew them at home — from childhood almost. Trained
governesses they were. But nobody wants governesses any
more. I wrote to them the very worst. Yes, I write and
receive letters sometimes through my agent in Bolivia. But
the worse I made it, the more they wished to come. So here
they are. Unfortunate? Well, they do not think so, bless
them! It compensates for a lot to see a people, naturally
good, coming back day by day from death.'

'No doubt you have been of much service to these inno-
cents,' said Father Hilario. 'But I must know what
doctrines you teach them.'

Carver stared at him.

'Doctrines? I don't know. Ask Janet and Sheila! Ardent
Anglo-Catholics, they are. Not very different from your-
selves, I believe. I will try to make them take a day off if you
want to convert them. Takes longer than that, does it?
Well, no doubt they will meet you half-way.'

The administrator, vaguely perceiving that there was no
common ground, returned the conversation to its point of
departure.

'You said you had brought them back from death, Don
Salomón?'

'Yes. There is no scientific justification. I am probably
quite wrong. But the Icuari had been very kind to me. So I
fear I forgot all my principles and settled down to raise the
birth-rate. Fortunately I have a chance to show you how I
do it.'

He called across the beaten earth of the village to the
sister whose plumpness suggested a far too easy conscience:

'Is the bride ready, Sheila?'

'Oh, yes, Mr Carver! I think they are all waiting for you. But hospitality comes first, doesn't it?' she added brightly.

Before Father Hilario could protest against the promised spectacle, Carver had risen and carried his two guests along with him. He stumped through the huts like a solid captain proud of his quarter-deck and entered a crowd of the Icuari which parted to let him through. The casual, contented movement was far more impressive than respect.

Under a shelter of boughs were standing a girl in a white tunic, a young pot-bellied savage with an immense navel and a wide grin, and what presumably were their families. Four old men squatted in a corner, wise, naked and unconcerned. They were the colour of rotten pineapples and had something of the same smell.

'Would you care to do a professional job on these two children, padre?' Carver invited.

The Diocesan Visitor did not reply. His set face was sufficient answer.

'Very well then, I shall carry on as usual. I assure you that you have no reason to object if Janet and Sheila do not. They have approved my translation of the marriage service into Icuari.'

'Then you do teach — all three of you!'

'I know. I should not do it. But it was unavoidable. Let me give you an example. The Icuari believe that maternal uncles become armadillos after death. That is of great interest. But once I had noted every aspect of any value to anthropology, I found the belief as inconvenient as they did. Defunct maternal uncles are a social nuisance. So I just outlined as much Christianity as a child of five could be expected to assimilate.'

'A child of five,' exclaimed Father Hilario, 'is not too young to be corrupted.'

'Really, father, you are most narrow-minded. We

94

cannot possibly do better until you send us a missionary. Now, we are going to approve the price of the bride first.'

Don Felipe swallowed a last mouthful, and stuffed half a potato into his pocket. His power over both contestants was in theory absolute — though in practice limited by a sincere desire to avoid trouble either with the Icuari or the Church — but he was aware that during the collision of such characters a civil servant would be wise to confine himself to his daily bread.

It was safe and proper, however, to put on the paternal face which he used for official occasions. Judicially and with his finger-tips together, he heard the bridegroom declare that six poles of seasoned wood, sheltered from rain and free of white ant, were offered for the bride.

Carver turned to the four old men.

'Am I to accept the six poles?'

They made a solemn pretence of consulting one another, but it was plain to Don Felipe that the committee's decision had been reached, much as elsewhere, before the formal meeting.

'It is too cheap. He must add a roof beam.'

'You hear?'

'I will add a roof beam.'

The bride's expression turned from slight anxiety to pride. She had cost her husband — considering his tools — months of patience and hard work.

During the ceremony Father Hilario kept silence, for it was simple and reverent. There could be no doubt that this heretic and his two women, however abominable their doctrine, had accustomed the Icuari to Christian ritual. It was not until dancing and drinking began, and the laity — if one could think of them as laity — had reverted to their primeval paganism that he demanded:

'Was that woman your wife, or was she not?'

'By tribal law she was,' Carver replied.

'And how long has she been so?'

'Sheila, how long was she my wife?'

'You bought her from her uncle when she was eight. No. 47 on the card index. A very obstinate case of worms. You ought to remember, Mr Carver,' said Sheila sternly. 'I do not know how you got on at all before Janet and I came.'

Don Salomón for the first time looked slightly embarrassed.

'It's the bad habit of trusting to your cards,' he said. 'Of course! Comes back to me now. Pretty little thing she was. She came in on that bad lot of skins. They rotted in six months. Shocking! I had to pay for her all over again.'

'With what kind of skins?' asked Don Felipe politely.

'Otter. The price of a wife is nine skins. Quite understandable. A mink coat, as it were. A very sound medium of exchange originally.'

'Sound, in heaven's name!' Father Hilario exclaimed.

'Originally, I said. When the Icuari were a river people it was a practical form of dowry. It proved that the bridegroom had enterprise and could handle a canoe. But after they migrated to these valleys they found few otters, and soon wiped those out. To get nine otter skins took years of hunting. And by the time the last was collected, ants or mildew had usually destroyed the first. A man like that—' he pointed to the aggressively dancing bridegroom—'had no hope of a wife till he was so old that he would care for nothing but sitting round a fire.

'That was the position when they received me as their guest. Too little money chasing too many goods. Result —no children. We are all conservative in these matters. The Icuari would not change from otter skins any more than we will change from gold.'

'And so you took advantage of that?' asked Don Felipe with an entirely neutral courtesy.

'Yes. There was nothing else for it. I gave a standing order for otter skins in Bolivia. No one else wants them. My agent thinks I am mad. But he collects them for me, and I go and fetch them twice a year.'

'But then you do not leave any wives for anyone else!'

'Oh, that's an exaggeration! But whenever I find a promising child with no hope of a husband, I marry her myself and sell her when she is fit to be sold.'

Don Felipe was ashamed of his past inactivity. What an exposure of his liberal administration! And under the horrified eyes of the Church!

'This passing through your hands enhances their value?' he asked.

'No! No! No!' answered Carver with forced academic patience. 'It reduces their value. That's the whole point. As a man of the world, you should understand it at once.'

The Anglo-Saxon shamelessness of the man was distasteful to Don Felipe. Any truly Christian gentleman would have clothed such a remark in more decent ambiguity.

'And how did you — to use a frank expression — get away with it?'

'Simple, once I had their confidence! Night after night with the old men. There they are! Just like politicians anywhere else — walking memories, but no constructive thought for the future! Chatter, chatter. I took it all down. Rivers flowing and maternal uncles, and quiet acceptance that the tribe must die. And then they came out with the tale of a custom permitting a husband to sell his wife for anything he liked to take. Quite legal, but half forgotten. Naturally! Who would want to sell a wife when it was practically impossible to buy one?

'Well, I saw my way at once. I could buy them young for otter skins and sell them for something sensible when they were fifteen. That is what you have just seen me do — sell a wife for the makings of a sound hut. I shall put the married couple in it, of course.'

'I have a liberal education,' exclaimed Don Felipe. 'No one can say I do not sympathise with temptation. But eighty-nine!'

'Yes, it's astonishing how my little family grew. I taught them a bit of sensible religion and tried to give them self-respect. Any man can handle a girl up to the age of eleven or so. But time passes. When my first batch of wives were close on twelve, I had to send for Janet and Sheila.'

'It is beyond belief!' Don Felipe cried, all the more angry because he was aware of a most improper jealousy. 'And then to introduce two crazed women to assist you!'

Carver stood up and, instantly, the old men with him.

'What the devil do you mean, man? Crazed women— those two angels? Come out of here immediately!'

The Icuari had perceived his anger. Don Felipe realised that they would strike out like frightened children if Carver made the least gesture of violence, but had a human faith that Carver would not. After all, he himself had sometimes been in a position to raise a finger. He scurried through the dancers a little ahead of his host, endeavouring to preserve an expression of the utmost geniality.

The Diocesan Visitor followed more slowly, smiling with inexplicable tenderness. He even blessed the bride as he passed her. It was extremely unfair, Don Felipe thought, that Father Hilario should leave the secular authority to interrogate this disgraceful debauchee and then shy away from the results. Typical of those black crows, it was! The Church, to start with, had been altogether too ready to bring in its thunders and, having made all the trouble, was now being exquisitely courteous.

'Don Salomón,' Father Hilario was saying, 'you have been in the forest how long?'

'Let me see now! Crazed women indeed! Let me see! A year before I found the Icuari. And six— no, no, over eight years since.'

'Verily what devotion! No wonder it was difficult at first for us to understand each other.'

'I cannot see why. Souls for God you want, don't you? Well— if I may use your terminology— when I began to love this people, so did I. Increase and multiply, that is what I am trying to make them do. Clear, I hope? Many thanks! No reason for a government officer to think we are all mad, is there? Look at that!'

Sister Janet, attended by two nursery maids in the white tunic of Carver's wives, was telling a story to a dozen or so of fascinated infants.

'*Suffer little children to come unto Me*,' Carver explained. 'I ought not to allow it. It is gross interference with their own folk-lore. But the fact is, padre, I have found in practice that if you want to raise a whole community from the dead there is nothing like elementary Christianity to do it.'

'That has been our experience, too,' said Father Hilario gravely. 'I'm very glad to hear it confirmed from such an—unexpected quarter. May I inspect the children, sister?'

'Of course, reverend padre,' Janet replied proudly. 'Their heads are beautifully clean now.'

Don Felipe, left out of the conversation in disgrace, also looked closely at the Icuari nursery class. He knew what Father Hilario was up to. Either of them, from long experience, could distinguish as little as one-eighth of white blood. There was none.

He ventured to reassert himself with a delicate question:

'Sister Janet, the bride whom we have just seen married—would you describe her as . . . well . . . inexperienced?'

'Certainly not, Don Felipe. She was one of my best pupils.'

The administrator blinked his fever-yellowed eyes under the impact of such innocence, but tried again.

'And you see nothing questionable in this second marriage?'

'No, Don Felipe. After all they are quite normal girls. They would be very disappointed if they had to belong to

Mr Carver's family for ever, wouldn't they?'

Father Hilario opened his arms in a jovial gesture which included the desolate, rain-sodden hill-top and all the children, old and young, upon it. His bark of laughter sounded through Icuari mists the sunlit trumpets of Europe.

'What's up? What's amusing you?' asked Carver suspiciously.

'My dear, noble friend! Ah, but you must see the jest of it!'

'I do not,' Don Salomón insisted formally. 'You must forgive me. The Icuari laugh seldom. One loses the habit.'

Don Felipe silently agreed. It was appallingly true — poor devils that they were out there in the uninhabitable. He himself, before this journey with Father Hilario, had for years seen no reason for any more than a melancholy smile.

'You have never any thought of the world outside — you and your two angels?'

'I must admit, padre, there are times when we think of home. But what with keeping each other alive and speaking the language to each other, we do tend to become single-minded — indeed, apart from our purpose, to have few thoughts the Icuari cannot share.'

'But they would not mind, I suppose,' Father Hilario asked, 'if the girls you buy were your wives in fact as well as name?'

'Mind? No, of course they wouldn't. Oh, I understand at last! Laughing at yourself, were you? The inquisitor descending upon Bluebeard! But, my dear fellow, it beats me that you couldn't see from your own experience how that sort of thing interferes with a mission.'

The administrator gasped at so uncompromising a rejection of opportunity.

'If you had any faith, Don Salomón, you would be a saint!' he portested.

100

'Don Felipe,' said Father Hilario, 'when God has produced the miracle before the faith, we should not, I think, be too ready to advise Him from our own experiments in mere trifles of administration which should come first and which second.'

Cancer

1

First Blood

SHE was a treaty cruiser, built for speed. Urgency was in her lines, urgency in the deep hum of the engines. Urgent were even the seemingly casual attitudes of the men in open shirts and grey flannel trousers who crowded her decks. She was jammed full as a refugee ship; yet this was no ragged cargo hysterical with relief and embarrassing the ship's company by their gratitude and misery. The men on deck were lean, well-fed Army officers returning hastily to the Middle East from their cancelled leave. They were not yet in uniform. War had not been declared.

Mr Avellion sat on a locker, watching the two huge curves of Mediterranean that raced towards the horizon from the cruiser's bows. There was no other movement on the water and no cloud but a dark patch of haze astern hanging over Marseilles. Ships, more sensitive to threat of war than of weather, were in port. The sea was an empty blue pool.

He was a civilian. In that eager warship, racing to deliver her packed human freight at Alexandria, there was a small group of businessmen, all specialists in shipping, oil and cables, or obscurer but imperial trades. None of them was important enough to command an unpurchasable air passage, but all were badly needed at their stations before Mussolini, if he meant to move, could delay their arrival.

There was peace in Avellion's heart; quivering and uncertain, but peace. He drew a deep breath as if to float this unaccustomed ardour of well-being more securely in an expanded soul, and coughed.

He was of use; he was wanted. What was it that the Board of Trade chap had said to him? *Mr Avellion, your local knowledge will be invaluable*. To ask him to leave in twenty-four hours was a bit stiff. Still, chaps like himself were important in times of war. Nobody could tell what value they mightn't find in his little business at Suez. He was sometimes hazy about the details of what he did there, especially in the morning with always a gaggle of silly Arabs shouting at him; but objectives became beautifully clear at sundown when his boy brought in more ice and the second bottle. Whatever he might feel for the rest of the day, there were two hours every evening when his life was full of interest. The dreams of those hours had, after all, been true. *Invaluable* — that was what the Board of Trade chap had called him.

He became aware of a voice.

'Eh? What did you say?'

'I said, "Not much chance if they catch us." '

The speaker, by profession a cable manager, was as obvious a businessman as Mr Avellion, but his fat was more neatly distributed throughout his person. Avellion was pear-shaped, with much of his weight far to the south of his belt; he cultivated a small white military moustache, above which was a powerful nose sprouting blue-grey buds like a tree in winter; his appearance was raffish and faintly disreputable, at any rate when compared to the plumpness, the round, clean-shaven face, the precise little mouth and nose of his fellow passenger.

Avellion's bloodshot eyes twinkled at him.

'They won't try, my boy.'

'First thing we'll know about it will be the whole Italian Navy on us,' grumbled the cable manager.

'They won't start till we do,' said Avellion, 'not they! They're still hoping we shall rat, like we did at Munich.'

'Hope you're right. But I don't like it,' replied the cable manager judiciously. 'I don't like it. The ship can't even fight. Do you know we have fifteen hundred passengers on board?'

'A fine lot of boys!' Avellion boomed. 'Proud to be with 'em. Well, how about a little drink?'

'There isn't any.'

'What?'

'There couldn't be enough, you see. So they've closed down altogether. We'll be short of food, too. Bound to be.'

'Bound to be,' echoed Avellion dully.

All around the after turrets the deck was strewn with men lounging on blankets, and reading, sunbathing, playing bridge, or asleep. The more energetic strolled back and forth, picking their way through and over the tangle of feet. The lifeboat against which Avellion leaned his shoulder was full of men; an orderly shambles in which everyone seemed to be unpacking and repacking kit. Scraps of conversation drifted past him, mingled of annoyance, indignation, and sardonic amusement.

'Thirty-six hours in the train, and we drank it all up. . . . No time to buy any. . . . Well, who the devil would think of packing his cellar? . . . Now you know what war is like, old boy!' Then laughter at the sorry plight of eight hundred officers on the quarter-deck and seven hundred men in the flats that did duty as troop decks, all torn at two days' notice from the delights of leave, and all without a drink.

Avellion had done just as they—packed his immediate needs and drunk them up. He was allowed only such baggage as he could carry; there had been no room for more than two bottles. They had left Newhaven on the night boat, sleeping wherever there was space to sit or lie, then spent an unshaven dawn at Dieppe, where the six special trains stood hissing in the sidings and the French children cheered and the adults watched with grim, set faces these forerunners of another war. So passed a day and a night, while they waited in sun-baked railway yards or trundled slowly southwards to Marseilles, until the trains emptied themselves into the cruiser and that weary, merry crowd sorted itself out on her decks.

It was magnificent, thought Avellion, a memory for ever. During the last war he had been out East, clerk in a merchant's office. He had since accused himself of — well, not funk but lack of spirit. He had been indispensable, they said; and it was true that, so far as the business went, he was. He had always told himself that next month the rush of work would ease, and that then he could enlist; it never did ease, and suddenly the war was over.

Yet now, twenty years later, here he was among these careless, loose-jointed boys and men, off to war with the first party of the professionals. *Followed their mercenary calling and took their wages and are dead* — that was one of the bits he would chant in his imperial solitude. And he was proud of himself. At fifty-five it wasn't so bad to have completed the journey and shared the hardships, such as they were, without feeling one penny the worse — except that, God, he couldn't endure many more hours without a drink!

Dusk fell. The blind turrets lifted their guns like the antennae of insects feeling for the night, and fired blank charges. The professionals jumped, and for a moment searched sea and sky for the enemy; then smiled as if they had known all along that these muted bangs were some naval ritual of active service. Avellion did just as they, but with effort. Though his mind was calmly convinced that there was no chance of war for at least another week, his nerves were uncontrollable. Thereafter he started at any sound at all.

A bugle summoned his mess to supper. He followed the notices which led him down, through hot and hotter boxes of steel, into the Marines' Flat. The ship's company seemed little affected by August in the Mediterranean. The soldiers blenched as they insinuated themselves between the steel walls, and the sweat leapt to their skins. Avellion felt faint. He slid on to one of the long wooden benches and smiled dimly at his neighbours across the table until he recovered. The meal was simple; there was tinned stew, tinned and now liquid butter, and marmalade. He pecked at them. There was warm water to drink.

The man who sat opposite him, sunburned as an Egyptian, said, as if apologizing for the shortcomings of the senior service:

'Not much in the way of grub, I'm afraid. They were given no warning that they had to pick us up, and it's a marvel how they manage to feed us at all.'

The speaker's silk shirt was open to the waist, and beads of perspiration trickled between the iron-grey hairs of his chest. Avellion knew the type. The man would turn out to be a colonel at least, when he changed into uniform in Cairo.

'Jolly good show, I call it!' said Avellion stoutly.

The military eye rested on him pityingly and approvingly.

'They shouldn't have sent civilians out this way.'

'It was the fastest,' Avellion replied. 'We have to be there before the balloon goes up.'

A good phrase that. He had learned a number of them in the train: to say 'browned off' for 'fed up,' to speak of 'armour' instead of 'tanks.' Thirty-six hours in the train. In his compartment one other businessman and four young chaps on their way to rejoin their units. All the whisky gone as well as some bottles of red wine they bought at a station. Whisky. It was hard to eat a meal without it.

The senior officer left. Avellion asked who he was, and immediately aroused enthusiasm. Yes, he was a colonel and certain to be commanding a division in a year, and had all sorts of new theories about armour. He had been invited to mess with the captain of the cruiser, but as soon as he saw how bloody uncomfortable everyone else was going to be, he insisted on coming along to share. Just like him! Grand fellow.

With this shot of romanticism in his water, Avellion

managed to drink two glasses of it. The liquid poured through his skin, leaving no satisfying body behind.

He staggered up on deck and retired to the space of forty square feet, between some ventilators and a pom-pom, where the civilians had drawn apart and spread out their bedding—two blankets per man issued by the ship, and whatever they could find in their baggage to mitigate the hardness of the deck. Once by themselves, the businessmen were outspoken in their condemnation of the cruiser, the discomfort, and the various government departments that had facilitated or demanded their voyage.

The ship raced southwards at thirty knots, and for a little while the contrast between the cool wind of her passage and the sweltering heat below decks was calming as whisky to Avellion. He took no part in the general conversation. His inflated imperial mood had vanished, but nevertheless he was disgusted with his fellow civilians. They were wrong, and he was weary, and the world was very wrong. If only he could sleep!

The night passed. It seemed an interminable twisting from one hip to the other; yet at times there was a glassy unconsciousness and at times a wild succession of half-wakeful thoughts, so mad that they could only be explained as dreams.

At dawn he watched his companions crawl from their blankets, ridiculous in untidy scraps of clothing or worm-like in nakedness. He stayed still. The dreams bothered him. There was no way of waking up from them; yet he was, he knew, awake. It was familiar enough, that feeling, but shadowed by the apprehension of some horror still unrealized.

The horror rose to the surface. There was to be no whisky that day and nearly all the next day. No whisky till Malta, thirty hours away, and no guarantee that one could land at Malta. But of course they would be allowed to land. He clung to that. Only thirty hours away. And of course

110

they would be allowed to land.

'Good morning to you.'

It was the cable manager. He had washed and shaved and extracted enough from a well-packed suitcase to give himself the dapper niceness of a holiday-maker.

'Got a touch of fever?'

Avellion tried to concentrate his thoughts.

'Fever? Fever?'

'You're shaking all over.'

Avellion held out his hand and looked at it stupidly. It did not seem to belong to him. It was dancing. He put the tips of his index and third finger on his knee and let them gambol like the legs of a ballerina. That was an old trick of his at parties—to wrap a handkerchief round his wrist to form the skirt and let his fingers dance. They danced now. His whole hand danced furiously, and there was nothing at all he could do to stop it. He felt a rush of anger at the man who stared.

'Nonsense! Nonsense!' he said. 'Always like this in the morning. Everybody is. Where the devil do I get a wash?'

He could not shave, but the cool water in which he dipped his face and wrists revived him. He dressed, and strolled round the deck, stepping with care over the penetrate bodies of the army. With many he exchanged smiles. They felt, obviously, that their discomfort was comic, that nothing whatever could be done about the inefficiencies of the War Office as a travel agency, and that one might as well enjoy the enforced idleness. For Avellion there was comfort in the prevailing bonhomie, and again a measure of calm in the exhilarating rush of the ship across a perfectly flat Mediterranean. He could not face breakfast or lunch, but it was not so bad. Not so bad. And he was four and a half hours nearer Malta.

In the afternoon he had trouble with a very primitive Avellion who wanted to scream. He kept him in order, but was driven to cadge—very decently—for drinks. Drink was

the subject of his conversation with all casual acquaintances. But the passengers' baggage was bone-dry. Everyone to whom he spoke was also hoping to God that Mr
Avellion — his nose looked so promising — would produce a
bottle and himself offer treat. A naval officer murmured
uncomfortably that the wardroom too was dry; they
couldn't, he said, very well open the bar for themselves
alone when the ship was full of devastatingly thirsty
soldiers. He moved uneasily away.

Avellion clung for support to that *invaluable local
knowledge*. He had it all right. His line had always been the
native trade, and he knew the dhow skippers from Oman to
Suez, their ships, their reputations, and their rackets; little
cargo could run the blockade to Abyssinia and no gossip of
it be repeated in his office. He looked forward to new, stern
friendships, more dutiful than his innumerable bar
acquaintanceships, more familiar than the strange attachments occasionally and passionately formed by Arabs for
those they could not understand.

No more of just making and losing money. At last, he
told himself, he had something to serve, and in good company like that colonel's. For an important man, an important man in good and gallant company, not to be able to
stand two days without a drink was absurd. Self-control!
Mustn't make a fuss.

Two more hours passed, long as the whole voyage. The
bugle summoned him to eat, but he could not face the mess
flat and sweating alleyways. The open deck was fresh and
cool as sanity.

The cable manager had pity on him and, suspecting that
the oily smell below had upset Mr Avellion, brought him a
sandwich. Avellion ate it and swallowed water. Nothing
had taste or even feeling.

'Bothered by the sea, old chap?'

Avellion shook his head. The confession broke from
him.

'I've got to have a drink,' he cried harshly. 'You don't understand. I've shifted a lot in the last twenty years. Not real heavy drinking. Only just what one needs in the tropics. It doesn't do me any harm, but being cut off like this—'

His hand danced in the air describing a vague figure of eight, a complicated gesture of emptiness.

'Ask the doctor for some,' suggested the cable manager. 'You ought to taper off gently. He'll know that.'

'Yes. Yes, I will. Of course.'

Avellion got up from his two blankets spread on the deck. He did not look back at them. There had been a queer shadow close to his ear, at the limit of vision. He scuttled off towards the sick bay, and then could not remember why he wanted to go there. He sat down heavily on a stanchion. To go to the doctor—of course that was it: to ask the doctor for a drink.

The cruiser hurled herself through the water, white ensign at the stern stiff with the wind of passage as the tin flag on a toy ship. The mercenaries of the Middle East strolled leisurely past Avellion; they could, he gathered, endure the steady diet of stew and marmalade; they could sleep well enough on blankets and the deck; they were ribald at the overcrowding, so close that one man's head was between the feet of another; but they still cursed bitterly at the lack of any alcohol to beguile the tedium of the voyage. It occurred to Avellion that he was not alone in his torment. He was again ashamed. He, too, was a servant of the state, and invaluable. If they could endure privation, he could. Good God, he had recaptured his youth during those long hours in the train! The doctor? It might be less than twenty hours to Malta at this speed. Then he could soak in it, and afterwards taper off gradually. That colonel, the one who sat and sweated into his marmalade, wasn't asking for special privileges. What? Go squealing to the doctor with all his comrades as thirsty as he? Comrades

—comrades—he kept rolling the young word through his mind as he walked back to his blankets.

The night was peopled with strange images. It seemed busier and less long than the last. Once he screamed.

'Sorry, chaps. Must have had a nightmare.'

It cost him a physical effort to say so. He wanted to go on screaming and tell them why. He screamed twice more —simply couldn't help it—but managed to make them sound like violent coughs.

In the morning he felt better. The shadow in the corner of his eyes had gone. He decided that he hadn't felt so well for a long time. That was what came from self-control, from really knocking off the drink. He had a pet, too. As soon as the others had gone to breakfast he played with it. It seemed quite tame, but stayed always out of reach of his hand.

When the cable manager came back, Avellion showed it to him.

'Look at him!' he said. 'Animals know whom to trust.'

'Look at what?'

'Here, man, here! See him?'

'See what?'

'Little black rat. His Majesty's rat! Look at him.'

The cable manager did not always appreciate jokes. He was therefore unduly willing to accept them when they were not there.

'Very good! Very good!' he said with an embarrassed laugh, and trotted away to take his exercise.

Several people watched, disturbed, the flitting of Mr Avellion's hands and listened to the endearing terms in which he spoke to the invisible; but he looked sane, though unshaven, and they gave him the benefit of the doubt—an eccentric passing the hours of idleness in his own way, with, undoubtedly, the help of a secret bottle.

In a dream Avellion waited for Malta. There was nothing clear in his brain but a longing and a prohibition.

'It will be all right when you get to Malta,' he said to himself. 'Do nothing till you get to Malta.' Desire was no longer so simple that it could be defined as wanting a drink. At Malta there would be an end to unknown agony.

The colonel sat down by Mr Avellion. He did not know what was wrong, or indeed if there was anything seriously wrong at all. He talked very casually with the eccentric businessman, and at last, as a good regimental officer, he understood and he admired the rat. He also said that Malta was in sight. Mr Avellion began to weep. He then screamed luxuriously, and kept on screaming while the colonel led him to the sick bay.

Mr Avellion got his whisky, but it was of little interest to him. He even reached Malta, or at least the launch which came out to carry him to hospital. The ship reported him as a case of delirium tremens caused by a habitual drinker's sudden want of alcohol. There were plenty of such cases in the books, due to poverty or isolation in desert or at sea. The ship was doubtful whether d.t. could be caused by sheer courage, but could give no other explanation of Mr Avellion's abstinence and death.

2

The Idealist

HE still used to finger his captain's uniform and wonder how the devil he had got into it without a major interruption of his life. There had been, of course, a sudden rush of unfamiliar incidents, but no break in the continuity of the self and the work which he knew, no chrysalis period of military training. At one moment he had been manager of a fleet of barges on the gentle Severn; at the next he was an army captain running lighters in a Mediterranean aflame with war. A deputy Assistant Director of Transportation they called him. It seemed a long title. He was used to being called the Young Boss. His father was the Old Boss.

And here he was in Piraeus Harbour, emptying into his barges the holds of the freighters which raced up from Alexandria; unloading on the quay or — if the weather were kind — at little ports on the other side of the Corinth Canal; storing and stacking; managing his Greek lightermen with the aid of a foreman who, sober, much resembled his old Severn-side foreman drunk; and commanding his small detachment of military through a sergeant-major who was the recoil mechanism between himself and the Army. The sergeant-major took and distributed the shocks so that the Young Boss — no, Captain Coulter, of course — could go on doing his job without disrupting the still unintelligible organisation of which he was a part.

Sergeant-Major Wrist was, in the eyes of Coulter, a character straight out of Kipling — pliant, resourceful, with as neat and tough a body as if he had polished and brushed it along with his equipment for twenty-five years of morning parades. He had managed to stay alive through one war already— not to speak of several expeditions which he described as picnics— and he freely expressed his intention of staying alive through this one. Coulter liked that. It was a proper old-soldierly way to talk. He felt that Wrist was wasted on a non-combatant job in the docks, and was sure that he must have pulled every possible regimental string to avoid it.

Their life of mere hard work was not, however, likely to continue undisturbed. That morning, April 6, 1941, Hitler had declared war on Greece. It was the end of five uncannily peaceful months while the Greeks fought only Italians, and the base had been free to pour in the seaborne supplies from Egypt. Coulter did not think the Germans were likely to bomb Athens. Their pedantic minds would conceive that, at least, as sheer barbarism. But they were bound to have a shot, instantly, at knocking out the Piraeus.

He was still in his dockside office when the stroke came, alone with the sergeant-major who never objected— especially when they had first had an informal meal together and some drinks— to staying at leisurely work up to any hour of night. There was very little warning. When the sirens screamed, Sergeant-Major Wrist at once enjoined his Captain to take refuge in the concrete shelter beneath the quay. Those, he said, were the Orders. A minute later, when they were at the door of the shelter, the raid began.

Coulter let the sergeant-major pop into the burrow, and himself stayed above ground and watched. This then was war. Flame. Noise. Space geometry of searchlights and tracer. The upward flowering of explosions. The hammering and tinkling and whining of bits of metal. A mind quite arbitrarily prepared to lay long odds that its body stood in empty air between flying objects.

He was fascinated both by the scene and by the fact that his curiosity seemed to be greater than his fear. He had been just too young for the first war, and all his life had been envious of that experience which had destroyed a fifth of his near contemporaries at school. At the age of seventeen he had been conditioned to the prospect of death. Three weeks was the average fighting life of a British infantry subaltern on the western front, and he had been disappointed that he was just too young to take the gamble.

He knew all right that he had been a young fool—it had seemed to him in peace utterly incredible, this desire to immolate oneself for the sake of excitement—and yet, when a second war came along, it appeared that he was merely an older fool. He could perfectly well have been running barges in the unraided Severn instead of a port which—if there were anything in all the military theories he had read—was doomed to absolute destruction.

So this was all. Well, but to endure it for three weeks needed, no doubt, such sustained courage that one might welcome the end foretold by the military actuaries. All the same, it was exhilarating to find—after twenty years of wondering about it—that one wasn't particularly afraid. Coulter was annoyed at himself for this sudden vanity. What were a few bombs compared to forcing oneself to jump out of a trench into the steady, calculated fire of 1917. No. No, this wasn't the real thing.

It was over in ten minutes. A lucky string of bombs had erased the northern block of sheds and set the s.s. *City of Syracuse* on fire. Her crew—those few of them who were on board—had tumbled down the ship's brow and bolted for the dock gates as soon as she was hit. It wasn't surprising. In her holds were two hundred tons of explosives and ammunition. The ship's officers of course would know it, though it was possible that the crew, up to the moment they were ordered to clear out, did not. For the sake of security and to avoid the risk of devastating sabotage in a port where there had been German agents at large till the

118

previous night, her cargo was officially described as mere military stores.

The *City of Syracuse* did not directly concern Coulter's office since she was discharging into the railway trucks alongside, not into lighters; but he had heard of the nature of her cargo and assumed that all the British working in the port were equally well informed. Security seemed to him to limit discussion rather than knowledge.

A naval launch was desperately trying to shift the ship into the outer harbour, but neither man nor rope could exist on her flaming bows, and the launch had not the power to tow her stern foremost. When the stern cable charred and broke, the Navy gave up. Very reasonably, too, thought Coulter.

The sergeant-major took his time in the shelter — and why not, since the all-clear had never sounded? — and missed such excitement as there had been. He now appeared, unruffled, at Coulter's elbow.

'Gone to fetch a tug, I expect, sir,' he said, watching the launch scatter red foam from her bows as she slid away from the *City of Syracuse* into outer darkness.

'Perhaps,' answered Coulter, giving the Navy the benefit of the doubt. 'But the nearest tug is in the naval basin. It'll take her a quarter of an hour to get here, and I think that's just ten minutes too long.'

'She does seem to be burning pretty fierce, sir,' Wrist agreed coolly.

Except for the occasional fountains of flame from the *City of Syracuse*, the docks were at peace under the moon. The tough central core of the northern sheds stood up sheer from a pile of rubble on which the dust was already settling. There were no troops about, for at that hour of night all of them, except the A.A. gunners, were back to their billets in the town. The duty clerks in the port offices were being marched away. The ambulances had cleared up the few wounded who could readily be found, and gone. The Greek fire brigades were presumably fully occupied in the town, for a glow over distant streets showed where another string of bombs had fallen.

As Coulter and Wrist turned to go, a staff car raced up the quay and stopped opposite to them. In it were the Area Commander and his Adjutant, perfectly cool, perfectly dressed. God knew what they hoped to do there! If it came to that, thought Coulter, God knew why he was still there himself! Theirs presumably was a moral duty, but he hadn't any duty whatever. Some of his barges were adrift in the harbour, but he could only let them stay there until the Navy brought a tug.

'Good evening, Coulter,' said the Area Commander. 'Barging in again, I see.'

It was a steady joke, which pleased the Commander very much. Somehow it pleased Coulter, too. It meant, after all, that the Commander recognised him, liked him, knew what he did and appreciated it. And that could stand repetition.

'Anything we can do, sir?' he asked.

'If I were you,' said the Area Commander, 'I should get out of here pretty damn quick. There's nothing any of us can do.'

He left his car and passed a pleasant word with the sergeant-major, even exchanging a casual reminiscence as one old soldier to another. Then he walked off on a tour of the docks to assure himself that there was no man in need of help.

'Well, he isn't taking his own advice, sergeant-major, but we will,' said Coulter, as if it were a foregone conclusion.

He started towards his waiting truck. Wrist pointed to the sliced cube of the northern building, outlined against the burning *City of Spracuse*.

'There was a gun up there, sir,' he remarked. 'I suppose they're all right.'

It seemed to Coulter exceedingly unlikely that the gun crew would have cleared out leaving any of their number alive on top of the building. Still, it was just possible that the whole lot had been hit and forgotten, and that there might be a survivor in no state to climb down.

'Shall we go and see, sir?'

What particularly annoyed Coulter was that he knew just where and when his sergeant-major was likely to be a bit of a fraud. Indeed he doubted if you could become a sergeant-major at all without a keen appreciation of the value of eye-wash. He did not believe for a moment that Wrist would have made his intolerable and officious suggestion if it hadn't been for the presence, somewhere in the docks, of the Area Commander.

But there it was. That was the way an army fought. That was the value of leadership. Even if Wrist did take good care that there was someone to commend his act of gallantry, it only reflected tremendous credit on the Area Commander who had inspired him. Scamps, these old soldiers? Well, if you liked. But, by God, they made the rules of their own game and enough of them had died at it!

The sergeant-major gave an indescribable hitch to his whole person, as if he were about to report to the Almighty that all, including his own well-polished soul, was present and correct. He then stepped out smartly towards the northern sheds. No, thought Coulter, of course he wouldn't run. Running, even forwards, suggested a sense of urgency and panic. That was not the way of the majestically professional British Army.

Captain Coulter found himself unconsciously lagging half a step behind. That wouldn't do at all, and he drew up and paced stride for stride with Wrist. He cursed his lack of any military training, aware as never before that he had only been carried along by observing traditions of which he had heard and read, by listening to the sergeant-major, by a romantic enthusiasm for those unrealised three weeks of youth.

What on earth was an officer expected to do in a case like this? Use his common sense, he supposed. The situation was not, in essence, very different from a pay parade when you followed all the absurd little ceremonies because it was expected of you, because it was that way a soldier liked to work. Alternatively, it was doubtless in his power to order the sergeant-major to drop this folly. Or he could go to ground in any solid cover there might be, and charitably watch Wrist trying to win his D.C.M. There was nobody looking to see what he did himself.

'Oh, blast!' Coulter thought. '*I* am looking.'

He found that he had grumbled the words half aloud, and was startled by his own voice as much as by his superb and unexpected arrogance.

'Sir?' asked the sergeant-major.

'Nothing. What the hell of a lot of bricks there are in four walls!'

They clambered over the rubble of the shed, keeping the mound so far as possible between themselves and the waves of heat from the *City of Syracuse*. To Coulter's right was the line of railway trucks waiting for the cargo they were about—and instantaneously—to receive. For what we are about to receive may the Lord make us truly thankful. Some of them had been loaded that afternoon. No stencilling on the boxes to indicate the contents. Security. Damned soldiers had learned that much if nothing else. At the tail end of the train, where there were neither building nor rubble between sidings and ship, the wood of the trucks was smouldering.

The flames over the *City of Syracuse* had died down. The plates of her upper works were red and the paint was curling off like wood shavings. All of her above the main deck was spurting and glowing. A subsidence or a melting anywhere would drop the furnace into the holds.

The cube of shed left upright was about thirty feet high. It stood because it had been reinforced to take the weight of the concrete gun platform on the roof.

'This will get us up, sergeant-major.'

A long strip of iron railing had been hurled against the trucks. It did not look as if it had fallen from anywhere, but as if it had been preserved on the ground for some calculable event of peacetime—to rail off the crowds at an embarkation of the royal family, or to fence a bit of welcoming garden in front of the customs-house. They upended the railing with some difficulty and leaned it against the wall for a ladder.

The heat of the burning ship seared eyes and face as Coulter looked over the top. On the platform was the gun, pointing at the scorched foremast of the *City of Syracuse* and partly wrenched from its mountings. There were two great-coats, forming a vaguely human-shaped pile which aroused and disappointed the gallant zeal of the sergeant-major. There were the long slender Bofors shells ready arranged to be seized by their partners in the complicated dance of loading. The place was deserted. Well, what else could you expect? The officer in charge would have ensured—and of that Coulter had all along been certain—that none of his men was left up there alive.

'Time we were going, sergeant-major,' he said irritably.

'We'll just have a look-round in the rubble, sir.'

'All right. It's possible of course.'

And he dutifully searched the hollows and dark corners where one of the gunners might have been blown. By this time he had become such a fatalist that he was jesting with the sergeant-major. To himself he said: chum, you won't know a damn thing about it if the ship goes up, so why worry?

He clung to that unreasonably comforting thought until

such time as Sergeant-Major Wrist decided that honour was at last satisfied.

Coulter offered him a cigarette, and walked back to his truck which was parked outside the port offices. He could have run now with a clear conscience, but it did not seem worth while. He was neither courageous nor cowardly; he was just empty.

As they drove out of the dock gates, he said to the sergeant-major:

'Well, Mr Wrist, if there are many chaps like you among the old regulars, I suppose we might win the war after all.'

'Thank you, sir,' replied the sergeant-major complacently. 'There's one thing we're taught early, if I may say so, sir, and that's our duty to look after the men, sir.'

They had gone half a mile from the docks when the *City of Syracuse* blew up. The blast cut a swathe through the houses packed on the hill above the port, but on the open sea front, along which they were driving, buildings merely spilled all their windows on to the pavement as neatly as if a stage set had fallen flat. Then a vast bulk, blacker than the night, swooped out of the sky before them and hurled up a water-like spout of trees, earth and grass as it plunged into a little public park at the cross-roads.

'Gawd, what was that?' the sergeant-major yelled.

'Must be the whole forepart of the *City of Syracuse*,' Coulter answered, fascinated by such a colossal show of violence.

The bows and forecastle had pitched right way up, and immediately looked as if they had been on the site for years—a fitting decoration for the park of a seafaring people.

'Gawd!' exclaimed the horrified sergeant-major again. 'She must have been full of ammo, and me muckin' about alongside like a bleedin' good Samaritan!'

'But I thought you—' Coulter began, and stopped.

Well, what was the use of saying that he thought Wrist

124

knew, that he never dreamed he didn't know? However he put it, it would inevitably look like boasting. And he was sure — indeed he well remembered — that any unnecessary dwelling upon danger had not been considered a soldierly virtue by that lost generation whom he could never hope to equal.

3

The Hut

THERE was a matter which they did not at first discuss, those two; for it was not until repeated doses of gin had deadened sensitivity that they were able to look each other in the eyes without uneasiness. Meanwhile their store of common memories, past misadventures that were always good for a laugh whenever two ex-security officers met, was rich enough to support unthinking conversation. Their enigmatic trade had been far fuller of the comic than of inhumanity. It was their job to suspect, but they were thankful when — with perhaps one yearly grim exception — their suspicions were proved lamentably wrong.

'Fayze was a bastard,' said the older man suddenly.

'He was. But I can't say he bothers me at this distance.'

Virian meant to say '*it* bothers,' but couldn't quite manage the word. The other, however, understood him.

'No. Nor me. But it did. Spoilt my sleep for a bit. I don't mind saying so now. How did you — well, get on afterwards?'

'Sat on it,' answered Virian non-committally.

He was obviously a man with a fine tradition of mental discipline behind him. His thin, dark face was mellow, and implied that he drew his strength from knowledge of human limitations and acceptance of human tragedy. He might have been twenty-five or so at the beginning of the war, that far-off period of which the two were talking, and a promising officer — a shade indecisive, perhaps, but slow to blame and much beloved by his men.

Medlock, the older man, was of a more plebeian type, with no more moulding about his face than the accidental contours of a chunk of rock. The hammer of fate could

126

smash him into smaller pieces than Virian, and he knew it. He was contented, however, to be as he was, and hadn't much use for complications. He was convinced — or once had been — of his own essential decency.

'I didn't like it,' he muttered. 'Didn't like it at all. I'd been a regular sergeant-major and just got my commission, you see.'

'That was why you didn't protest?' Virian asked.

'What about yourself?' Medlock retorted, catching the irony. 'And why didn't *you?*'

'Oh, obedience,' answered the other easily. 'As an amateur soldier I felt I had to do what I was told. It's a bit hard to analyse. The enemy outclassed us in skill and material. Well, all that was left in which we could equal him was an obstinate Teutonic obedience. His not to reason why, his but to do and die. A good many of us felt like that. You, as an old soldier, were far too sensible to find romance in mere obedience any longer.'

'Hell of a thing to do,' grumbled the ex-sergeant-major. 'Order us to go out and shoot a civilian.'

'They only asked us to see that he *was* shot,' Virian corrected him.

'Wouldn't do you much good to tell that to the judge! We were present at a murder. Accessories. You get hung just the same.'

They began to go through the happenings of that day all over again, proper old soldiers (or old murderers) recalling every foot of the terrain, every hour of agony and disapproval since they had emerged from Colonel Fayze's secretive office with set faces and a feeling that their integrity, their little personal shares in Christendom and civilization had been outraged.

The newly-commissioned sergeant-major had been the more horrified of the two. He was accustomed to see his instructions in black and white before he paid serious attention to them. War had to be orderly, and not for nothing was his temple called the orderly room. He claimed now, ten years later, that he had been on the verge of refusal, that he hadn't seen any necessity for violence at all.

'You did. You saw it,' Virian insisted. 'Don't make things worse for your conscience than they need be. It had to be done. What was the name of that fat crook we bumped off?'

'God, you don't have to put it like that!'

'But what the devil *was* his name?'

'I don't remember,' Medlock answered impatiently.

'Nor do I. Revealing, isn't it? Gallant memory, always in the breach, always protecting us from night starvation! Well, it was some very common French name, so let's call him M. Dupont.

'Dupont had betrayed—and don't you forget *that!*—a whole honeycomb of French Resistance cells. As a direct result, the Gestapo shot twenty-seven men and women, and sent Dupont to Spain for his own safety. Fayze's organization kidnapped him there, and brought him to England in a submarine chaser. You knew that. And then they dressed him up in uniform and put him in a military prison as if he were an allied soldier being held for suspected espionage.

'All very neat work! Secret service stuff right out of the books! But Fayze and the fool who did his dirty jobs in Spain hadn't worked out what was to happen next. They couldn't bring Dupont to trial because he hadn't committed any offence under English law. And they couldn't intern him because at that period in the war there wasn't any quiet spot where no questions at all were asked. So they had to get rid of him, and persuade the Free French to do the shooting. I don't wonder you forget why Dupont's death was necessary. He was a sacrifice to inefficiency. But inefficiency is a much more potent factor in war than logic.'

'Do you remember that dam' tough with the blood on his boots whom they sent with us?' asked Medlock with a movement of the shoulders that had been turned from a shiver into a shrug.

The dam' tough had been the only man in the party who really looked as if he had been employed on this sort of mission before. A mysterious commando lad. At least they supposed he was commando, or from someone's private army—though he wore a gunner's badges on his neat, new battledress. He never said a word about himself, and asked no questions. The uniform, which lacked the individuality given by daily use, made it difficult to guess what he had been in civil life. He had a simple, unimaginative face, knocked about a bit by boxing or some other violent exercise, and it was firmly set to the job in hand. Virian and Medlock had been glad that they were accompanied by an apparent professional to whom as much as possible might be left.

They knew him only by the assumed name of Smith, and it was he who drove the car—a big, black saloon with two extra seats in the back. There were five of them altogether in the car when they went to fetch M. Dupont; Virian, Medlock and two Free French. One of the Frenchmen, who was the—well, it was understood that he had a personal score to settle with M. Dupont—was a small, sad, determined man in civilian clothes; the other, in uniform, was very much an officer of the French regular army. He was of their own sort, keyed up to the inevitable sense of duty, and with distaste clearly mapped upon his humane and honourable countenance.

They drove to the prison. Medlock and Virian signed for the body of M. Dupont, who was officially being held as a doubtful Free French soldier until his antecedents could be investigated. Dupont had gladly accepted and lived up to this fiction. He was clever enough to realize that the longer he was kept, the harder it would be to dispose of him.

When he was in the car, Dupont's nerve began to fail. He asked Virian hesitatingly what their intentions were. They had the answer ready for that. Dupont must be reassured. If he were to put his head out of the window and yell for help, the law of England would automatically be on his side, war or no war. Keep him quiet till the end — those were Virian's and Medlock's orders.

Virian told M. Dupont that he was being handed over to his compatriots: that they were driving to a rendezvous out in open country where a Free French detachment would take charge of him. This made Dupont less apprehensive. He could have little doubt what his own countrymen would do to him sooner or later, but he was also very well aware that, being good Frenchmen, they would have to invent a show of legality — which would be difficult when they were guests in a country with a tender conscience. A formal handing over meant, for a time, reprieve.

M. Dupont sat on the back seat between Virian and the French major. Facing them, on one of the extra seats, was the sad, determined personage, looking determinedly out of the window. In front were Medlock and the uncommunicative Smith. Dupont and Virian kept up a polite and desultory conversation.

'Never been able to understand, I haven't,' said Medlock, 'how you could sit there chatting away. In French, too,' he added, as if an assassin's proper language should be English.

'It was easier than sitting grim, and saying nothing,' Virian explained. 'And Dupont helped. He was a very civilised creature. He didn't like social embarrassment. Good Lord, if I hadn't known his record, I should have put him down as just a bland, fat Frenchman! All for peace and decent living, he was. That was probably what made him take the Vichy side — that and money.'

They drove away over the sweep of the Wiltshire Downs in the direction of Bath. It was a golden day of late autumn, with just enough wind to ripple the massed spearheads of dying grass and to check the high-hovering clouds from ever settling on the sun. M. Dupont, released from the discipline and scrubbing soap of a military prison, was enchanted, and lavished courteous praise upon the English countryside. It reminded him, he said, of Picardy.

Their destination was a disused mine-shaft with a tumbledown building above it. Colonel Fayze had given them the map reference, assuring them that Smith had visited the spot already and that the building was unlocked. Two of the planks which covered and completely hid the mouth of the shaft had been loosened, said Fayze with an obscene wink, and could be lifted out. He had shown pride—a legitimate pride from the point of view of his office chair—in the excellence of his arrangements. The disposal of Dupont on paper had had his personal attention.

After an hour's run, Smith stopped the car below the mine-shaft. Nothing was to be seen but an isolated hut of timber and corrugated iron, with a strong door from which the padlock had recently been wrenched loose; no derrick or abandoned machinery revealed the purpose of the building and the dark emptiness beneath the floor. Fayze had well chosen his theatre for the operation. There was no need for any bumping through country lanes into a suspicious remoteness, or for scrambling on foot through dense woods with a reluctant victim. The hut was within fifty yards of a main road. A car full of men could stop on the verge for a short while without arousing uneasiness in Dupont or other curious but less essentially interested travellers.

The only disadvantage was the frequent passing of traffic on the road which ran, level and clear, for a hundred yards past the hut and a little below it. At one end of the straight was a blind hill, and at the other a corner. To ensure privacy, both those points would have to be watched.

Dupont was left in the car with Smith, while the four

others got out for consultation at a decent distance.

'If Medlock stays at the corner,' said Virian, 'and I go to the top of the hill, we shall be able to signal to you when the road is empty.'

The French major appeared suddenly forlorn, his face that of a man who had known all along that he was an unreasoning optimist.

'I thought that you . . .' he began.

'No,' Virian answered firmly. 'My instructions are just to keep the ring. It was definitely understood that you . . .'

'I could not myself . . . my honour as an officer . . .'

'Naturally, *mon commandant*,' Virian replied, and looked questioningly at the other, so sad and wirily small and determined.

'I have had my orders,' that second Frenchman murmured, 'to accord to M. Dupont the justice he has so richly merited. I shall obey. I beg you to believe that I do not say it with pleasure. But'—he sought their eyes with a simple honesty that, in the circumstances, was monstrous—'he is a heavy man, and I shall need some help.'

'This Smith,' Medlock suggested. 'The colonel said he was to make himself useful.'

True, Fayze had airily assured them that the mysterious driver was ready to do whatever he was told; but Virian was unwilling to force such responsibility upon any human being till there was some evidence of a real lack of sensitivity.

'I'll get hold of him and see what he says, if you'll stand by the car, Medlock, and keep an eye on Dupont.'

He took Smith a little apart, and asked him what exactly his orders were.

'To assist you in every possible way, sir,' Smith answered.

Virian was uneasy. There was a light in the young eyes which looked uncommonly like hero worship. Yet Smith's expression was tough and set. The very smoothness of the skin hid emotion more absolutely than the mobile lines of an older face.

'You understand, of course, just exactly what the job is?'

'I did the reccy with the colonel,' Smith assured him.

He produced the word 'reccy' with a certain pride, which suggested to Virian that he had not been long in the army. Well, God knew what some of these young commando chaps, quickly, violently trained, must have seen and done already!

'Then will you go up with that gentleman and the prisoner to the mine-shaft? He, of course, is going to—to take the necessary steps. And, look here, Smith, refuse if you want to! This is no part of your duty as a soldier.'

'I understand that, sir.'

There wasn't any shaking that firm professional. His attitude was so matter-of-fact that Virian began to doubt the value of his own scruples. He gave full credit to Fayze for choosing a murderer's mate whose cold-blooded morale was an example to them all.

They took Dupont out of the car. The polite smile with which he had brightened his formal conversation was fixed at half its full extent. He looked at them, his eyes searching each face in turn with the uneasy instinct of an animal at the shambles gate.

The French major reassured him with deliberate ambiguity.

'This is the rendezvous,' he said. 'It is here that you will shortly meet certain Free Frenchmen.'

Dupont again anxiously reviewed the faces. What he saw relieved him—for their orders were to keep him quiet, and even their eyes were obedient. His smile returned to its natural mobility. Two big drops of sweat trickled down his fat cheeks, shaved to a pig-like smoothness for the morning inspection of his person and his cell.

Smith, Dupont and the executioner walked up over the

grass towards the hut. The French major remained by the car, torturing a cigarette between his fingers. Medlock went to the curve of the road; Virian to the top of the hill. So long as both held their hands in their pockets, the road was clear. When their hands were exposed, it was a sign that traffic was approaching. Smith stood by the door of the hut, relaying their gestures to the interior.

Virian could see a quarter of a mile of empty road. He put his hands in his pockets, dismissing quickly a thought of Roman thumbs. On a distant slope was a small convoy moving down towards him, but the job would be over by the time it arrived.

Medlock, at his end, kept his hands very plainly in sight. A baker's van came round the corner, along the straight and up the hill past Virian—who now also revealed his hands, for the approaching convoy was too close. A motor cycle, a truck and six heavy lorries bumbled interminably past at regulation intervals and twenty miles an hour, adding to Dupont's store three more minutes of October noon.

Medlock put his hands in his pockets. Virian waited for a far-away car, and damned the wheels that flashed in the sunlight for not turning more slowly. They passed, and he found his hands playing noisily with the coins in one pocket and keys in the other. He waited for the shot. It didn't come. He was furiously angry. What were they doing inside the hut? After all this trouble! Why couldn't they get on?

Ten minutes went by with no movement on the road but the lumbering, swift shadow of a carrion crow impatient to return to his perch. Then Medlock's hands came out with a gesture as if he were flinging at the hut the contents of his pockets. An oldish man, instantly recognizable as a retired colonel or general, deprived—and no doubt uncomplainingly—of petrol, drove round the corner in a dog-cart with his two little grand-daughters. He called in cheerful comradeship that it was a lovely day. Bitterly, Virian put him down as a merciful and honourable man. He could afford those virtues in the simpler wars that he had known.

Again both ends of the road were clear for long minutes, and again there was no shot. Medlock came striding back from his corner, his face that of a sergeant-major who was about to tell his paraded and incompetent squad exactly what he thought of it. Virian, too, hastened back to the car in fear lest his companion should hurl some blunt protest or, worse still, some unfeeling denial of protest, into so delicate an occupation.

'Man doesn't know his job!' Medlock stormed.

'Would you expect him to?' retorted Virian.

The French major at the car turned on them, illogically angry as themselves. Some cutting irony at the expense of the English came beautifully shaped from his lips and died away as he became conscious of the brutal absurdity of any blame.

While they were staring at the hut, a melancholy procession came down the hill towards them—Dupont, Smith and the Frenchman, more sad than ever. Even Dupont looked disappointed. Very likely, he was. The Free French detachment, the larger public among which he would, for a little while, be safe, had not turned up.

Dupont was again left with Fayze's tame tough, while the other four went aside.

'Couldn't Smith relay the signals to you?' Virian asked.

'Yes,' the French civilian replied. 'Yes.'

'Well, then? Well then, for God's sake?' the major demanded.

'The hut is too small. I cannot get behind him. Perhaps he will not let me get behind him. And to draw the pistol before his eyes—no, I cannot do it.'

'Well, we daren't hang about here any longer,' said Virian. 'Someone may get inquisitive, and start watching us. We had better drive off now and come back later.'

The party packed into the car, still unexpectedly six.

Dupont conversed with polite, tacit sympathy, identifying himself with the unknown derangement of plans which all had suffered. He behaved as if he were an embarrassing but useful prisoner—a double agent, for example, about to be sent off on some dangerous journey. He may even have persuaded himself that such a destiny was possible.

He addressed himself particularly to the French civilian, perhaps trying to allay his own suspicions. Dupont was a type to be successful, Virian decided, as minor business man or major traitor, for he had an insistent cunning. He talked and talked, closely watching with eyes that held a decent pretence of geniality the impact of his words. The failure in the hut was very understandable. Dupont was tiresome; Dupont's fat face was that of a crook; but it was impossible to treat him with anything but courtesy. To draw a gun before his face was a task as awkward as to get him out of the office without giving him a small order.

Smith had been pale and self-controlled when he returned from the hut. He now returned to his puzzling and case hardened temperament. He asked sharply where he was to go.

Well, where? Just a drive. Out for a drive. A pleasant occupation for a family on Sunday afternoon. Such aimlessness was intolerable. An order had to be given, some destination found.

'Oh, stop at the first pub when we're off the downs,' Virian replied, his voice military and exasperated.

It was a considerable place, more of a roadhouse than a pub, which had no doubt been gay enough before the war with thirsty and fast-driving youth. Now, however, the long lounge was vacant and frustrated of purpose. Fireplace and imitation beams had been excitably decorated with paper flags and regimental badges. All this dust-laden patriotism, exposed to sunlight, had the depressing unreality of a night-club on the morning after. Smith, Dupont and the Frenchman sat down at once and together, as if bound by a hard, common experience, in a corner of the room.

'I won't drink with him,' Medlock whispered. 'God damn it, there are limits!'

Virian carried three drinks to Dupont's table, and himself remained with Medlock and the French major at the bar. For once he found himself in wholehearted sympathy with Medlock. A curious atavism, to refuse a drink with a man you were about to kill. He couldn't remember that there was any such law of hospitality in the Christian religion; it was wholly pagan—a rule of Viking hovel or Arab tent. Where the devil, he wondered, had he inherited it? And why should Medlock observe it, too?

The French major seemed also unwilling to join Dupont, either from the same scruples or because he was busy disassociating himself from the whole affair and its mismanagement. The three of them drifted through the door to a bench on the clean stone flags outside. After a while the other Frenchman joined them, confidently leaving Smith along with Dupont.

'I must offer my excuses,' he said. 'I did not anticipate—'

Here, away from the victim, his character no longer appeared of any extraordinary determination. He admitted nothing (and one could hardly put the direct question), but plainly for him as for them this was a first experience.

'Look here!' Virian exclaimed, suddenly as compassionate for the civilian as for Dupont. 'I am prepared to go back and report that this can't be done.'

'But, alas, it must be done.'

'Why? We can keep the blighter in prison for you. If they can't find a way of holding him, it's their business to think of one. What do you say, sir?' he asked the French major.

'Me? I have not the right to interfere. It is your service

which took Dupont, and your service which had requested us to get rid of him. Sooner or later our duty as Frenchmen must be done, but I admit I should prefer it to be by due process of law.'

So, even to him, there was no point in immediate punishment. There was a more complex, far more insistent motive for Dupont's death than mere justice. Fayze and his precious colleague in Spain were terrified lest their too impulsive act should become known to the enemy, with whom they had a rogues' agreement that kidnapping and assassination were barred. Such unsporting practices would have interfered with the daily game of collecting information. The end of all fun and promotion — like placing a bomb on a football field. Fayze didn't at all want his agents kidnapped by way of retaliation; so Dupont could never be allowed to mix with other internees, to appear on any list, to write a letter or answer a question. He had to vanish for good.

It was the uncleanness of this necessity which revolted Virian. For this, for the sake of what in the end was nothing but inefficiency, he and Medlock and young Smith — it was the youth of Smith which appalled him, whether or not the man was callous — were to be turned into murderers.

'What about our orders?' Medlock asked.

'Damn our orders! If we report that the thing is too risky, they must accept our opinion. I'm not saying that Dupont doesn't deserve to be shot. I'm saying that we can't take the responsibility.'

'That is between you and your superiors,' the French major remarked unhelpfully.

'And mercy — doesn't that come in?'

'One can have too many scruples,' added the other Frenchman, his voice bitter with longing for the simplicities of peace.

He, at least, had no doubt that Dupont's sentence was just. He had become more deeply obsessed than they by the demands of war and civil war, so that in his eyes this killing served a spiritual purpose which transcended its vileness. It was only the incapacity of his own hand which tormented him.

'Well, we've got them. So why not admit it? We hate this. We can't go on expecting you to do it, and looking the other way. We can't go on testing Smith to breaking point by making him drink with Dupont just as if the man weren't a ghost come back from the grave. Why not admit that we do have scruples and take the brute back to prison?'

Virian let himself go. A limited and painful eloquence. It couldn't be for the defence, since his client—they all acknowledged it—was guilty; it couldn't even be for miti-gation of sentence, since that sentence, though highly irre-gular, though the motives behind it stank to heaven, was just. No, it seemed to him in retrospect that he had preached the virtue of mercy in futile abstract, as any poet or parson.

'The defeated cannot afford mercy,' cried the tortured executioner.

It was astonishing that a man could pronounce so neat and closed a phrase with such emotion. Evidently it was the profession of faith with which he comforted his soul— and unanswerable by citizens of a nation which did not for a moment believe itself to have been defeated.

Virian got up—it would do no harm to let the leaven of mercy work in his absence—and went into the lounge to look after Smith. His conscience was raw on every surface.

Smith was playing shove ha'penny with Dupont, like an old, experienced warder in the condemned cell.

'All right?' Virian asked. 'How are your glasses?'

'Don't mind if we do, sir'.

Virian went over to the bar and ordered two stiff gins. He beckoned to Smith to join him.

'Would you like to go outside for a breath of air?' he asked.

'I'm all right, sir,' Smith answered, with a strong, impatient accent on the 'right'.

Hidden in the impenetrable sternness of youth he carried the drinks away to his corner, and resumed his game with Dupont. Virian returned to the others, telling himself that he was the only man among them who was not fit to be a soldier.

The French civilian, with the quick sympathy of his race for emotion, put a friendly hand on the Englishman's shoulder and said:

'I cannot permit Dupont to live. The responsibility is mine.'

'But what do you suggest?' Virian asked harshly. 'Are we to go back to that damned mine-shaft?'

'No. Somewhere else, I beg you.'

'I can't take you anywhere else. My superiors have worked this out very well. I'll say that for them at least.'

'In the hut I cannot — arrange it.'

'But that is only what I am saying,' Virian insisted. 'It can't be done — for the reason that it's humanly impossible for us.'

'You would report that?' asked the French major.

'Certainly. Without hesitation.'

'We should appear to be cowards.'

Medlock gave a grunt of scorn. As an old professional soldier, he had no objection to appearing a coward so long as the situation called for cowardice. Only amateurs and Latins bothered about appearances.

'And who the hell cares?' he said.

'Alas, it must be done,' repeated the civilian.

'But you've just said it can't be done.' Virian almost shouted.

'I say the hut is too small,' the other insisted. 'You are slow. You wait for traffic. I wait for you. And then by that time Dupont is not where I want him. I say that I cannot' — and his voice, though it was low, vibrated with

140

agony—'I cannot raise the pistol before his eyes.'

It was the note which Virian had already heard, for a single instant, in Smith's voice also. Through the door he could see him still playing his forced and melancholy shove-ha'penny with Dupont. The situation, futile and mismanaged, was intolerable to all of them. They were like children who had broken the back of an animal by brutal thoughtlessness and then were without courage to put it out of pain—and he himself the worst of them.

This couldn't go on. Mercy. No mercy. It can't be done. It must be done. That civilian and Smith had first call on any mercy. If this infirmity of purpose went on much longer, one of them would hysterically free Dupont, or take him out and shoot him before the eyes of some astonished farm labourer.

'Damn Fayze! Damn his precautions!' he cried. 'Listen! We get out of the car. You walk at once up to the hut with Dupont in front of you and Smith behind you. Medlock and I go to our posts on the road. We shall all arrive at about the same time. Unless there is traffic right on top of us, we shall give no signal. As soon as Dupont is over the threshold—do it! He'll have his back to you, and he will never know a thing.'

The decision was instantly and gratefully accepted. Virian had fought for Dupont's life and Virian had condemned him to death. He himself was well aware of what he had done. Inconsistency be damned! If one couldn't have heaven, then hell was preferable to chaos.

'Well, Dupont,' he said, breaking up the shove-ha' penny game, 'let's have another shot at it.'

The sound of his own voice in that unfortunate phrase, which he had cheerfully pronounced without thinking, made him wince and turn away.

Dupont hoped politely that the luck would be better, ingratiating himself like a circus pig that had been trained to smile. He left the board, and took down his coat and hat.

He had plainly decided that for this day at least he had nothing to fear. The drinks, the genial delay and the resolute acting of his companion had put him at ease.

As Dupont heaved at his tight overcoat, Virian caught Smith's questioning eye and beckoned to him to remain behind for a moment.

'Same positions, but it will be done through the back of the neck the moment he steps into the hut. A few seconds, and all over.'

Smith ran his tongue round his lips, and seemed about to speak. There was no longer any light of adventure in his sturdy, blue eyes; they had matured, as if searching deeply, far down beyond the presumed limit of his vision, into probable consequences.

'Yes? What is it?' Virian asked, trying to put into his smile the eagerness which he dared not show in his voice.

'O.K., sir,' said Smith.

He drove the party back to the mine-shaft. The journey had the nightmare quality of life in reverse. Pub to lowland hedges, to grey villages under the downs, to clean sweep of hill turf, to the crest of the road and first glimpse of the hut — all the way back, inevitably, to the hated beginning that should have been left for ever.

The French civilian told Dupont to get out and walk up to the hut. He himself followed a pace or two behind, and Smith strolled purposefully after.

Medlock hurried to the curve of the road; Virian up the blind hill. There was a car approaching which would be on them in twenty seconds. He made no signal. That was time enough if all went smoothly.

He looked round. Dupont was just entering the door of the hut. He saw the Frenchman's pistol sweep up in a curve and cross the threshold alone, as if it were some tenuous body independent of those before and behind. The shot, too, was thin and strained. Louder and more final was the double thud of planks thrown back into place. When the car passed, Smith and the French civilian were already walking down the hill.

On the way home they all talked very heartily. Someone laughed, and there was a sudden silence. After that, they all laughed if there were reasonable excuse. Smith put his bravado into his driving. It was brutal. He didn't seem to care whether they ever reached London or not.

'God, he put the wind up me!' Medlock said to Virian, obsessed by his companion of ten years before. 'And that blood on his boots—'

Smith hadn't noticed the blood. He had only heard it when he lifted Dupont's shoulders. They made him get out and wash it off in a stream.

'God, he was a tough, and no mistake!' Medlock persisted. 'I don't mind telling you—he used to chase me around in my dreams.'

'He said the same of you,' Virian answered.

'Eh? What do you mean? What do you mean? I thought you didn't know him.'

'No, I didn't know him. But I saw a letter of his.'

'He wrote about me?' Medlock barked indignantly.

'About you . . . and me . . . and especially Fayze. Smith was just one of his civilian clerks. Temporarily unfit for general service, worshipping his boss and longing to work for him on a real secret mission. Fayze wasn't the man to lose a chance like that; so he used him, and put him into uniform for the job. He told Smith that it was a trial trip, that if he had the nerve to *assist us in every way* . . '

Medlock put down his drink and retched.

'That bastard Fayze!' he shouted.

'Yes. But, if it's any comfort to you, in *his* dreams there are two of them to chase him around. Smith killed himself a week later. It was his letter to his parents that I saw. Fayze got it before the police. I need hardly tell you that it went no further.'

4

The Battle of Mussolini

TIME had dealt fairly kindly with both of them, thickening the loose limbs once burnt and slendered by desert sun but leaving them their fine-drawn regard for duty and each other. War was still a vividly remembered way of life, though now being recorded by historians too young to have experienced it. They had the facts right, Tarmer said, but not the day-to-day feel of them.

The old friend with whom he was lunching—and had once lunched, if you could call it that, every day for two oppressive years—received this remark with one of his personal silences as if a fuse were slowly burning down into sensitivity.

'A chap in the paper,' Bill Avory exploded at last, 'was actually complaining that nobody ever entertained the public with a good story of an escape from an Italian prisoner-of-war camp.'

'There were mass escapes when Italy packed up. A lot of fellows got clear away as we did.'

'Before that, he meant. He said that an officer's duty to escape had been less obvious in the casual climate of Italy than when subjected to the melancholy emptiness of German discipline.'

The fact that Avory exactly remembered the precious and exasperating phrase proved that it cut, and that he found truth enough in the slander to spoil the image which two prosperous, middle-aged citizens conceived of their adventurous youth.

'I wonder if it wasn't far harder to escape in Italy,' Tarmer suggested.

Avory insisted that it couldn't have been. There was no denying that the climate had been casual—so casual that a monk had been readily allowed to come into the camp for cocoa, and there had been goats in the outer perimeter.

'It seems absurd that we couldn't just walk out,' he said.

It did, in retrospect. Even Tarmer, whose conscience was far tougher than his friend's, felt a shade of guilt as he remembered the failure of tunnels, of impersonations, of attempts to stow away in ration carts. On the face of it, both of them were examples of the lack of enterprise which that young critic of war on paper had mentioned. Prisoners in Germany did seem to have been more ruthlessly determined.

But Italians had more imagination than Germans and were less bound by routine. It had been impossible to calculate in advance where any of the guards would be idling at any given time. If you laid plans to take advantage of the usual genial but quite effective chaos, you would hit a night when discipline was of cold, Teutonic standard; and if you timed exactly . . .

'We could never time exactly,' he reminded Avory. 'We had to work out an average.'

And even when they had averaged for week after week the guard changes, the movements of the Ditch Patrol, the interludes when illicit litres of wine were hoisted up by string to the five watch-towers, they would find all their ingenious calculations dislocated because Colonel Colonna's wife was giving a party and in need of orderlies.

The Colonel—that flamboyant old chevalier of the Mediterranean who commanded the camp—undoubtedly would have liked to invite all his prisoners, accepting their parole in the politest manner of the eighteenth century. He deplored the military honour of the twentieth which compelled them to make nuisances of themselves to him and his government.

'Your journalist sounds like that pompous ass, Fantle,' Tarmer protested. 'He always made escape sound easy, too.'

Wing-Commander Fantle had been the Senior British

Officer. He took his responsibilities so seriously that he had no time for manners. Nothing ever prevented him from saying what he chose to his fellow prisoners, but to Colonel Colonna he could only speak through an interpreter. He had therefore chosen Captain Tarmer to be his adjutant in preference to more submissive officers. Tarmer could translate his imperial protests into fluent Italian.

Fantle's sole concern with Europe had been to drop explosives on it — useful enough at the time, but leading to contempt for the languages spoken underneath. Thus it was easy to maintain a cordial atmosphere in spite of him. When the Senior British Officer started off a protest with: *Tell that dam' organ-grinder*, Tarmer had been able to insert some compliments and a proper respect for rank. Translating the other way round — for the Commandant's interpreter spoke Italian-American which Fantle wilfully pretended he could not understand — it delighted him to make Colonna sound terse, cool and British.

When either of them accused him of making sentences too long or too short, he sold the myth that it was impossible to be polite in English or precise in Italian. Since eyes could express themselves without any interpreter he had no hope of persuading the Commander and the Senior British Officer to like each other, but at least he ensured as much tolerance as could be expected from two different animals separated by the bars of the cage.

'It may have been my fault that we couldn't work up enough resentment,' Tarmer said.

'You couldn't help it! In a place like Medina Fort one was forced to have some military manners.'

It was a little gem of seventeenth-century fortification — nothing but a museum piece until it occurred to some imaginative Fascist official that a stronghold designed to keep the enemy out would be equally effective to keep him in.

The heart of the fortress where the prisoners were

confined — housed partly in huts, partly in the renovated and white-washed quarters of old blue-and-gold artillery-men — was a blunt-angled pentagon measuring about three hunded yards across. Formally delimiting this area was an inner perimeter of low wire. A prisoner who stepped over or vaulted the wire could officially be shot at. He never was. The Italians, with their sound grasp of essentials, realized that the momentary infringement was not worth the trouble of cleaning a rifle.

They could afford to be generous. Beyond this inner perimeter a stone glacis sloped down to the broad, green ditch around the fort. The far bank of the ditch was a thirty-foot sheer wall, topped by a further fifteen feet of heavy wire fence. The prisoners had at last been forced to admit that the smooth, well-fitted ashlars of the wall were unclimbable.

'Anything is climbable,' said Bill Avory, still smarting from the accusation made by his older self against his younger self.

'But not in a hurry,' Tarmer replied.

He remembered the ropes, pitons and ladders which they had ingeniously made. Time to use them, however, could not be fabricated. The whole circuit was commanded by five watch-towers, one near each angle. At night the great ditch was flood-lit from the towers. An escaping prisoner had as much chance as an actor on a stage of avoiding interested — almost friendly — observation.

Bill Avory had been convinced that the only way to get out was by the gate, nonchalantly strolling past the guards at the barrier, over the seventeenth-century bridge and across the barrack square of the garrison. He was very nearly successful, disguised as the monk who came in for cocoa; but the Italians had guessed somebody would try that one. They were so delighted to have foreseen every detail of Lieutenant Avory's plan that they returned him to the cage in fairly comradely fashion and with snatches of song. Colonel Colonna was bound to punish, but saw to it that bread-and-water and solitary confinement meant wine-and-rolls and a card party in the afternoon. Cavalry panache appealed to him. He was fascinated by the cherry trousers of the 11th Hussars which Bill still wore, even under his home-made cassock.

As soon as three goats were turned loose in the fort ditch, all plans for escape immediately took this new factor into consideration. During the day the animals were free to browse where they pleased; at night they were penned under the bridge. Inevitably they became pets. The convention which prohibited the crossing of the inner wire was being continually violated.

Colonel Colonna, very bothered lest his orders to shoot might possibly be obeyed, protested politely to the Senior British Officer. Fantle retorted that the wire ought to be put in reasonable repair, thus preventing officers from crossing it to feed the goats or to retrieve articles of clothing which the goats were eating. To this the Commandant replied that it was unsoldierly to use the wire as a washing-line.

Tarmer thought so, too. He was a Guards Officer, and his training occasionally overwhelmed him. He therefore translated the bit about the washing-line correctly. The Senior British Officer snorted that the Commandant wouldn't know a soldier if he saw one. Tarmer, pulling himself together, interpreted this as a mere harmless comment that gentlemen in captivity could not be expected to keep up the high sartorial standard of Italian officers. Colonel Colonna at once sympathized, shook hands all round and allowed a manly tear of pity to sparkle for a moment in his eye.

Over-petting was thereupon reduced; but the habits, characters and potentialities of the three nanny-goats were recorded by the escaping clubs with the devotion of psycho-analysts. The camp had time for patience, and one could never say that any scientific study was wholly useless.

The goats were of marked individuality. Each reflected its upbringing — or at least seemed to do so when scrutinized by rampant imaginations. Tecla belonged to the Commandant's wife; she was black, supercilious and inclined to bleat at the harsh necessities of her life. Lucia was a gentle, modest job in brown and white, owned by a neighbouring priory. Beatrice, who belonged to the camp doctor, was pure white but a liberal; she disliked the Church and the Military.

Fra Giuseppe — the monk who came in for cocoa — used to milk all three. Indeed it was almost certainly he who had conceived the economical thought of pasturing goats in the green ditch. When attending to Lucia and Tecla he always looked round to see that Beatrice was fully occupied. Her horns were slightly deformed; when her head was lowered, they pointed forwards. She tended to be attracted by any bent backside clothed in black, whether cassock or breeches.

'Fantle used to swear that the anti-Fascists were always ready to help us,' Avory said.

'Like hell they were! We never saw an anti-Fascist except the doctor.'

A genial and comforting soul! But it would have been absurd to ask him for help in an escape. He would have replied at once, with sound common sense, that they were much better off where they were than wandering round the countryside.

'Even Mussolini wasn't anti-Fascist,' Tarmer went on. 'He was just pro-British.'

So far as one could judge the political opinions of a goat, that was the literal truth. Mussolini's pro-British sympathies were obvious from the day he was introduced, black, weighty and gambolling with anticipation, into the fort ditch for the sake of roast kid and the future of the milk supply.

The prisoners at once christened him Mussolini, and the name stuck. Their guards, watching with approval the potency and cavortings of the animal, failed to see any grave insult to their Head of State. Disrespect there might be, but they themselves were far from reverent—though showing more subtlety than could be expected of the enemy.

'Just imagine the row in a German camp if everybody had started to call a billy-goat Hitler!' Avory exclaimed.

'There you are, you see! Germans go blind with anger—which must have been a great help when one wanted to get away from them. Your man who made that crack about the casual climate of Italy didn't know that it made escape harder, not easier.'

Mussolini adored the prisoners—possibly because he took the cheering of the enemy as more of a compliment than the sardonic encouragement of unfrustrated guards. He recognized affection in the voices, and looked to the British for approval of his revolting preliminaries, his tender approach and his decisive attack. During the days of Mussolini's attention to Lucia, Tecla and Beatrice the camp's morale had been high and joyous. There was something fresh to talk about, something to exaggerate and a new and promising source of noise.

Noise in the ditch—plenty of it at the right place—was essential to the escaping scheme registered in the names of Avory and Tarmer. The plan was born from a tunnel dug practically single-handed by a vast Marine who had been picked up by an Italian destroyer while optimistically trying to swim from Kithera to Crete. His tunnel ended, as they all knew it would, where the massive masonry of the fort met bedrock. But there or thereabouts he dug up the remains of a cross-bow.

This inspired Avory to a flight of imagination which Tarmer carried into the world of reality by finding a mechanic to work on it.

'I wonder what happened to Tommy Robins,' Avory said. 'He was as good on materials as you are on men. Getting the feel of them, I mean.'

Pilot-Officer Robins had manufactured from old car springs two cross-bows of formidable power. Tested for silence, weight of projectile and range, they were accepted by the committee of four as fully developed secret devices and stored for use when the perfect occasion arose.

The target was the cable which sagged from post to post above the high wire fence of the outer perimeter. A rocket-shaped grapnel, with four deep hooks at one end and a rope at the other, was to be shot like a whaling harpoon across the ditch and over the cable. A hearty pull on the rope should then either break the cable or drag it off the insulators. Immediately after the watch-towers had been plunged in darkness a second grapnel would be fired over the fence. The hooks were bound to catch somewhere at the top of the wire, and the party would then climb wall and fence by means of the hanging rope.

So far, so good—always assuming that the nearest watch-tower did not notice the first projectile and its rope soaring through the air. But if the four partners were to be able to put a reasonable distance between themselves and Medina Fort by morning, there must be no suspicion that any escape had taken place. The camp, therefore, had to appear quite silent and peaceful in the accidental darkness, and there had to be a simple explanation of the scrapes and scufflings as the party swarmed up the rope.

That was where the goats came in; the most promising way of creating a diversion was to let them out of their pen. But it was far from fool-proof. A sleepy Beatrice could not be absolutely trusted to put in a personal attack on the patrol; and those docile creatures, Lucia and Tecla, were certain to do nothing but browse.

The constant activity of Mussolini, however, added new and exciting chances of success. A couple of days after the patriarch's arrival, Avory called a committee meeting in one of the old galleries beneath their quarters.

'If we could set Mussolini free in the ditch,' he had said, 'and if he got tangled up in a coil of wire or some tin cans or something in the dark, the Ditch Patrol wouldn't look for any other explanation of noises.'

'He might hurt himself,' the Marine objected.

'He might,' Tarmer agreed. 'And if he does I will ask the Senior British Officer to send some flowers. But the Geneva Convention says nothing about damage to goats.'

Tarmer remembered speaking with some bitterness. That very morning Wing-Commander Fantle had declared that Colonel Colonna, his half-battalion of decrepit ice-cream merchants and the four half-witted apes perched up in each watch-tower were quite incapable of keeping an enterprising rabbit in a hutch. Meticulous planning could get a man out of anywhere. Look, he said, at all the empty-headed crooks who escaped from Dartmoor!

That meticulous planning! God, they had spent hours and months of hours at it! But Mussolini — reminding them forcibly of the outside world and their own Lucias and Teclas — was an inspiration to still further planning. How to let the goats loose? Tarmer had a vision of finding a use, at long last, for the damned monk who swilled their cocoa. The full details could wait. For the moment it was enough to ask Tommy Robins to make a twenty-foot pole smoothly tapering to a short, sharp spike at the end.

'Not for Mussolini?' the Marine had implored him.

'For Beatrice — through the casemate.'

Out of the subterranean galleries opened casemates which had once held the guns to sweep attackers off the glacis. The mouths were blocked by iron bars and coils of wire, frequently checked by the Ditch Patrol. Even so, prisoners had crawled through them—but only into the glare of the lights and immediate arrest.

One casemate, close to the bridge, was just above the pen of the three nanny-goats. It was quite possible to spoil Beatrice's sleep and temper by working a pole through the entanglement and poking. Yet only the combination of Mussolini and Beatrice could really be trusted to raise hell. The committee pointed out to Tarmer that Mussolini was shut up out of reach in a pen of his own.

'Even if we talk Fra Giuseppe into letting the nanny-goats out,' Bill Avory objected, 'he won't let Mussolini out, too. The girls have to rest some time.'

That was true enough. It looked as if Mussolini would have to be kidnapped or invited into the camp, and then concealed until the moment came to make use of him.

No contact with Fra Giuseppe was possible on the following day. The escape committee was despondent, for Mussolini, having generously fulfilled the purpose of his visit, might at any moment be driven back to his home. Preparations, however, were complete. The cross-bows could go into action at ten minutes' notice.

On the next evening Fra Giuseppe was seen in the ditch, all pastoral in the last of the twilight, while the four goats walked peaceably in front of him to their respective pens. Tarmer shouted to him that parcels had arrived with a fresh supply of cocoa. He suggested, as if it were the most natural thing in the world, that Mussolini ought to come too, to say good-bye to the boys.

'But he smells!' the monk had protested.

'So do we! Be a sport, Fra Giuseppe!'

He was. Over the bridge, past the laughing guards at the barrier, trotting happily and poisoning the air for fifty yards around him, came Mussolini followed by Fra Giuseppe. The goat sat down with his four legs curled under him: a black, contented bulk upon the cooling paving of the fort. Somebody served him the scrapings of the evening's spaghetti; someone else wreathed his horns with paper flowers left over from such Christmas celebrations as the camp had had. He looked straight from hell, but he was in heaven. Mussolini brimmed over with affection for human kind, and yet was continually deprived of the petting he adored owing to his penetrating odour. He shared to the full the emotions of those girls in the advertisements whom men won't dance with.

As soon as Fra Giuseppe had become gently inebriated by the smell of cocoa, Tarmer asked him why his Lucia had been limping and hoped that she had not cut herself on the wire of the inner perimeter while licking salt from out-stretched hands. The monk had noticed no limp — reasonably enough since she hadn't got one — but promised to have a look at her before he went home to his priory. Tarmer's eloquent Italian rippled with anxiety for Lucia. Meanwhile the cocoa failed to appear. Fra Giuseppe at last realized that he was being subjected to gentle, almost ecclesiastical blackmail, unspoken and perhaps not even deliberate. He agreed to go down to the ditch and report back immediately on Lucia's condition.

As soon as the monk had strolled off towards the barrier and the bridge, leaving the delighted Mussolini where he was, Avory raced to the casemate and started to arouse Beatrice's brisk temper. The twenty-foot pole was already through the casemate, its point free and commanding the little pen. The cross-bows were set up and loaded.

'Cocoa,' Tarmer murmured, the imagined scent of it almost as vivid as the real scent twenty years earlier.

'Now?' Avory asked in surprise, sharing step by step the train of thought except for that sudden nasal memory. 'Wouldn't coffee and a brandy be better?

Yes. Yes, they would indeed. One couldn't recover the taste of cocoa brewed in a POW camp. It was as hopeless as to try to re-enter the paradise which brown sugar had been at the age of five.

Bill Avory beckoned to the waiter, and chuckled.

'I always wish I had been watching,' he said. 'All I saw at my end of the pole was Fra Giuseppe unlocking the door of the goat-pen. And then Beatrice charged.'

The monk shot out into the flood-lit ditch with the doctor's anti-clerical goat a yard behind him. It looked as if his initial burst of speed might carry him clear out of the operational area; but, fortunately for the plan, Beatrice caught him.

Her butt went home just above the right knee. The desperate monk, screaming for help, swerved, spread his cassock like a bullfighter and received the next charge in the cloth. Beatrice's horns bruised painfully but were not sharp enough to penetrate loose clothing; cloth stretched tight, however, was another matter. The monk's excellent technique resulted in a heaving tangle of black and white. When it became possible for the eye to separate one from the other, Beatrice was dressed in the lower half of the cassock and Fra Giuseppe was embracing her hind legs in a frantic attempt to prevent her cantering away with the rest of it.

'It was more than we dared hope for,' said Tarmer. 'We could hear the sentries cheering and laughing in the towers.'

The monk was between Towers 1 and 2, and it was certain that the guards were looking at nothing else. The Bridge Tower to the west and No. 3 Tower to the east were unsighted by the angles of the pentagon. Tommy Robins fired the grapnel over the cable. The Marine heaved on the rope. After a moment of resistance the grapnel returned to hand, flying back into the camp on a lower and more violent trajectory than the curve of its outward journey.

The darkness shocked by its sudden totality. Not only were the flood-lights extinguished but all the camp lights as well. There was an instant of astonished silence on the part of both guards and prisoners, through which echoed the exclamations of Fra Giuseppe, now rendered hysterical by the kicks of Beatrice and his incoherent gratitude to the saint whose miracle or the soldier whose Christian charity had put out the lights.

The second grapnel sailed over the ditch and caught. With the interested assistance of Mussolini, escape was now nearly certain. Tarmer stood by the affectionate head, Avory at the stern. They lifted him over the inner perimeter wire and dropped him on to the glacis between the Bridge Tower and No. 1. He had an old leather shoe tied to his tail by a yard of cord. Its mysterious leaps and scufflings ought to be enough to delay and deceive the Ditch Patrol for the half minute required to climb wall and wire.

Tarmer and Avory raced back from the disposal of Mussolini to find Robins and the Marine still testing the rope. Resistance was soft and unreliable. The grapnel seemed to be caught in a weak loop of wire which it was pulling out along the top of the fence; it felt as if it could not be trusted to support bodies climbing furiously up the rope against time.

It stuck firmly on something hard, evidently the top of a post. But a last jerk was indecisive, though nothing appeared to break or yield. Tarmer and Avory added their weight to the rope and had to take a step backwards as it gave. In the darkness it was impossible to see what was happening; there was nothing for it but to keep on pulling in a desperate attempt to recover the grapnel and try again. Another yard or two of rope came in, and its angle was not so steep. The sensation was baffling. They felt as if they were the winning team in an obstinate tug-of-war. Then thirty yards of that formidable outer perimeter fence fell over into the ditch, forming an impenetrable trampoline suspended from the leaning posts at each end of the wreckage.

There was another terrifying moment of silence, which ended in the almost musical twanging and tearing of wire as the grapnel was worked loose by brute force and recovered.

The guards on No. 2 Tower turned their attention from the bleating of Beatrice and the monk, and challenged. They then opened fire with rifles on the ditch and the collapsed fence. Since their eyes were still unused to the blank darkness, they found it hard to judge the correct angle of depression. Some of the shots strayed across the protruding angle of the camp and sang past the ears of the defenders of No. 3 Tower.

'I've never understood 3 Tower,' Avory said.

'They swore afterwards that they thought parachutists were trying to rescue us. But I know what happened. They had a light machine-gun which they'd never had a chance to use, and they weren't going to be left out of whatever excitement there was.'

3 Tower put down a curtain of fire on the ditch and at least hit the glacis. Ricochets from that smooth stone slope howled across the camp — some of them on a trajectory low enough to tear splinters off the wooden roof of No. 2 Tower.

On the still peaceful western side of the camp Mussolini behaved as if he had been in on the plan since the beginning. Loyal and single-minded, he charged down to the quietly grazing Tecla and tried to console her loneliness. Tecla at any time was a dignified goat, her expression always making it clear that Mussolini's were unwelcome attentions to which it was her duty to submit; so now, approached by an importunate lover at, for goats, an unreasonable hour, she fled for her pen under the Bridge Tower.

The Ditch Patrol, which had been idling its way from No. 4 to the Bridge Tower, clearly decided that the eastern side of the camp was well covered by fire from Nos. 2 and 3, and was also extremely unhealthy. It therefore cautiously continued its round until alerted by the bouncings of

Mussolini and his shoe. It didn't stop to investigate at all. It took such cover as there was and plastered the ditch with automatic fire. Most of it was high. The guards on the Bridge Tower, nervously searching the impenetrable darkness for the unknown enemy which had attacked Nos. 2 and 3 Towers, briskly engaged the Ditch Patrol.

By now Mussolini was in safety with Tecla under the bridge. But Tecla must have made the most of the difficulties and protested that the pen was not nearly large enough for Mussolini too. Her excuse was acceptable. He was always a free and easy goat who liked plenty of space and publicity. He therefore trotted off beyond the bridge on the scent of Lucia. She had half-heartedly followed her master, the monk, and was now browsing close to No. 1 Tower.

No. 1, hitherto deprived of an opportunity for heroics, at once opened fire on the mysterious noises. Since the ditch ran straight between No. 1 and the Bridge Tower, without any protruding angle, the gentle slope of the glacis was murderous, and the stuff came off with the accuracy of tennis balls. The terrified Lucia joined Tecla under the bridge. The guards up in the Bridge Tower, attacked from both sides and hearing beneath them the sinister rattlings and scrapings of the final bloody assault, surrendered to Mussolini.

'I suppose it was funny,' Avory said.

'It was damned dangerous. Nobody felt like laughing till Fantle appeared.'

Dodging from cover to cover the Senior British Officer had joined the prostrate and fascinated group just as the cross-bows had been dismantled and concealed. He demanded a situation report from his adjutant. Tarmer replied that the goats had got out, that the guards had mistaken them for escaping prisoners and that in the general confusion part of the fence between Nos. 2 and 3 Towers had fallen into the ditch.

'Then what the hell are you still doing here?'

'Personally, sir,' Avory had said, 'I am waiting for the lights to go on so that I can finish my book.'

Hardly fair, perhaps. But the disappointment was bitter. As for a mass break-out in the confusion, it couldn't be launched into an unseen tangle of wire through which nothing but artillery could blast a path.

The firing and the distracted cries of *Mamma mia!* died away. Searchlights and the head lamps of trucks illumined the ditch, revealing not a single corpse, not even of a goat. All was painfully quiet except between Nos. 1 and 2 Towers where the Ditch Patrol, having clothed Fra Giuseppe in a blanket, was fearlessly meeting the challenge of Beatrice.

When the break in the power line had been repaired, Colonel Colonna at the head of a full company marched into the camp and paraded his innocent charges. To his astonishment not one was missing.

It was then that resentment should have been shown, that the prisoners should have jeered at their captors and established such a moral ascendancy that a mobile battalion would have to be rushed in to control them. But only four knew what had really happened. The rest were gasping between laughter and bewilderment, and inclined to hope that a revolution had broken out in Italy.

As soon as the parade had been dismissed and only the senior officers remained, the Commandant observed in a tone of mild distaste rather than rebuke:

'I am informed that some joke was played upon Muss . . . upon the he-goat.'

'We all sincerely hope he came to no harm, sir,' Tarmer answered.

'Thank you. Apart from a sprained tail he is unhurt. May I ask you, gentlemen, to accept the apologies of myself and my command for disturbing your evening?'

'Tell him that it was a disgraceful, cowardly episode,'

Fantle stormed, 'and that we don't give a damn for his apologies!'

Tarmer's conscience stung him a little as he remembered how he had translated that one. But Colonna was no German commandant bristling with suspicion, fury and punishment. In spite of what he must be feeling, he still cultivated a friendly atmosphere full of human acceptance of the tasteless tricks of young officers and the liability of troops to panic in the dark.

'The Senior British Officer assures you, sir,' Tarmer had said, putting an extra formality into his voice so that the change of tone would not be too obvious, 'that between gentlemen of good will all apologies are unnecessary.'

No, he had not been wrong. Unmilitary, perhaps. But if there were anything whatever to be said in favour of war Colonna represented its spirit better than Fantle. He said as much to Avory.

'Just what that damned journalist meant by the casual climate of Italy!' Avory replied.

'But it cuts both ways. In any German camp the posts would have been set in concrete with decent efficiency. And then all four of us would have got clear away.'

5

Immoral Trade

THE only murderer I ever knew was a personal friend. Yet I had to admit that his sentence was absolutely just, legal and merited. Even the military police were kind to Valdes. They assured him that it did not hurt at all to be executed by a firing squad. Valdes politely agreed with them — not that he cared about pain. He was as used to that as a retired boxer, and looked a little like one, too.

He wanted to live as eagerly as the rest of us, but he realized that his death, like any other military ceremony, had to be performed with dignity. He was a soldier all through. He made one understand the character of that handful of men who conquered the Americas. Yet the luck of war had landed him in a non-combatant unit.

He was an Andalusian, sturdy, of middle height and with the type of face which the Spaniards call *chato* — looking as if it had been flattened out by a road roller and come up smiling. It must be common in the Peninsula. I had three other toughs with much the same lack of features.

Valdes had fought right through the Spanish Civil War and been interned in France at the end of it. In 1940 some of those internees were evacuated before the Germans could grab them, and formed into a Spanish commando. A good idea on paper. What they didn't know about bloodshed wasn't worth knowing. And yet their commando was unusable — too fierce, too desperate. They hadn't the flair of the British for discreet, deadly action.

When the Spanish commando was disbanded, Valdes, with a few of his mates, was posted to the Pioneer Corps. What an outfit that was! We had docile labourers recruited

161

from Africa or obscure islands in the Indian Ocean, and able-bodied poor of every colour in need of work and regular rations, and always some Q men, as they were called — habitual army criminals who had learned by experience and low cunning to anticipate the psychiatrist's next move and to get themselves registered as psychopathics. My own company was a mixture of Arabs, Q men and vaguely oriental beachcombers. Corporal Valdes and his section of Spaniards formed a solid island of sanity and hard work.

In 1944 the company was with Eighth Army in Italy, cleaning up close behind the advance. My main trouble was Italian hospitality. The men were not accustomed to red wine in that quantity. Valdes and his Spaniards, who were, acted off duty as nursemaids in the cafés. The amount of rape and murder those fellows prevented was astonishing. They were proud of the reputation of the British Army — yes, proud of it, even in the Pioneer Corps. For them there was no other army in the war at all. Of course, when they joined up, there wasn't.

'My captain,' Valdes said to me one night, 'we cannot all be in the Guards. But we wish to assure you that we know how to die with decency.'

They were going out beyond the front line with a Field Company of sappers to fill up craters in a mountain track which was going to be badly needed next day. It was late in the evening when they volunteered for the job, and they were all, I suppose, at the third litre; but there was no telling where the generosity of wine ended and Andalusian pride began.

Pride. Perhaps murder is never very far from it. There didn't seem room for either when one morning I sent Valdes and his section down to railhead to collect a consignment of picks and shovels. Nothing but picks and shovels — but to Valdes they were Toledo steel. I had seen him use them under shell fire with such nonchalance that even the Q men didn't find an excuse to run back to safety.

That hardware was important to my Spaniards—so important that when a young French sergeant told them to get to hell out of the way and let him load his truck with warlike stores they ignored him. Unfortunately Valdes, after two years of internment, spoke French. Unfortunately, too, he had that unreasonable Spanish contempt for the neighbour across the northern frontier. At last he told the French sergeant to pipe down and wait his turn.

The sergeant replied that he was not going to wait for any non-combatant bastards who were not fit to shovel—well, you can imagine the number of uses that an angry and imaginative Frenchman could find for a shovel. Valdes did not lose his temper. He rose with dignity to the occasion and developed his favourite creed: that if there were no shovels the luckier men who had fighting to do would never get near enough to the front line to do it. The Frenchman—so much we had in evidence—remarked that all the British Army ever did was shovelling while their allies did the fighting. Corporal Valdes quietly picked up a rifle belonging to the French detachment, and shot the sergeant dead.

It was astonishing how correct and soldierly Valdes's movements then were. The only authority handy was the railway transport officer. While the startled Frenchmen were busy with their sergeant, Valdes marched up to the R.T.O., saluted smartly, gave his name and unit, handed over the rifle and reported the incident. The R.T.O. wiped the sweat off his elderly brow—he had been naturally disconcerted by the approach of a murderer with a loaded rifle—and sent for the military police. The section, still an island of proud discipline, returned to camp.

There was nothing I could do. If it had been a British soldier Valdes had shot, I think I might have got the court-martial sentence reviewed and had him punished by a long term of imprisonment. But he had had shot an ally, and allies were touchy. It was more essential for the war effort that Valdes should die than that the French should suffer a sense of grievance.

He admitted as much himself. He did not regret the murder at all; he only regretted that it had been unavoidable. He pointed out that he had paid no attention to personal insults, but that an insult to the British Army was not to be borne. For three years, he said, we had treated him as a friend and a gentleman. The least he could do in return was to protect our honour.

I was determined that Valdes should not be executed. Somehow I, a mere captain, reached the French G.O.C. I speak reasonable French — that and a bit of Arabic and the remains of several tropical diseases were my qualifications for the Pioneer Corps — and I nearly won him over. I insisted that there was no need to prove Valdes mad; to shoot an unknown and gallant Frenchman he must be mad. The general was exquisitely courteous. He knew that these were mere empty words, but they pleased him. Speaking for himself, he said at last, Valdes could be reprieved; but for the sake of the suffering mothers of France and the damned politicians — he dared to couple the two together with the irony of a man who was absolutely sure of himself — he regretted that he could not interfere. I came to a dead end against French obstinacy.

I tried the corps psychiatrist — with whom, thanks to the curiosities among my Q men, I was on excellent terms. He told me that Valdes had the only faultlessly healthy human mind he had met in years, and that if hard scientific lying could help him, helped he would be. He did his dishonest best, but the big shots above him refused to play. About ten per cent of my company had deserved a firing squad at some time, and Army H.Q. were tired of finding excuses for their behaviour. They refused to distinguish between Q men and emotionally primitive Spaniards.

I had no military ambition. I was just a grey-haired

captain, only fit enough for the Pioneer Corps. So my plans for saving Valdes were quite uninhibited. I seriously considered every trick one reads of in fiction—down to supplying the firing squad with blanks and bribing them to say nothing. But not a single one of my ideas was practicable.

Valdes' section was equally desperate. They took it for granted that I was on their side. They had no more logic than women, and were just as right. Their experience of impossible escapes in the chaos of civil war was to the point, but such plans in a more formal army were unworkable. Private Moreno, who was some sort of relation of Valdes from the days when they had possessed homes and wives, wanted to get inside the jail and substitute himself for the condemned man. He couldn't very well be shot instead, and a court-martial—always merciful when its collective sense of humour was aroused—was unlikely to give him more than a year.

I thought about it night after night. I even trained Moreno to imitate Valdes's voice and accent. But he was a good inch too tall; and, though he did have a similar type of squashed and wrinkled features in the same tint of deep tan, common sense insisted that one could never be mistaken for the other unless they were heavily made up or bandaged, and then only in a crowd of Arabs or Englishmen.

Valdes was in the jug at Bari. I used to drive down and see him whenever I had a spare moment and could invent a reasonable excuse. On what would have to be my last visit, two days before he was due to be executed, I ran into the corps psychiatrist being let out through the formidable gate as I was being let in.

'Another of your beauties,' he said to me.

'Who is it this time?'

'Pidgegood. There's nothing wrong with him whatever except that he knows as much of our routine as I do. You can have him back when he's served his sentence.'

Myself, I knew all along that there was not a trace of mal-adjustment in Pidgegood; he had merely been born without a sense of shame. But it had taken a long time for over-conscientious psychiatrists to realize that jail was the proper place for him. He was a gipsy—or said he was. He had found in peacetime that wild eyes and dirt and a general air of rural eccentricity always intimidated house-wives and farmers, and he trusted that the military were just as easy.

They were. Pidgegood couldn't read or write, but he had the cunning of the devil to make up for it. By the time he had been dismissed from his battalion as an incorrigible and cowardly rogue, he knew enough psychiatry to fool any solemn doctor. He put on an act just sufficiently unbalanced to make sure that his crimes would land him in a mental ward rather than a cell, but not enough to get him invalided out of the service. He preferred the army—what little he saw of it—to being drafted into a factory.

Courts-martial had no effect on him; he always came back to me with a careful letter of advice from the psychiatrists. But my chaps found a use for the man. If there were any enquiries about missiong pigs or chickens and no chance of the company's innocence being believed, they always put the blame on Pidgegood. He was perfectly willing to accept it, even on the rare occasions when he wasn't guilty, and was rewarded by privileged idleness.

I was far from fond of him, but he was a part of my company to which we were all accustomed. So I asked to be escorted to his cell. I went there before my visit to Valdes. It was going to be the last time I should see my corporal, and I knew I should want to be alone afterwards.

Pidgegood would talk of nothing else but Valdes. He reproached me to my face for not getting him off. There wasn't a man in the company, he said, whatever his colour, who wouldn't have died for Valdes, except me. I didn't attempt to explain. Pidgegood never understood the army machine.

'Have you seen him?' I asked.

'Gawd, yes! We runs round the yard together.'

They did not have a condemned cell, you see. Firing squads were hardly ever used in the humane army of the last war. I suppose the proper procedure for dealing with Valdes was laid down, but it was not a matter of everyday experience and nobody wanted to be too formal.

And then, corrupted by the mere presence and criminality of Pidgegood, I suddenly saw a remote chance.

'Do you want to go back to the psychiatric ward?' I asked him.

'They won't 'ave nothing more to do with me,' he said.

'Ever tried attempted murder?'

'Not worth it. Touch one of them warders, and they'll 'alf kill you and swear it was done resisting constraint.'

'It wasn't one of them I meant,' I explained.

He got it. He got it instantly. His gipsy mind took him right to the point before I had done more than feel for it myself.

'I couldn't do 'im any 'arm with my bare 'ands,' he said, 'before they'd separate us.'

We were alone in the cell. The warder was outside, but he didn't bother to supervise interviews between a prisoner and his long-suffering commanding officer. I took a handkerchief from the pocket of my battle-dress trousers and blew my nose, looking away from Pidgegood. When I had replaced the handkerchief and done up the button I noticed that the familiar lump against my thigh, which was my powerful pocket knife, had disappeared. I swear I felt nothing. It only occurred to me later that the unaccountable loss of several of my treasured possessions had always taken place when that scoundrel was with the company.

'The face, if possible, Pidgegood,' I said, getting ready to go. 'And if there is anything I can do for you at any time, you know I will.'

'Thank you, sir. But I reckon I won't be coming back to the company this time.'

167

Then I went on to see Valdes. There was a sergeant of military police present throughout the interview, and I couldn't drop a hint of what was brewing. When I left the cell I returned Valdes's salute with the tears running down my face. I was sure I would never see him again. Pidgegood seemed a frail ally against the imposing formality of military justice.

Not till the morning when Valdes, we all assumed, had been executed did I hear what had happened. The Spaniards of his section came babbling into the orderly room all at once and for the first time in their lives had to be reminded by a roaring and indignant sergeant-major that they were soldiers.

Did I know the news from Bari? No I didn't. Valdes had been attacked in the exercise yard by Pidgegood and carved up with two strokes of a knife. The first had slit him from mouth to ear and taken the ear three-quarters off; the second had ripped open the artery of his left arm. Did I know that it was not the custom to execute a hospital patient? Did I know that he must be nursed back to health before he could be shot?

I showed as much pleasure as could be expected from an unemotional company commander, and asked how Pidgegood had come by a knife. That did not seem to bother anybody. Pidgegood could not be imagined without a knife. They forgot the regular searches of cell and person. In fact it was very fortunate that Valdes, Pidgegood and their fellow criminals had been doubled out for exercise within a few hours of my visit.

Through the correct channels I asked whether it was permissible to visit Valdes in hospital, not being quite sure whether he was officially dead or not. Nothing against it. He was very glad to see me. His head was swathed in bandages, and the pale oak colour of his face had changed to yellow. He could not understand what had come over Pidgegood. He assumed that the doctors must have been right about him after all.

Military justice was now following all the rules of the game. Valdes had a guard continually at his bedside — or at least playing cards not more than three beds away. He was not even allowed to attend to the needs of nature alone, though his escort remained outside the swing door. I took a fatherly interest in all these arrangements. I also took note of the exact measurements and windings of his bandages.

I gave liberal leave to the Spaniards of his section — with the exception of Moreno. The hospital doorkeepers became accustomed to their cheerful arrivals and chattering departures. Valdes soon looked his normal self and colour. The surgeons, knowing what was in store for him when they released him, kept him as long as they mercifully could, and even wasted time in removing the scar of Pidgegood's knife — or mine, rather — by the latest plastic operation. But at last the week arrived when he had to be passed fit for execution.

I allowed four of the section to take a company truck and pay a good-bye visit. I met the truck on the road and put Moreno in the back of it, holding a saint of painted wood on a rather large base representing a rock. Inside the base was a sort of cap, made of bandages wound over the thinnest possible mould of plaster of paris. It needed only one more wind and a safety pin to be an exact replica of Valdes' bandage. Parcels brought by visitors were examined at the door, so we had to use this subterfuge. We felt sure the saint would have no objection to taking part in an errand of mercy.

Beyond providing the party with very precise operation orders which I made them learn by heart, I had nothing else to do with the proposed felony. Whatever happened I knew they would never give me away or even refer to the matter again.

At 14.15 hrs. the detachment passed the lavatories on Valdes' floor. Moreno whipped the cap out of its hiding place and entered No. 3 lavatory. The rest went straight on to Valdes' ward and presented him with the saint. At 14.18 hours Valdes, accompanied by his guard, also entered No. 3 lavatory, sidling in and not opening the door too wide. It was a stable door, but so long as Valdes and Moreno kept their heads down they could not be seen. We simply had to trust that the guard would not look under the door and see four feet instead of two.

Valdes put on Moreno's battle-dress, and shoved his bandages in the pocket. Moreno put on the cap, and Valdes' pyjamas. Groaning a little and holding his tummy to disguise his height, he trotted back to bed and dived under the bedclothes. His four visitors made a little doleful conversation and said an emotional good-bye. Then they picked up Valdes and drove like hell for our camp, passing close behind the French sector of the front where they dropped their corporal. I wasn't sure that I had not been too impudently ingenious there. But the plan worked. After all the last place anyone would look for Valdes was among the French.

He changed into ragged civilian clothes—also provided in the truck—and spend the night crawling through the French forward positions until he was sure that only enemy patrols were ahead of him. Next morning, pretending to have escaped from a German labour battalion, he came in. The French believed him, or said they did. They were always short of good men and pretty unscrupulous how they recruited them. Six hours later Valdes had enlisted in the Foreign Legion.

Moreno had a much better run for his money than we ever thought he could. He kept up the deception till dawn of the following day, and very gladly accepted what I had prophesied—two years reduced to one when the sentence came up for revision. The others swore that they had never known that the man in bed was not Valdes, and the prosecution just failed to prove beyond a doubt that they did.

170

Pidgegood enjoyed a happy and idle war in the mental home. As for me, the worst I had to bear was an interview with my colonel who told me privately that I was strongly suspected of knowing more about the escape of Valdes than I had stated in evidence. He had sworn to my character and assured the military detectives that their suspicions were impossible.

'It's an immoral trade, command,' he said, looking me straight in the eye. 'One becomes far too fond of one's subordinates.'

6

Woman in Love

IT was the nearest he had ever come to sending an agent to his death. Her death, rather. He admitted that he shouldn't have taken the risk, that a man with his experience of women should have known better; but there he was with the enemy order of battle—or ally's peaceful deployment, according to how you look at it—all along the southern fringe of the Iron Curtain from Bratislava to the Black Sea. The list was complete, and accurate up to the previous Saturday; and there wasn't a chance of getting it out to the west. No handy secret wireless. No landing grounds. Not a trustworthy agent who had the remotest hope of being given a passport in time to be of use. Theotaki had found his job much easier when operating under the noses of the Gestapo.

He was a Roumanian of Greek origin, with all a Greek's hungry passion for the ideal freedom which had never in practical politics existed, and never could. He had also the Greek's love of adventurous intrigue for its own sake. One gets used to the trade, he would say. Steeplejacks, for example. They couldn't be thinking all the time about risk. They took, he supposed, meticulous care with all their preparations—blocks and tackle, scaffolding, belts—and then got on with the job. It was only when a man had scamped the preliminaries that he need worry about risks.

Normally there was no need to scamp them, no disastrous demand for hurry. Cold war wasn't like hot war, and there weren't any impatient generals howling for immediate results. So caution, caution, caution, all the time. It was a bit dull, he said, but the main objective had to be to keep his organization alive.

He admitted, however, that this had been an occasion for desperate measures. The only chance he could see of getting that enemy order of battle into hands that would appreciate it was D17. D17 was going to the very next day to Stockholm to be married. She would never have been allowed to leave for less neutral territory; but it was hard, even for communist bureaucrats, to think up a really valid excuse for preventing a citizen—an entirely useless citizen whose parents were living on the proceeds of their jewellery and furniture—from taking herself off to Sweden and matrimony, when a firm request for her had been passed through diplomatic channels.

Alexia—D17—was a very minor agent: somewhat too enthusiastic, said Theotaki, for her sister had been mishandled by the Russian advance guards when they entered Bucharest and had died the following week. The unfortunate incident had had some effect on Theotaki's ideals of freedom too. But he never confessed to emotion. To judge by his jowled, dead, decadent face, you wouldn't have thought him capable of feeling any.

Since he had moved before the war in the social circle of the parents and their two daughters, he knew Alexia very well. She had, of course, no idea that he was in any way responsible for the occasional orders received by D17. She couldn't have given away more than the three names of the other members of her cell—at least she couldn't up to the time when Theotaki was forced into gambling against his better judgment.

He kept her under observation all the morning. She was shopping for a few clothes and necessary trifles that she could much better have bought abroad. But she didn't know that. Alexia visualized the outside world as seething with unemployment and economic distress. Of course she did, of course she did, exclaimed Theotaki, defending this absurd shopping. Even when you are aware that all your news is tainted, you have to believe some of it. For all

Alexia knew, the shops of Stockholm might well have been looted by starving rioters or bought out by dollar-waving American troops.

She was obviously happy. Well, why wouldn't she be? She was a tense and luminous woman in her middle twenties escaping to her lover and doing a bit of buying to please his eyes. When, however, she sat down, alone, in the huge barren hall of a cheap café, she was ashamed of herself. Theotaki guessed it from her bearing, from the uncertainty of her eyes. He was clever as any woman at guessing mood when not a word had passed. To be ashamed of yourself for being happy was, he explained, one of the most damnable, minor, nagging aches of political tyranny. Your personal tastes and joys could not be altered by the common discontent, yet you felt they should be. Love and the flighting of duck at first light and the relish of wine to a man and the feel of a dress to a woman — they don't come to an end because your country is enslaved and terrorized.

So that was the position — D17 sitting in a café, thinking of her beloved with one half of her mind, and with the other her duty to hate; and Theotaki moving behind her to find a table, not too far away, where she couldn't see and greet him.

He took one of the café's illustrated papers in its cane frame, and began abstractedly to write a poem across the blank spaces of an advertisement. When he had finished his drink and his casual scribbling, he paid his bill and sent the waiter to Alexia with the paper. He then vanished from his table and stood talking to a casual acquaintance by the door, whence he could watch in a mirror the effect of his inspiration.

The waiter suspected nothing. It was a quite normal act to send a paper to a customer who had asked for it — especially if the customer were a pretty girl. At least it appeared quite normal when Theotaki did it. That he was alive at all was largely due to his naturalness of manner.

Alexia received the paper as if it were expected. Theotaki approved her presence of mind, and well he might. Any gesture of surprise could have led—if the waiter earned a little extra money by giving information to the police—to prolonged questioning of both of them. He admitted that he had been apprehensive. He hadn't been able to arrange much training for her and her like.

She glanced idly through the coarse rotogravures of factory openings and parades, and found the doodling of some previous reader. There were girls' heads, and jottings for a very commonplace love poem to sweet seventeen. Among the half lines, the blanks to be filled in, the notes for promising rhymes, was a phrase *your garden at three in the morning* continually repeated, toyed with and crossed out because no order of the words could be made to scan. Then came a row of capital D's, as if the lovesick doodler, failing to succeed as a poet, had tried to design the most decorative letter with which to begin his work.

D17's garden at 3 a.m—the message would have been instantly clear to Theotaki who never read anything that was misplaced, even a printer's error, without wondering why it was misplaced. But he didn't expect the same alertness from D17; he only hoped. As a man of imagination he had, he insisted, the keenest sympathy for romance, and therefore thought it more than likely that Alexia would be too absorbed by justifiable dreams to notice his vulgar scribblings. He was very pleased with her indeed when her hand began to fiddle with ash-tray, saucer and salt-cellar arranging them into a group of three to show, if there were anyone watching her, that she had read and understood.

D17's garden—or rather her parents'—was a reasonably safe spot for a rendezvous. A high but climbable wall separated its overgrown shrubbery from the state-disciplined bushes of a public park. In happier days Alexia and her sister had been very well aware of its advantages.

High-spirited young ladies, said Theotaki. Yes, and they

had had their own uproarious methods of discouraging unwelcome suitors. When he dropped over the wall that night, for the second time in his life, he remembered that ten years earlier there had been a cunning arrangement of glass and empty cans to receive him, and a crash that woke the uneasy summer sleepers in four blocks of flats that faced the park.

This time there were only silence and soft leaf-mould. Theotaki in a whisper reminded the darkness of his last visit and of the two excitable policemen who had burst with Alexia's father into the garden. Even in those days he had been skilled at evading policemen.

The darkness did not answer. Very rightly. This might be a trap. D17 had not received her orders through the usual channels.

Theotaki sat down with his back against the wall and waited. After a while he again addressed the dark shapes of the bushes. He warned them that if they were not alone they had better say so, for he was about to speak of the relationship—the 1951 relationship, that is—between himself and Alexia.

Alexia detached herself from her background, and assured him that she was alone. As proof of his authority, he told her the names and numbers of the other members of her cell and what their recent activities had been.

'Will that do?' he asked, 'or do you want more details, D17?'

She murmured that she couldn't know . . . that she would never have believed it possible . . . that never in all her life had she respected him—or anyone—so much. . . .

Theotaki apologized for being desperate. Caution—caution, he told her, was the only road to success. There was no hurry, no room for either risks or enthusiasm. Still, sometimes—regretfully—one had to improvise. Where was it safe to talk?

She led him away from the wall into a tunnel of green

darkness, and begged him to say what he wanted from her. Always that dangerous feminine enthusiasm. Yet it was a little forced. Theotaki could tell by her voice that she was uneasy at the unexpected mixture of her social life—such as it was—with her very secret service.

He apologized again for his inefficiency, for the urgency—there should never be any urgency—which had compelled him to appeal to her directly.

'It isn't fair to any of us,' he said.

'Whatever happens to me, I shall not talk,' Alexia assured him in a passionate whisper.

Theotaki considered the eager, small-boned body with the pitying eye of a professional. It would be capable of exquisite suffering, but he was inclined to share Alexia's faith in its resistance. Torture had little effect upon a flame. Better technique was to confine it closely and have patience until it went out. He reckoned that about three months would be enough to draw out full confession from an Alexia who by then would be Alexia no longer.

Three months. Or much less, if she were caught without possibility of blank denials. Good God, when he thought, afterwards, how nearly it had happened, how but for the most amazing luck . . .

'You are in love?' he asked.

'Doesn't it stand to reason?'

Theotaki quickly answered that he hadn't doubted it for a moment. Nor he had. She wasn't the type of woman to marry, just to escape from the country, without love. No, he wanted to know what she would answer—to hear, as it were, the worst from her own lips.

He remembered the man who taught him his trade. He liked to remember him very carefully, for, since the man was dead, there was no other method of consultation. This teacher of his used to say that a female agent was every bit as good as any male. What she lacked in attack, she made up in human understanding. But never, the dead man had insisted, never choose a woman in love!

Something of this, by way of warning, he repeated to D17.

'I think your friend did not understand women,' she answered.

Theotaki explained that his friend had been talking only of women of character, who worked for patriotism, not money. He had not implied that such a woman's devotion would be any less because she was in love, nor that she would be likely to sacrifice the cause to her private happiness. No, he had only meant that any woman of outstanding intensity was, when in love, Love Itself. She became possessed by hormones and happiness, and ceased to bother with details.

'And I wouldn't choose any woman but a woman in love,' Alexia laughed. 'Because until she is, she's only half alive.'

Theotaki admitted there was something in that. The will of a woman in love dominated her environment, though it couldn't perhaps, burn its way through armour plate, it would certainly try.

'But don't forget my friend's experience,' he warned her. 'He was a man of very wide experience. And so be a little more careful over details than you would be ordinarily. Just to compensate.'

He gave her the precious sheet of foolscap, closely typed over with the positions, the strengths, the armour of corps, divisions and independent brigades.

'Learn that by heart,' he said, 'and then burn it. Burn it and crush the ashes. When you get to Stockholm, make an excuse, as soon as you reasonably can, to be alone, and go straight to the address you will read at the bottom of the sheet. Say you come from me, and recite your lesson. That's all. Then you can be happy with a good conscience. I, your leader, tell you so.'

When she had vanished silently into the house, Theotaki

flowed, inch by careful inch, like the battered tom-cat he resembled, back over the wall. He walked from the park to his flat through streets deserted by all but the police. Several times during the journey he showed his papers. He was a privileged person, kept rather contemptuously by the Ministry of the Interior for the sake of his general usefulness. Nobody could possibly have suspected Theotaki of any idealism.

D17 — well, what D17 did when she was alone in her bedroom could only be reconstructed from his knowledge of her and the story that reached him weeks later. She had a quick, reliable memory, and in the grey hour before dawn she learned those dull military numerals as conscientiously as she had learned poetry for school examinations. She would remember, said Theotaki — who had practised, earlier in his career, the same exact and desperate memorizing — every fact and figure for the rest of her life. That done, she would have been relaxed and beautifully at ease. The last service had been asked of her; she had an honourable discharge. She could give her whole attention to dreaming of the joy that would begin next day.

She must have sat down about sunrise, in the last of her spare time, too excited to sleep, to write to her fiancé. That was like her. She was rich in forethought and expedients. Her departure might still be delayed by some incalculable change in the official mind. If it were, her lover would have a letter to comfort him. If it were not, they would read the two pages together, and laugh for relief from their common fears which had not come true.

Then, when the letter was in its envelope and stamped, came all the fuss of leaving, the weeping mother, the insistence that she should have enough breakfast, the last-minute closing of her four suitcases, the drive to the station.

At the frontier Theotaki took up direct observation again, for, if D17 should walk into trouble, he wanted to

have first news of it. He was astonished at the ease, the gallantry of her departure. The Roumanian officials searched
two of her cases and left the rest unopened. It was the
starry-eyedness of her and youth and her own infectious
certainty that no one could stop so innocently blissful a girl
which carried her through. A perfect example, Theotaki
pointed out, of the woman in love dominating her environment. That grim frontier post, on both sides of the line,
was all bows and smiles.

Theotaki could go no farther. That he had been allowed
to come so far, and on the flimsiest of excuses, was a severe
test of his nuisance value to his Ministry. He hastened back
to Bucharest, very relieved but unable to get rid of an
aching nervousness. He put it down to his dislike of breaking
the rules of the trade. By short-circuiting his own organization, he had hopelessly committed its safety to the hands
of D17. He assured himself that she could have no further
difficulties, but she had still to cross a frontier between
Budapest and Prague; and at Prague, before she took the
plane to Stockholm, there would be a last, thorough and
envious examination of her papers and her baggage.

Theotaki spoke of Alexia's journey as if he had been on
the train with her. In thought, hour after hour, so he was.
He knew to the minute — though that of course was mere
calculation of schedules — when the blinds of the train
would be pulled down so that no passenger might see the
possible presence and activities of Russian troops; 136th
Assault Division, she would say to herself, and inevitably
her mind would run over the bare details of its strength and
its experimental bridging equipment. She wouldn't be able
to help this silent recitation, and would try to stop herself
forming the mental words lest they might be magically
overheard.

All that was true enough. Nevertheless Alexia, as he
heard afterwards, had passed most of the journey in a
dream of romantic confidence. It had been broken, while

she sat in the train, by moments of vague inexplicable worry; but whenever she and her baggage were in contact with the enemy, she treated officials as if they were as gay and careless as she herself, in twelve hours more, hoped to be. She turned the future into the present with an audacity that no mere man could have imitated and which she didn't even recognize as unreal — with the result that when police and customs and their informers on the train gave her a look, they saw only a girl neither immorally rich nor suspiciously poor, and much too happy to have anything in their line of business upon her conscience.

At Prague, however, the solid and bad-tempered Czechs turned her inside out. They flung the upper layers of her bags aside and angrily rummaged the bottom for anti-social contraband. They interrogated her. They gave her a fresh batch of forms to sign. And when they had punished her so far as they could for wanting to leave the Russian orbit at all, they had to allow her to leave it.

After that it was all plain sailing. She was met by her fiancé on arrival, and Swedish smiles passed her straight into their country, and let her loose in a blue and white Stockholm which sparkled like her mood. No, not sentimentalists, Theotaki explained. They had merely done their investigation of Alexia at the proper time, and once her visa had been issued there was no further point in annoying her. That was the mark of a civilized country. Communists hadn't yet learned to make up their minds and stand by the decision.

It must have been very difficult for D17 to shake off fiancé and future parents-in-law and the odd score of hospitable friends who were determined to cherish her; but she did it. She had, after all, long experience in concealing her intentions. Somehow she established her right to a moment of privacy, and claimed it. She delivered her message, word perfect, and kept the taxi waiting and was back in her bedroom in half an hour.

Then she started, said Theotaki, to unpack. He heard of that unpacking when he met his Stockholm correspondent in the quiet course of their business, and even then they couldn't laugh. He was right. He had never come nearer to sending an agent to certain death. On the top of the first case Alexia opened was her writing-pad, just where she had hastily thrown it in the unworldly light of dawn, after finishing that last letter, that all-absorbing letter, to her fiancé. The bag was the only one of the four that had never been examined by Roumanians or Hungarians, and the Czechs had gone like burrowing dogs for the bottom while scattering out the top between their legs. In the writing-pad, hidden only by its flimsy cardboard cover, was the sheet of foolscap, gloriously forgotten, not crushed at all to ashes, not even burned, which Theotaki had given her with such delicate precautions.

7

Moment of Truth

SHE begged me for it. You know how divinely exalted young women can become. Begged for a cyanide pill as though it were her right, as though I should be doing her out of a great spiritual experience if I hesitated. Men don't behave like that at all. A man accepts the means of death without looking at it, hides it in his smallest pocket and examines it with loathing when he gets home or wherever is serving him as a home. No, martyrdom for us has no attraction—not, at any rate for the more active type.

You never dreamed she had that sort of past, did you? And I would not have told you, if you hadn't made that unjust remark about her: bright and beautiful as the vicar's daughter in a Victorian novel. Pah!

There's nothing artificial in her character. It's not an attack of poise brought on by reading too many women's magazines. Dina impresses everyone, even on first acquaintance, with her extraordinary inner happiness. It's real, and only an unromantic mind like yours could have thought it was not. She adores her husband. Can't see anything ordinary in him. And she is convinced that there were never such children as hers. Nothing exceptional in that, of course—except that she happens to be right. Dina is entirely without any sense of guilt; that unnecessary, unjustified sense of guilt which takes the spirit out of so many of our highly civilised women. She is in love with life and she can't forget it.

I suppose you know that Dina is of pure Polish blood and breeding. By 1944 there was nothing left, of all she believed in, but patriotism. War and politics had made her an orphan, and the little legacy which would have taken her through the university was reduced to nothing. So when she was about to become a charge on public funds she was shipped off from Warsaw as a foreign worker, and found herself in a factory at Dusseldorf making sights for guns. The Germans are a most extraordinary people. Can you imagine any other nation filling up their country with enemies in wartime? They couldn't believe that Europe really disliked being conquered by nice, comfortable, honest Nazis.

In Dina's factory I was a very favoured person, working on special lenses. That's a job which trains a man to infinite patience and readiness to accept disappointment. It married in with my real interest, which was to interfere in every way open to me — very minor ways — with the production of munitions. I was not suspected. The whole of my political past in Austria made me a very probable Nazi sympathiser. My reason for loathing Hitler and all that he stood for was simply good taste. That's a motive quite outside the ken of policemen, and I didn't go out of my way to explain it.

Dina was reported to me as promising material. Among so many worn, shabby, still pretty girls she was inconspicuous, but she had the advantage that even in the rain and smoke of Dusseldorf you could always spot her, if you were looking for her, a long way off. I had her watched for six months before I employed her.

I became fonder of her — in a fatherly way — than was strictly professional. She was so graceful and slight, with a corona of fair, fine curls and big brown eyes burning to shake the world, or at any rate that part of it governed by Hitler. And so very, very young. If she had been born ten years later than she was, all that emotion — well, it might have found an outlet in crazy worship of some crooner or other. As it was, she had as single a mind as a tiger cub on its first kill without the help of mother.

I had not the heart to use her for much except messages; and once or twice, when it was reasonably safe, she accidentally left a little parcel of explosives — disguised as a packet of sandwiches, for example — in contact with a machine lathe. She had little to fear from any ordinary questioning. She could readily admit that she ran innocent errands for me.

The less one knew, the better. But I had occasionally to deliver material to another organisation — a suicidal outfit of Poles, led by a Colonel Lipski who passed himself off as a sturdy blacksmith from Posen. Communication with him was difficult — we were taking our orders from different sources — and I had recourse to Dina. She could disappear into the wet, black streets and become part of the drifting smoke and drifting masses. It was quite natural for Poles to foregather. We all had so much freedom.

That's an odd view of wartime Germany, isn't it? But sometimes, after working hours, the streets seemed to hold more foreigners than Germans. The situation must have been a nightmare for the Gestapo. They did their best. Efficiency was impossible, so they made up for it by terror. In our factory alone they tortured and shot four men for sabotage. Two were loyal Nazis. One was their own agent. And the fourth, a very conscientious foreman. A little too conscientious. In that fog of suspicion we were remarkably successful at faking evidence against anyone who was better dead.

Still, human nature was on the Gestapo side. Their agents, sharing a street corner or a café or just a damp patch of shadow with weary foreigners, were bound to make friends. Those war slaves were simple people, straight from tenements or villages. Five per cent would betray whatever they didn't understand for money; and twenty per cent couldn't keep a secret without telling a neighbour. That made a full quarter whom it was lethal to trust. And into that sullen, formless mass I had to send Dina. She must have a felt a little like your Victorian vicar's daughter then.

Some such murderous rumour, something whispered and overheard in the dusk at the factory gate, enveloped Lipski and his organisation. I don't suppose the Gestapo knew at first what would come out of the arrests. But Dina and I knew. Lipski hated too passionately. If they really went to work on him, he was likely to spit in his interrogator's face and boast of his past and what he had done — naturally taking all the blame on himself. He was a very gallant man, but not clever. A trained Gestapo expert, with such a spirited confession to work from, could lead the blacksmith-colonel much farther along his line of contacts that he ever meant to go.

It was then that Dina came to my workshop. She had every right to be there. She was employed in the storekeeper's office, and I used to pass my indents through her. My assistants just grinned whenever I invited her into my little private office. Not unpleasantly. The smiles merely commented on the sentiment of a middle-aged Austrian for a waif as tense as the glass on which he worked.

'I shall be next,' she said.

She gloried in it. Think of your own daughter in her most unaccountable and resolute mood—that was Dina! She might have determined to run away and get married. A grim bridegroom. Not to be feared if he embraced her instantaneously. But the Gestapo might ensure that the honeymoon was protracted.

It was a wonder that she had not been arrested already. Lipski was possibly unconscious for the time being.

'Try to believe that you know nothing,' I told her. 'Why shouldn't you have taken messages for me? My assistants, the foreman, the office boy—they are always trotting about the works with notes from me. I have a passion for writing notes. Forget down to the bottom of your soul that what I gave you had any more significance than what I give them!'

She refused to be put off.

'It's not the messages among ourselves,' she answered. 'I am the only person who could lead the police from Lipski to us.'

'But you will not,' I assured her.

'How can you know I won't?' she cried. 'How can *I* know? We must make sure—both of us.'

I pretended not to know what she wanted. She was so young, and death is so irrevocable.

'You promised,' she said.

Well, I had—to all of them who worked directly under me. Yes, I had explained to them that instant death was quite painless, reminded them that soldiers seldom had that much luck, told them that the only thing to fear was betrayal of a comrade. All very suitable. No doubt there were thousands of commanding officers handing out the same line on both sides of twenty different fronts. But that did not make it less true.

I had the pills locked up with my personal instruments, marked Aspirin. Hold one in your handkerchief, male or female, convey it to your mouth and crunch. A remedy that no one should be without, as the advertisements say. It was a pity that the establishment behind Lipski had never distributed free samples. But they were doing sabotage on a shoe-string.

Dina was bound to be questioned. Lipski would not give her away—not even spitting at them. Poles are always chivalrous. But nothing could prevent them finding out, by a process of elimination, that she was among three or four suspects who came into the story out of darkness and vanished back into darkness. And Dina, of course, could lead them to me. Not that I mattered. I had cyanide, too.

I gave her what the situation demanded, remembering—oh, what she was alive and all she wouldn't be if she were dead.

Dina was arrested next day. She did her duty. Only eighteen she was when her teeth met in the pill. Don't they say that all his past life revolves before a drowning man? Well, before her, in the second that was left to her, revolved all the future she might have had. The lovers, the husband, the children, the peace which somehow, some day, would bring long unimaginable years.

Less than a second, I had told her. But there was time in it for a moment of truth when the fifty or sixty years which might have been could advance her, on account, their visions of fulfilment.

Just as real, perhaps, as a glimpse of heaven to the old and pious. But she was too young. No harps or angels or Nirvana for her. Life—that was the heaven which Dina saw unfolding. Yet she crunched and she swallowed, and her heart raced so that she thought its last fluttering was on her. But still the heavy boots marched on each side of her, and she with them.

All men are much the same. My duty was to see that she died before she could talk. Theirs was to exterminate the saboteur. Yet they were quite content to question her decently for a day, and then put her in Ravensbruck Camp as a highly suspicious character against whom nothing definite could be proved. Even in Ravensbruck the commandant made a sort of pet of her. When for a few seconds you have longed to live with a passion that most of us never know in our whole existence, your joy thereafter is bound to make its mark on those around you.

And so on to this day. What we see in her is a woman whose every cell is still rejoicing because it is alive. There's little room for hurt after a rebirth like that, and none at all for guilt. And love of husband and children is an unexpected Gift of God that goes far beyond the hackneyed phrase, even beyond her dreams of them while crunching cyanide. That is the explanation of Dina.

A miracle? No, I gave her real Aspirin, of course. There are times when the preservation of an individual is more important than any good reason of state. Isn't that what we were fighting about?

8

The Case of Valentin Lecormier

M. LE CONSUL:

I ask you to excuse the paper upon which this is written. Where I am, the necessities of civilisation do not exist. Even the poor devils of police who patrol the frontier do not normally carry paper. In order to write to you I had to capture an assistant-inspector of customs, and relieve him of his spare account-books.

This is not a begging letter. You cannot help me. Whether I live or die depends entirely on myself, and I do not know which I deserve. In any case one rarely receives what one merits. No, M. le Consul, I write to you only to establish the nationality of my wife and children.

We were married by the priest of Ferjeyn on April 15th, 1944. The marriage is recorded in the church register; and also the births of my three sons. They are French and, though so young, they know it. In twelve years they will be ready and willing for their military service. I shall be grateful to you if you will enter their names upon the register of French citizens. As for my wife, she is a simple Christian Arab. Syria is her country, and without me she would be lost in France.

M. le Consul, my name is Valentin Lecormier, formerly sergeant-major of cavalry. I am a deserter. It is very rare for a warrant officer of the regular army to desert, but I will explain it as best I can. There may be some record of me in your office files, but it is probably considered that I am dead.

I joined the Army in 1932. For me it was a profession as congenial as any other, and, to tell you the truth, what most attracted me was the pleasant life of our little garrison

190

towns. I was not such a fool, of course, as to suppose that I should spend all my years of service under the trees of the main square; but we export our civilisation with our soldiers, and I knew that I should seldom be far from a shaded pavement upon which to spend my hours of leisure.

When that damned Hitler unleashed his war, I had already passed four years in Beirut as a corporal-instructor training Arab levies. I assure you I had no ambition. I merely applied for every post which suited my taste for small towns, and pretended to have the requisite qualifications. I persuaded my superiors that I spoke Arabic. And if you are young and make a show of accomplishment which you wish you had, it will not be long before in fact you have it. That's life.

After the fall of France, when our army and government in Syria declared for Vichy, I rode over into Palestine with my troop to join the Fighting French. It was not a question of choice. I have never made a choice for myself more than any other man. Choice? There is no such thing. One follows events, and gets out of the mess as best one can. That is, I believe, what they now call existentialism. A long word for the practical philosophy of every soldier.

No, I did not trouble my head with de Gaulle or Pétain, or faith in France or the lack of it. I considered only my affection for Colonel Collet. A mountebank. One admitted it. Still, a soldier must feel love like the rest of us, and he cannot be held responsible for where he places it.

After that there was no time for decisions. The campaign against our own countrymen in Syria. A harsh interval while we exchanged our horses for armoured cars. The Western Desert. Bir Hachim. And believe me, M. le Consul, the world was wrong to make such a fuss of that battle. I was there, and I tell you we could not run away because the Boches were all round us. And then it was hardly decent to surrender when there had been so much surrendering in France.

And so, better men being dead, I was hoisted up to squadron sergeant-major, and on we went to Tripoli (where one saw a town and a square and a civilised café again) and into Italy and back to Syria for rest and reorganisation.

In that narrow strip of Syria between Turkey and Iraq, which is called the Duck's Bill from its shape, there was some fear of a rising of Moslem fanatics. So they sent me out in charge of a detachment. A captain was in command, of course, but an old soldier was needed to see that he came to no harm. Since I now spoke fluent Arabic, it was an excuse to present myself with a deal of liberty. I used to pass my days at Ferjeyn, which, being an island of Christians set upon a mountain in the middle of two hundred thousand Moslems, was the right post for a man of tact.

At Ferjeyn, M. le Consul, I fell in love. She was the daughter of the headman, John Douaihy. What else could you expect, given eight years of foreign service and no hope of France? Our regiment had not been picked for the invasion — for there were not enough of us left to be any use to a higher formation — and so we comforted ourselves with the thought that it could not possibly succeed. I repeat, we had no hope of France.

I should not like you to think that my love for Helena Douaihy was that of a soldier who marries, in a moment of supreme boredom with interminable male society, the first decent girl he had seduced. No, as a responsible warrant officer, I used to warn my lads against such unsuitable attachments.

I did not seduce her. I have nothing of which to accuse myself but the strange and bitter chivalry of the French. Since it has persisted in our nation through five centuries of common sense, it is not surprising that in a poor devil like myself it should outlive those many years when my only choice was between celibacy and army prostitutes.

It was her rags, I believe, that aroused in me an over-whelming desire to cherish her. Her father was by no means badly off. But you know the Arab. He does not waste money on daughters, unless they must be curry-combed and clipped for church or a party. Yes, it was her rags. When Helena was working in the fields or drawing water, she seemed to me like a fifteen-year-old princess of the romances, dressed in the clouts of the kitchenmaid. She had worn her one frock so long that the stuff had become threadbare over her breasts, worn away by the continual sharp pressure from within. Well, that is not a pheno-menon which repeats itself in later years; but her face has kept its delicacy. I assure you that one would turn round and stare after her even in the streets of Paris. And she has been a wife without reproach. That is what I wish to impress on you. In her way she is a true bourgeoise, and she has helped me to bring up our sons so that France can be proud of them.

It was not then — on detachment in the Duck's Bill — that fate made of me a deserter. In the spring of 1944 we were ordered, for God knows what reason, to Cyprus, where we found ourselves among a lot of damned Englishmen and Greeks. Of the two I preferred the Greeks. They have inherited the culture of the Roman Empire, whereas the English have no idea of what a town should be.

There we were. More training. For ever training. It seemed to us that we were destined to nothing but camps, year after year of camps, till we were old and grey.

It happened, M. le Consul, that the major wished to buy some wine for the officers' mess, and I for the sergeants. The wines of Cyprus are fairly drinkable, but merchants are inclined to sell any filth in their cellars to soldiers, since the English, whose palates are rotted by beer and whisky, do not know good from bad. So we decided to go out in civilian clothes. The major pretended to be a French diplo-mat on leave, who had rented a villa in the hills, and I — I dressed myself as any poor and decent Syrian who might be his cook or butler.

We settled down in a cellar by the quay to taste what was offered. The wines were good and, to tell the truth, we forgot all differences of rank. The patron did not bother us. He slept behind his counter, and only woke up when we called for another bottle. The major was not a bad little chap, but of the right wing of the de Gaullists. He was a royalist and thought of nothing but some damned Henry V who was to come to the throne of France. As for me, I am a republican. True, the Third Republic made me vomit. But being what we are it is the best we could do.

Well, at three in the morning we began an argument. It was foolish. A sergeant-major should not talk politics, and least of all with an officer. But he was as bored as I. We were two Frenchmen, isolated among Englishmen and Greeks, with no hope of home. I cannot remember at this distance what was said. No doubt there were faults on both sides. Our nerves were exasperated. And so I found that I had hit my commanding officer over the head with a bottle.

I examined him. I had enough experience of wounds. I said to myself that he would not die, but that he would need a comfortable week in hospital. The patron had not woken up. In his trade, if one is to get any sleep at all, one must not pay attention to a little noise. I bandaged my major and wrapped him in blankets, and walked out on to the quay.

M. le Consul, I had made no plan whatever. Choice, as at every turning in a man's life, was forced on me. It was that hour, with dark turning to grey, when no one takes a decision, least of all a soldier. He stands to, and obeys. As for the general who issued the orders the night before, he is fast asleep.

I walked on the deserted quay, regretting that I should

never see my Helena again, for she would have married some village notable long before I came out of gaol. True, they might treat me more leniently. We old soldiers of the Fighting French were charitable to one another. But the best I could hope for was the mental hospital. And indeed I had well deserved that I, a sergeant-major, should spend five years sewing rabbits upon babies' nappies under the eye of the occupational therapist.

The black mass of Lebanon showed up against the red of dawn. It was not a cloud. It stood upon eighty miles of steel sea and striped haze, and so solid it was that I prostrated myself like a Moslem praying upon the quay, and bowed my farewell to Helena and to Ferjeyn and to Asia. I must admit that I was very drunk.

Then a voice hailed me from the dock:

'Brother, that is not the direction of Mecca!'

I looked up. A caique was drifting out on the dawn wind, her captain at the great tiller. Her sail was half hoisted, and she was painted blue and yellow. I asked the captain where he was bound.

'To Beirut,' he said, 'if it pleases God. Come with me, brother, and learn the difference between east and south!'

He took me for a fellow Moslem, you see. And they do not care about passports and police controls, those chaps in the caiques.

All the same, he intended a mere sailor's jest, I suppose, rather than a serious invitation. But I did not wait for him to change his mind. I would have obeyed any sensible suggestion from any quarter. I dived in, and he luffed and picked me up. I told him with much detail that I was a Turk who had escaped from an English prison. That amused him so richly that he did not ask too many questions.

And there I was condemned by a single impulsive act to the life of a deserter, and presented at the same time — for luck cuts both ways—with a chance of permanent freedom, since it would be assumed for at least a week that I was still in Cyprus.

The west wind was fresh and steady, and by sunset we were close under the land. Part of our cargo, like that of any caique in wartime, was contraband. In the night the captain rowed his crates ashore on the beach of Batroun. Half an hour later he had resumed his voyage to Beirut, and I was walking to the coast road through a darkness that smelt of the spring rains.

By bus and lorry—and detours on foot around the control posts of military police—I reached Damascus, where I had banked for years the economics of my military pay. It was a little account which I had kept quiet. Not that it was dishonest. Far from it. Custom demanded that when an Arab trooper was posted to the squadron of his choice or recommended for promotion he should give a little present. That was something which everyone knew, but of which no one spoke. So it was only decent that I should not flaunt my bank account before the eyes of the military authorities.

I was sure that there would be no enquiry for me yet in Syria. After all it was only forty-eight hours since I had deserted. So I presented myself at the bank without fear. There was a clerk on duty who knew me, and it was not the first time he had seen me in civilian clothes.

The sum was small. It would not have bought a decent tobacco stall in France; but it was enough for a house and farm at Ferjeyn, and something over. Provided I presented myself as a prosperous man, well-dressed and careless, I had no doubt that John Douaihy would give me his daughter. They are easily impressed, the Syrians. So long as nothing is stinted at the marriage, they do not much care what happens to a daughter after.

The journey along the edge of the desert to Hassetche was arduous. I had no papers—beyond a good French military map — and so it was essential to avoid all roads and public transport. Stained with dust and salt water as I was, I resembled the poorest of Arabs. I bought a camel and pretended to be taking it to market — always at the next town along my route. I have had charge of many animals in my time, but I tell you a camel is the only one it is impossible to love. One receives a more civilised response from an intelligent jeep. Sometimes I rode my camel and sometimes I led her. She was only a stage property and of little use to me. Perhaps she knew it.

At Hassetche I sold my camel and bought a fine pony and dressed myself decently. Then I rode to Ferjeyn and was received by John Douaihy with that superb hospitality which the Christian Arab reserves for the elder European brother — provided, of course, that he behaves like a brother. John knew what I wanted from him, though we did not yet mention it. There was a difficulty to be disposed of first. He expected me to tell him that I had enough of the war.

I should explain to you that our commune, isolated for centuries among hostile Mohammedans, saw nothing at all disgraceful in being a deserter. No fighting had ever counted for them but the long bickering between Christian and Moslem, which in their soil was native as the mulberry. War between Christian nations was to them as irresponsible as the jealousy between the House of France and the House of Anjou must have seemed to a sensible Crusader. A free fighting man who withdrew himself from participation in any such lunacy was not to be blamed.

But why tell them at all, you will ask. Because I had to prevent them from chattering far and wide that there was a real Frenchman in Ferjeyn. If they understood that I had deserted and was wanted by the police, they would be as untruthful about my past as if I had been one of themselves. And it was not difficult for them to accept me. They think in terms of religion, not, as we do, in terms of nationality. I was Christian. I spoke Arabic. Therefore, if I wished to be, I was one of the commune. It is true that they were Maronites and I (according to that enthusiastic socialist, my father) was an atheist. But Ferjeyn and Helena were well worth a mass.

M. le Consul, I married Helena and I bought my few hectares of good land. My father-in-law—for, being headman, he had the right—gave me the identity card of a man of Ferjeyn who had gone to Morocco twenty years before and never returned. I am no longer Valentin Lecormier. I am Nadim Nassar. I permit myself to bore you with these details, since I hope that you will wish to check the truth of my story. My sons, though they bear the name of Nassar, are in fact three little Lecormiers, and, I repeat, they look to France and to you to claim them in due season.

You have no interest in a renegade? M. le Consul, I plead my long service, such as it was, and I would beg you to understand that there is not all the difference you would think between Ferjeyn and a mountain village of France. I was happier there than I have ever been. True, I was ravished by my little Helena, but ravishment is not necessarily content. I will try to tell you how I could be content, and still remain a Frenchman.

Where there is stone for wall and paving, one is not wholly a barbarian. My house was well above the commune, and three hundred metres below the top of the mountain. In a hard winter the lowest tongues of snow felt for the limit of my land and melted into the stone channels that irrigated my terraces. When the sluices were open, the water ran on an even slope, quite silent and without foam; but the rush was so fast and smooth that a leaf falling into the channel vanished to eternity as swiftly as a human life.

When you looked up from the plain of Duck's Bill towards Ferjeyn, you saw nothing but stone, and strips of green. Terrace rose over terrace, and above each was the bare rock from which the earth had been stripped, and packed into the narrow fields that girdled the mountain. But when you looked down from my house over the grey walls and flat roofs of Ferjeyn, there were only green tops, falling in steps, of orchard and vineyard and olive and wheat. I find that civilised, M. le Consul.

The life — well, it was a little primitive but not unfamiliar. We had our group of village notables, and the café where we gathered at the end of the day's work. True, when I first knew it, our café was nothing but a hole in a ruin furnished with bench and counter. So I set into the pavement three tables which I had made with my own hands, and planted a vine to give shade. There we played our games and drank our wine and araq — as good fathers of families, of course — and watched the life of the commune on the flag-stones of the little square. There were John Douaihy and his brother Boulos, and the priest, the saddler, the grocer and myself.

The square was my delight. On the north side was an ancient, tumbledown colonnade with a roof of red tiles supported by slender pillars of stone. It had been built by a Greek architect exiled from Constantinople to our remote province. In your travels for France, M. le Consul, you must often have lived in some alien and melancholy spot which, all the same, became a home for you because of an avenue of trees or the satisfying proportions of a single house or perhaps a garden. You will know then what I felt for our square. It was the link with my civilisation.

I cannot say that outside the square the streets resembled those of France. To tell you the truth, they did not exist. The houses were separated by mud in winter and dust in summer. As an old sergeant-major with a taste for tidiness, I did my best for proper streets, but without success. All the same, I persuaded Ferjeyn to establish a rubbish dump and pay a collector and a cart. That was a triumph. Admittedly he was the village idiot, but he was the only garbage man within a hundred miles.

You will have gathered, M. le Consul, that my advice was respected. I gave it rarely. If there were anything I wished to change, I was well content to spend a patient year in changing it. Peace — that was all I asked. Peace for my Helena and myself.

After Syria was given her independence, the first thought of the simple Moslem peasants around us was to raid the Christians. A sort of celebration. It was very natural. Had the Christians been in the majority, they would have endeavoured to raid the Moslems. But the government, in those early days, was determined to be as efficient as the French. They strengthened the garrison at Hassetche, and they reminded the fanatics that Syria was a land of many religions, all with the same rights of citizenship. A massacre — even though a little one and carried out for pure sport — could not be permitted.

Then, as you know, the honeymoon ended and the politicians returned to the making of money. At Damascus there were revolutions. Over here, in the lost corner of the country, there was discontent. And with us when one is discontented, one distracts oneself by taking action. The gendarmerie is weak and scattered, and there is little to prevent a criminal from escaping into Turkey or Iraq. For my part I prefer Turkey.

Day and night Ferjeyn began to talk of danger. I have never understood how the Arabs can be called fatalists. In a crisis they are hysterical as women. One must admit that there was a little danger, but only of stones thrown, of rifles fired too high to do much damage, of a house burned and cattle stolen and a woman raped — an excitement of spirit which two of my old Arabic-speaking corporals could have extinguished by mere calm and authority!

We, the notables, met at night conspiratorially, behind closed shutters in my house or the house of John Douaihy or the priest's. That made a good impression on the village. But my venerable colleagues had no more sense than children. They wanted me to make a fortress of the mountain.

'Willingly,' I answered. 'If I have twenty men who shoot to kill, I will hold Ferjeyn from one harvest to the next.'

Ah, yes, I could have them. What did I think? That they were no soldiers? Of course I could have them, and the boys and greybeards too—

But they knew and I knew that this was all talk. The truth was that they dreamed of constructing an impassable Maginot Line, for they wished to hold Ferjeyn with the least possible bloodshed. And they were right. We were sixteen hundred men, women and children, surrounded by two hundred thousand Moslems. The only tactics by which I could hold Ferjeyn—cunning and ambush and ruthless slaughter—would have meant blood feuds with the Christians that might endure a hundred years.

When I had pointed out that even a Chinese wall would not stop Moslems unless we had men on top of it trained to kill, the priest begged me to go to Palestine and buy a tank. For him a tank was a piece of magic that would make Ferjeyn invincible. He might have been talking of a sort of beetle that could move itself and fight.

I soon had enough of these councils of war which were only exclamations. I refused to take command. I wasn't having any. I was content to eat and drink and till my land. That was my life.

They did their best to persuade me. The priest waggled his fingers at me as if I had been a child he were about to baptise, and told me to fight for my religion. I was polite, for I had to appear impressed. But I could not share his opinion that it was a service to God to murder Moslems. All my life I have been unwilling to anticipate the intentions of the high command.

Another night John Douaihy warned me that he and I might lose our property. He was at his most dignified; he spoke like a governor of the Bank of France. I shrugged my shoulders. What could we lose? We were not rich. And a crazy band of Moslems is not an army of occupation. They do enough damage to boast about, and then go home. They cannot take away the soil in wheelbarrows.

Then the women and children. I must defend them. That was the excitement of the saddler, who, in his old age, had married a wife nearly as pretty as Helena. Well, the appetites of radiers are not a matter upon which one should let imagination rest — unless one is the wife of an old man — but someone has to be sacrificed, and memory is short.

'Brothers,' I would say to them, 'let us endure the chastisement that God sends us in the firm faith that it will quickly pass — so long as we have bribed the civil administration, given feasts to Moslem notables and assured the interest of the gendarmes.'

All that we had done. We knew how to look after ourselves. Without any government at all, Ferjeyn would have got on very well with its neighbours. No need of proof. We Christians had been on our mountain since the Arab conquest. The flagstones of our little square were Roman. That was the strength of my argument. I appealed to history.

But, alas, we had a government of politicians and they took a hand, withdrawing all troops from the district. Their intention was obvious. They meant to divert attention from their misdeeds by allowing a raid on the Christians, and then to punish those who were responsible. Thus they could imprison a number of their political opponents without having to admit the real reason.

Down on the plain the harvest was over and the peasants were idle in the heat. Any day the attack might come. It tried our nerves a bit. Helena would sometimes scream at me from the courtyard because I was calm. When a woman's pride in her husband is hurt, she wishes all the world to know it. It is not so very different in France. I remember the wife of a colonel who would rush out on the barrack square whenever he came back late from Paris, and address him from a wholly unnecessary distance. As a result we had pity on him, and made him no more trouble than we could help.

You will say, M. le Consul, that I was unworthy of the hospitality I had received, and that I had become a coward. No, I have never been extravagantly afraid to die. But one wants to know for what. We of the Fighting French died because there was nothing much to live for, and it was easy to form the habit; but in peace that won't do. One's duty is to keep under cover.

And then I and mine were safe. I did not share Ferjeyn's hatred of the Moslems. All the surrounding country knew that I was born or had become a Frenchman, and that I was only a Maronite Christian by courtesy. A man such as I could be killed any time, free of charge, if he were disliked; but if he had won affection he would be spared, raid or no raid. I was not a hereditary enemy to be treated according to the rules of the game; I could be judged on my merits. God knows I have few enough, but I have always made friends among the simple.

My only preparation was to buy myself a good rifle. For eight years I had had no need of arms, and I was convinced I should not need them now. Still, I took care to have a whole case of good ammunition. It is idiotic to find oneself short.

We knew twelve hours before the Moslems of the plain began to stir that the raid was coming. How? M. le Consul, the Syrians cannot tell you how they know anything at all. They tip out before you a vast manure-heap of rumour. It is potentially fertile, but before it can be of use it must be spread so wide that no one can discover from what cartload the green shoot of truth has sprouted.

It was the native custom to spend only one happy hour among the Christians, attacking before dawn and leaving at sunrise. Those of us who had strong stone houses in the town, with the stables below and the living-rooms above, barricaded themselves in and demolished the outside staircases. Those who had houses of one story, more or less European and quite unfitted for defence, sent their women and children up to the top of the mountain.

Helena wanted to go with them. I forbade it—but not, I beg you to believe, as an Arab husband who receives obedience as of right. A woman, frightened or in tears —one ignores her or distracts her attention by caress and compliment. That was not my way. I treated my wife as an equal, but I did not forget that a happy child obeys without knowing it obeys. I infected her with my confidence. It may be that she was the only woman in Ferjeyn to sleep a little.

I was sure that the raiders would not waste time in climbing as high as my house. At three in the morning, however, as a sensible precaution, I stationed myself upon the high roof of a ruined storehouse from which I could command the path. There, under cover of the parapet, I could speak with any of my Mohammedan acquaintances who might be out for sport. In case my friendliness were not immediately understood, I had, of course, my rifle.

They do not come on silently, the Arabs. It was that which first made me feel disgust, both as a soldier and a European. Good God, if one wants to surprise and kill, one should move like a tiger—whereas these poor barbarians yapped like a pack of dancing jackals! They were drunk with their religion. I understood more clearly the nature of the raid. For them, it was a sort of revival meeting.

I have no patience with fanatics. I am far from the convinced atheist that my father wished me to be, but I must admit that unbelievers have their uses. A little mockery compels the religious to behave themselves. In France it is enough to set the tone of public opinion. The same for alcohol. What prevents us all from drinking ourselves incapable? The fear of ridicule.

But mockery is a townsman's weapon. That yelling mob of half-wit peasants called for something stronger. How many of them there were I could not tell. Over five hundred. Enough, at any rate, if one turned a Hotchkiss on them, to make the houris of paradise work overtime. Their torches showed the black masses skipping up the tracks to Ferjeyn, with the flankers leaping from terrace to terrace. They might have been a great herd of goats with the spring fever on them.

The two streets that led into the village were defended by our young men. I do not think I malign them if I say that the chief object of each was to escape with life and with a sword cut or two to show that he had fought bravely. That was what we had known all along, but it was indecent to admit it. They were overrun. Of Christians and Moslems there were five dead — persons of no importance who could be easily forgotten when the affair was patched up and speeches made and compensation paid. The leaders, as in our own wars, were well behind the front line. It is curious when you see a vagueness, a mere way of thought, translated into action. Ferjeyn did not mean to kill. Some defence was necessary, both for self-respect and to discourage raiding in future, but unforgivable losses had to be avoided.

The horde skipped and gambolled through our deserted streets, with their dirty rags floating behind them and yelling for Christian blood, just as we do, at times of crisis, for that of bankers or politicians. Here and there, in the light of the torches, I saw a face I knew. It was rather the shadow of a face, so distorted by frenzy as to be unrecognisable. They set fire to whatever would burn. That was not much, for the old houses of Ferjeyn had walls a metre thick. My poor village idiot was chased and sacrified. And somewhere they burst into a house. I heard the cries of the women.

The light was growing. They did not attempt to climb to the higher farms; there was enough for them to do in Ferjeyn. They burst into our café and sacked it, breaking the bottles of araq and emptying out the wine barrels down the hill. Among them were drovers and pedlars who, when they came up to Ferjeyn on a friendly errand, would toss down a drink like anyone else and take the more pleasure since it was forbidden; but now our poor wine became a symbol of the unbeliever. So they tore down the whole shop, and set fire to counter, shelves and barrels in the square.

From my roof-top I could see all — the fire, the dead and the bodies of two women upon whom they had used their knives. That was their habit, and it was Ferjeyn's to forgive. There would be apologies and then peace for another twenty years. A Moslem raid was a risk of our life. In civilised countries there are worse risks and more of them. A woman who has been run over — she is not a pretty sight either.

Then they started on the church. I should have liked to see our priest stand in the doorway with his Cross. That indeed would have been religion. And it might have worked. The Arabs are easily made ashamed by dignity. But he was up the mountain, comforting the women. Well, if it was not his business, it was certainly not mine.

They should have gone home, for there was light enough now to recognise every lunatic among them; but they were still not content. They began to knock down the stone pillars on the north side of the square, and to lever up the pavement. That, M. le Consul, was not religious mania. It was jealousy of our common heritage.

Do you know the Moslem villages in our corner of Syria? They are mud huts built upon a mound of their own filth, ten or twenty metres above the plain, which has accumulated through the ages. Well, that men who exist in those conditions should kill and burn and rape is very natural. It even astonishes me that they should lose patience only once or twice in a generation. But they cannot be permitted to outrage all the decencies.

In that moment I saw Ferjeyn as our possession, yours and mine. I will try to explain. It was a part of France or Italy or Spain. A little Christian town. It is true that the inhabitants were Arabs, and the society upon our square did not amount to much. Nevertheless, town square it was. And even in France one does not expect profundities from the comrades with whom one plays dominoes at the Café de la Gare.

M. le Consul, I repeat that no man can take a decision at dawn. He obeys orders and that is all. I made no choice. Being what I am, I was incapable of acting other than I did. I took, if you like, my orders from the stone. It was a part of Europe which was being violated, and that was not to be endured from barbarians who lived in mud, whose souls were brittle as mud.

I assure you that I remained calm. I was not affected by the women lying there nor the child impaled upon a banner nor my poor village idiot who was hardly distinguishable from his own garbage. But when they hurled down the slender drums of a pillar, I told myself it was time to act. It is true that I should have been more cautious for the sake of my wife and children. But, M. le Consul, what is the use of a family if you have not your little piece of civilisation in which to put them?

I lay down regretfully upon the parapet. From the square below, my roof-top was confused among others. They could not see who was shooting nor from where. I do not pretend to be a crack shot, but I am an old soldier who can do damage even when he is under fire. Being forced into the role of avenging angel, and equally invisible, I could not miss.

First I picked off the poor fools who were tearing down the pillars, and then the banner bearers and then any man who appeared to be well-dressed. That saved the government the trouble later. I had only just begun on my third clip when Ferjeyn emptied. The light was now growing faster than they could run. I shot them down on the road and in the gaps between the ranks of olives. I had for a little while the illusion that they were Boches; it was as if I were finishing the war from which I had retired. In any case there were resemblances. The peoples of the north and of the east — they have always been the enemies of our way of life.

On the edge of the plain, thinking they were out of range, they stopped to wave their bloody ironmongery and shout defiance. I bagged two more at twelve hundred metres. I blame myself. It was a waste of ammunition that I should have rebuked in a recruit.

When the sun rose I went down into the square of Ferjeyn with my hot rifle under my arm. I might have been the only man alive. The fire was going out. The shelves and barrel staves had burned, but the counter of our café was only charred. It stood like a town altar to good humour. I do not say it had never been abused, but less than most other altars.

The banner bearers lay on the pavement, together with the child and the two women. There was also a fanatical sheikh from the biggest village of the plain. He would cost Ferjeyn a shocking sum in blood money, that one. A single pillar was all we had lost. Two dead men lay among the fallen drums. And then there was the debris where they had jammed in the alleys trying to escape. Well, men being what they are, every square must be washed with blood in the course of its life if it is to remain inviolate. I found a broken bottle with a cupful of araq at the bottom. That did me good.

And so up the hill to my house. Eyes no doubt were looking at me from behind barred shutters. But nobody called to me. Nobody ventured out. They did not know what to believe, or whether the raid was indeed over. They were good, simple souls, inclined to put faith in the supernatural whenever explanation was difficult. They had no means of knowing that the only saint concerned was my rifle.

I found Helena praying, with a child on each side of her and the eldest behind. All four were very stiff and imploring, like the figures in one of those pictures in the Louvre which are all red and blue and gold. I had allowed her to teach the boys what she wished. It was not right, perhaps; but I assured my conscience that the teachings of such a woman as Helena could do only good.

I told her the raid was finished, and that it was not likely to be repeated in our lifetime. I did not yet explain what had happened. She had to be allowed her moment of joy. Two or three such moments to give strength, and one can endure one's seventy years of kicks up the backside.

The boys, of course, demanded if I had killed lots of enemies. They were disappointed when I said I did not know. What do they have in their heads, those little people, that they should think killing is so difficult? And why do their eyes shine, when they themselves cannot eat a lamb killed for the Easter dinner if they have known it alive?

Well, I cleaned my rifle and made a good breakfast. I was thoughtful. As an old sergeant-major, I am naturally a bit of a politician and I began to see what was on the way to me. There are times, M. le Consul, when one apprehends with absolute certainty the fate that is approaching, yet one chooses to think it has no more reality than a bad dream.

All four of us went to work on my terraces. It is not a bad life, that, when the family works together without paying or receiving wages. Each one knows that the others—even the smallest—are doing their best. And at the end of the day there is the little town in which the father of a family can relax with his companions.

My harvest was not yet in, for on the mountain we were six weeks behind the plain. As I swung my scythe—I could not bring myself to use a sickle like my neighbours—I wondered if I should ever eat the bread that Helena would make from our wheat. There is no bread in the world like our flat loaves. It even makes you forget the crusty rolls of France. But you will have eaten with the Christians high on Lebanon, M. le Consul, and you know.

Well, at eleven there was a civic procession to my land—John and Boulos Douaihy, the grocer and the saddler (whose wife, no doubt, had now decided that she really had not missed much). I led them to the house. Helena brought us meat and wine, and retired. The Arab woman does not intrude on the society of men; she is perfectly capable of upsetting afterwards whatever they have decided.

We congratulated ourselves upon the courage with which we had so brilliantly dispersed the raid. We talked for an hour, showing nothing but fine Arabic and goodwill. But at last there was a shade of embarrassment. Not one of them knew for certain what had happened.

I explained, deprecatingly, that I had perhaps fired one or two shots and that, seeing it was the will of God, the bullets had not been wasted. They were so puzzled that they took me literally and asked who fired the others. No way out! I admitted that all were mine.

'But how many have you killed?' John asked.

He was so appalled that he forgot his manners. A direct question like that is not asked—unless, of course, one is encouraging a good story-teller to exaggerate his exploits.

'Perhaps a dozen. Perhaps two.'

I had not counted. There were six in the square, all dead. There were eight where I had fired into the crowd (the wounded they had carried off). Then there were those in the orchards, who may have amounted to two dead and four able to crawl away. And, by the way they fell, I might count two as a result of my little lesson to them upon how far a good rifle in the hands of a French sergeant-major will carry. At least eighteen in all. I swear to you that I was shocked. It was a little too close to assassination.

John stared at me with his tarboosh jammed on his bushy grey eyebrows. He much resembled a well-fed owl. His beak was powerful, and he was of even thickness down to the point where his shanks appeared from his wide Turkish breeches. His brother, Boulos, I used to call the little owl. He had perhaps more sense, but lacked dignity. Both of them were bound in decency to exclaim their amazement and felicitations; but I knew what they were thinking. In the eye of the mind they saw the blood money we should have to pay. One cannot massacre true believers in a Moslem country. It is not enough to say, as children do, that the other began it.

We decided to keep our mouths shut. The Christian Arab is accustomed to be discreet. He has the experience of twelve hundred years behind him. There was no reason at all to tell the truth to the other inhabitants of Ferjeyn, who only knew that I had been the first to venture out into the square and that I was armed. But that much was to be expected of a man who had been a soldier.

Helena had been listening from the next room. That is the custom, and very useful — for a silent audience always gets more sense out of a debate than the participants, who for half the time are not listening but thinking of what they will say next.

When the party had gone she asked me why I had fought. To my fellow-townsmen that was no problem; they all liked to imagine themselves doing what I had done. But Helena was puzzled. Of course she was. During those weeks before the raid I had tried hard to make her understand that it was ridiculous for a man such as I to shout and wave a gun and run away with honour satisfied. And at last she had agreed that, if I would not do that, it was reasonable to keep out of local quarrels.

I could not attempt to explain to her that it was the stone which changed my mind. She would not have understood. Her home was sacred to her, but not the commune where she lived. Helena would have been quite content, provided she had her children and her husband, to inhabit a desert island.

I told her, therefore, that I had lost my temper. That was something wholly alien, but to which she was accustomed. I hasten to say, M. le Consul, that with my family I rarely lost my temper. But at inanimate objects—like, for example, an obstinate tree-root in the field or the rusted split-pin of an axle—it was my custom to curse like a madman. Such impatience is wholly European, so my outbreaks were a complete mystery to Helena. She took all as explained when I said that the stupidity of a Moslem fanatic affected me like an inanimate object. And it is possible that I was telling more truth than I knew.

In the evening a whole troop of gendarmerie rode clinking and stumbling up the track to Ferjeyn. They had come, they said, to protect us from the vengeance of the Moslems. That was mere courtesy. They knew as well as we did that those poor beggars down in the plain had had a bellyful that would last them for years. What they wanted was the truth, and they were going to stay with us until they got it.

They were good material. I could have used some of them myself in old days. And they behaved decently. That was understandable, since we fed men and horses as if they had been our invited guests. The captain was an old grey fox in his fifties, with thirty years' experience of Syrian lies. We couldn't fool him and we did not try. Every man and woman said honestly where they had been during the raid, and of course their stories tallied. There was only one liar in Ferjeyn, and that was I. I told him the truth, too, up to a

212

point—that I was not afraid of the Moslems since I had many friends among them, and that I had stayed at home and taken no part in the defence. My papers were in order, and he had no reason to doubt that I was indeed Nadim Nassar, who had spent twenty years in Morocco and France before returning home. My fellow townsmen did not talk of my origin; they were not asked. In any case I think they had all forgotten my real name. As for the Moslems of the plain, they only remembered that I had once been in the French Army—which was nothing extraordinary.

For a week the gendarmerie gave us no peace. We were always being visited by the sergeants, or summoned to the captain. They interrogated us separately and together, and confronted us with each other. As policemen, they were not bad at all. They had been trained by us, and some of them, during the war, worked with the British too. But their task was hopeless. No one had seen the shots fired. Everyone could say where he was, and had witnesses.

Then the whole investigation was bedevilled by a message from the magistrate who had been taking depositions among the Moslems. They insisted that they had been fired on by a machine-gun. It is probable that they believed it. In any case they could never admit that they had run in panic from a single rifle.

The captain started on the machine-gun. It is not difficult for an experienced man to tell whether Arabs are lying or not. I do not say he will get the truth in the end; but he will know whether or not it is being told. The gendarmerie searched for that machine-gun, and did more damage to our houses than the raiders. And all the time the captain watched our faces. At the end he could have no doubt there was no machine-gun.

Then the old fool of a priest, who was not in the secret, suggested that perhaps a band of fellow Christians had heard of our danger and ridden three hundred miles from Anti-Lebanon to help us. I have more respect for the

Church than my father had, but one must admit that they can never let well alone.

It was a most improbable suggestion. Such a thing was unheard of. And how could a band of Christians have crossed the plain and hidden themselves on our mountain without being seen? But the captain was so puzzled that he did not rule out this preposterous miracle. He searched the whole mountain, looking for the tracks of horses and the empties from the machine-gun.

At last the gendarmerie left us. Horses and equipment in good order, they rode off down the hill. Considering that they had been five years without a French officer, they were well-disciplined and a credit to their training. Nor did they lose interest in us. They chose their agents cleverly; during the next month there were several strangers who visited Ferjeyn to buy or sell — all of them Christians, one a distant relative of the priest. But not another fact did they learn. I repeat: the whole village, except myself, had only to tell the truth.

Meanwhile the Moslems of the plain were overwhelmed by the consequences of their little outing. Not only had their losses been staggering for such a raid, but the government, having now sufficient excuse to arrest anyone it liked, made a clean sweep of all political opponents. The plain swarmed with police and troops. The Moslem headmen were not allowed to bargain with us or to threaten feud. It was evident that the affair was not going to be settled by our immemorial methods, but by administrative action as in Europe.

On the face of it this suited Ferjeyn. We should not have to kill half our sheep for a week's feasting while peace was made, nor pay the ruinous blood money expected. But we were not altogether content. Red tape and good order were as unfamiliar to us as to the Moslems. And we did not like the silence of the authorities.

John and Boulos Douaihy went to see the provincial

governor. They were very well received. He apologised to them for the lack of police protection, and assured them that the history of raids between Christian and Moslem was now closed for ever. That was welcome, so far as it went. But John and his brother had the impression that they were being treated as the chiefs of a wild tribe. The governor was polite, but supercilious. And, what was worse, he appeared to believe the rumour that Ferjeyn had somehow received aid from a secret society of fellow-Christians.

A month later the shock arrived. No fines, no punishment. A civilised solution. The inhabitants of Ferjeyn were to be moved right across Syria to the south of Damascus, and to take over a village of Moslems which was entirely surrounded by Christians. There would be an exchange of population as just as could be arranged, hectare for hectare and house for house. It was an act typical of the modern state. Any brutality is permissible if it simplifies the work of government servants—exception made, of course, of diplomats, M. le Consul, who maintain always the highest traditions.

Even then there was no question of handing me over. They were very loyal, my two owls. But I could not hesitate. Another man, less sceptical than I, might have spent a week of sleepless nights under the illusion that he had a decision to make. To me it was perfectly clear that what I feared had arrived, and that I could only obey my destiny.

I summoned the four notables of Ferjeyn who knew the truth, and told them that I would confess. They were astounded. I swear it had not yet occurred to them as a solution. My father-in-law and his friends were proud men, and it was not in accordance with their traditions to hand over a citizen of the commune to justice, even if he were a French deserter.

Well, but it was the obvious way out. And at last they agreed that I should tell the truth—on condition that a sure way of escape for me could be found. They promised to cherish Helena and the children, and to send me some of the proceeds of my land if it could possibly be done.

I noticed that John, though he exclaimed with the rest, was not altogether sincere. I thought that perhaps he doubted whether my confession would put off the fate of Ferjeyn. I assured him that it would. I know the Syrian officials. Even when they are determined to be Western, they do not want more work than they can help. If they were certain that the slaughter at Ferjeyn was the work of one man and that the Christians, there and elsewhere, were just as tame as they had always been, all this exchange of population would be too much bother.

Yes, John agreed to all that. It was not the question which was troubling him. He took refuge in his owlishness, and said that we had discussed enough for the day, and he would tell us what he thought another time. The fact was that he did wish to spoil an evening in which everyone had expressed such admirable and generous sentiments. In a French town he would have been a born chairman of committees.

We all insisted that he should speak out. He was the oldest of us and, when it came to local customs, by far the wisest.

'My son, Nadim Nassar, has killed forty men,' he said—the total had become a little exaggerated. 'We shall watch day and night. We shall turn ourselves into soldiers, and Ferjeyn into a camp. But even so we cannot be sure of protecting his children from revenge. The Moslems know how to wait. One year. Two years. And at last we shall find my grandchildren dead and mutilated.'

It was true. I might escape or the government might imprison me. But in the end my boys would fall to the bullet and knife.

'If only it were possible for us to swear by God that he was mad, and be believed!'

It was the saddler who thus regretted my sanity. But he was on to a good idea. There is no blood feud against the children of a madman.

To pretend to be a lunatic! M. le Consul, the more I thought of it, the more I liked it. And in that case the Moslems would no longer feel disgraced. They would be predisposed to accept the explanation. To run from a madman with a rifle — well, who wouldn't?

It was clear to me that one only needed a little cunning. I have no faith in plans, which are always worthless, but when it comes to putting on a comedy I am in my element. Any experienced sergeant-major has acquired a sense of stage management.

I told the four to keep silent about my intentions, and that in a day or two I would have something to propose. At work and in the silence of the night I rehearsed the scene in my imagination, and when I had convinced myself that it would succeed, I talked to Helena. She was appalled when I told her that to save our little town I had determined to confess. Since Ferjeyn had not demanded the sacrifice, she saw no necessity for it at all. She was quite ready to exchange her house for some filthy Moslem hovel. When she had cleaned it for a month, she insisted, we should not know the difference.

And then she relieved herself with tears. She could not sleep, she told me — myself I am always drowned in sleep — for terror of what might happen to the boys if ever it became known to the Moslems that I alone had been responsible for so many deaths. I think it was she who put the idea into the head of her father.

She claimed the right of wife and children to go with me, if I must confess and escape. But that was impossible. She had no conception of the life of an outlaw. To cross, all of us, into Turkey or Iraq was easy. And what then? A man accompanied by his family must have open dealings with strangers and foreign police. I was a French deserter. I could not account for myself—unless I gave my identity as Nadim Nassar of Ferjeyn. And if I did that, we should never have an hour when we could feel safe.

No. Alone I could vanish and perhaps remake a life. Meanwhile she would be living in comfort on her own land with her father to protect her.

Then I explained to her how I meant to save the children from blood feud. She was wise in the ways of her country, and she agreed that my scheme was possible. But not in one single detail must it fail. Raving and clowning, she said, would not be enough. To convince my public I must commit some horror that no Arab—if he were only pretending to be mad—would ever dream of. And that was to shoot her.

We were a model couple. The wives of Ferjeyn would hold me up to their husbands as a paragon. That was easier for them than to try to imitate Helena. If I could have brought myself to do so, I would have beaten her once or twice just to make the lives of my friends more peaceful. Even the Moslems spoke of Nadim Nassar and his wife. And so, if I were seen to aim at her and shoot, there would be no doubt that I was mad.

She insisted. She had no fear. She thought that a soldier such as I could pick his target, and even in a moment of emotion separate one toe from the rest. But she knew her people. There does not exist an Arab—unless trained by Europeans—who could aim at his wife and be sure of not hitting her. For them it would be an act of homicidal lunacy impossible to feign.

It was only the four notables of Ferjeyn whom I let into the secret. The rest of my fellow-townsmen continued to be left in ignorance. John Douaihy was certain that they too would be convinced I was mad. He had no fear for his daughter. It is extraordinary how the Arabs, who are always letting off firearms, never trouble to find out what is practical and what is not.

218

We sent messengers to the headmen of the villages in the plain. Nothing was said of peace-making and compensation. We hinted—in a courteous tone of regret for old times—that the government would not allow us to take the initiative. All we wanted was an informal meeting to settle up our business affairs with old Moslem friends. We said, too—to tempt their avarice—that we might be selling some land and stock before the exchange of population.

The notables of the plain sent us back an answer which was reasonably cordial, for none of them wanted us to be removed from our mountain. An interest would be gone from their empty lives. Besides, they preferred people they knew to people they did not, whatever their religion.

The day fixed for the meeting was very hot. That's understood, of course. But it was an afternoon when even the rock lizards sought the shade. The plain was indistinguishable from a desert, and on the mountain the dust rose in eddies from our terraces and reddened the leaves of the orchards. Eight of the notables came, with their principal relations and retainers. After talks (which had no content but politeness) the cushions and carpets were spread under the pillars of the square, and some thirty of us, who were the most important, sat down to eat. The women served us. Helena had put on her native costume. She was like the girls of the Crusaders, flowing in robes and embroidery. There was certainly plenty to hit without touching flesh.

It was more dignified than gay, our feast. Naturally there was still some reserve. But manners were effortless since our customs were the same. Sometimes it seems to me a pity that Arabs ever divided themselves into Christians and Moslems. They should have remained idolaters like the Hindus.

I had hidden my rifle on a roof-top across the square. None of us carried arms beyond those for pure decoration. Between John and me was sitting an old fool of a Sheikh, a man of the utmost stupidity and kindliness. He resembled

French generals I have known. He was so harmless that it was incredible anyone should outrage his feelings. A great dish of rice and placed in front of him. At that moment I seized him by the back of the neck and plunged his face and beard in it. For good measure I emptied the cream salad over my father-in-law. Then, shouting and laughing, I leaped over the heads of those who sat opposite me on the ground, and lost myself in the alleys on the other side of the square.

When I reappeared upon the roof they had not recovered from their surprise. John Douaihy was screaming apologies, and swearing that I was more Frenchman than Syrian and that I had lost my wits in the sun like any dog of a European. Bareheaded and clothes torn, I capered upon the roof-top firing shots. The Moslems were in panic. It was an unmistakable echo of the night of the raid. I think it had occurred to them, minutes before my friends took oath on it, that I might have been their only serious enemy.

I began to curse Ferjeyn and the wife who had brought me there, and I shot in the general direction of Helena. It was not difficult to miss her, but to appear mad and to miss all the other women too — well, I doubt if that scene alone would have been convincing. But Helena acted magnificently. She ran like a terrified chicken. And then, according to our arrangement, she stood still in the middle of the square and raised her arms to me for mercy.

It was a moment more tense than any crisis of war. I forced myself to concentrate. I found afterwards that my teeth had bitten deep into my tongue. I fired. She fell like a dead woman. I shall never forget how the cries of the people in the square were all at once silenced. I watched her face, which they could not see, and she made me a little smile of congratulation. Another second, and I should have blown my brains out.

She told me, when I saw her again, that the bullet had

passed through the great wings of her arms as she lifted them, and close to the body. And then what did she do, my well-beloved? She passed her left hand under her robe and ripped the flesh from a rib with the nail of her middle finger so that it would appear she had been grazed. That will seem to you barbarous, M. le Consul, but it was for her children.

They chased me, but not too close — for John and Boulos deliberately led the pursuit up the wrong alley. Meanwhile, I dropped to the ground in front of the saddler's shop. He had left his stable open, as if by accident, and his horse saddled. A pretty price he charged for it, too. But he had the right, and one must not ask too much of one's friends.

I rode through the olives and up across my own land by a little path, where no one who did not know every stone of it would dare to follow at the gallop. There were several shots fired after me — perhaps by our guests, perhaps by men of Ferjeyn who were horrified as much by the breach of hospitality as by my treatment of Helena. I passed my house and waved to my boys. Their dear faces were full of conflict as those of men. They were wildly excited by my speed, but they could not help knowing that the bullets which cut the leaves and whined were meant for me.

By God, when it was all over, I think my four friends themselves were mystified. There had been, I must admit, a certain gusto in my acting — in all, that is, that did not concern Helena. It was a relief, for once, to be permitted to have the manners of an apache and push a venerable beard into the eternal rice. There is no doubt, M. le Consul, that in the long run it is a strain for us to behave as formally as Arabs. I am ashamed of it, but I cannot deny it.

All the night I rode east towards the frontier, skirting the foot-hills of the Jebel Sinjar. The western end of the range is in Syria, and at the tip of it is the isolated mountain on which stands Ferjeyn; the eastern end is in Iraq. I had no idea what would happen or what pursuit there would be. The only certainty was that the notables of Ferjeyn would inform the authorities, and that the gendarmerie would be on the look-out for a madman with a rifle. I laid a trail that they could follow into Iraq.

On the second night I travelled north along the frontier and crossed back again into Syria. Then I rode north for a third night and forded the Tigris. Once over the river, a fugitive has only to follow the tangle of tributaries up into the hills. He is in country as green and wild as the Auvergne, but far less inhabited. And there is nothing but the uniform of the frontier patrols to tell him whether he is in Iraq or Turkey.

The little money that I had was enough for my necessities. I slept on the ground—which is no hardship in August—and I bought my bread in the villages, telling lies to account for myself. Up there one does not ask questions of a man with a rifle if he can pay his way.

But a rifle is more valuable than any gold. If you are to keep it, you must sleep on it. When I was in Weygand's Army of the Orient, I remember that at night we chained our rifles to the tent-pole. Well, there were eight weary men sleeping in a tent. A clever Arab thief loosened the guy ropes and lifted the pole without waking one of them. In the morning there was not a rifle among the lot.

I tell you this story, M. le Consul, that you may not think too hardly of me, a sergeant-major, for nearly losing my own. I was sleeping under the trees at the bend of a stream. Unlike the fast water on my land, it made a noise, that stream. It was impatient for the Tigris and the Persian Gulf. I surrendered myself utterly to the grass that was my bed. I was not over-weary, but I longed for Ferjeyn and Helena and my boys. When one is unhappy one takes refuge in sleep as in a drug.

He had taken my rifle from under my body without waking me, but at the last moment the trigger guard caught on the buckle of my bandolier. I was festooned with cartridges like some damned Russian dancer in a cabaret. He pulled and ran for it, but I, I was only five yards behind. When he stopped to fire at me from the hip I dived under the barrel and drove home my knife in his stomach.

I am no Good Samaritan, I assure you. But it grieved me to kill an honest man who was only stealing a rifle. I might have done the same, if I had had the skill.

'When did you eat last?' I asked him.

My interest was technical. If there was anything in his stomach, he was a dead man.

'The day before yesterday,' he answered.

'God is Great, brother!' I said to him, and put him on my horse with his head-cloth wrapped round his guts.

We were, I think, in Turkey, but the nearest town where there would be a doctor was Zakho in Iraq. It was not far — about thirty kilometres. And I knew the track. He was all skin and muscle like a dried herring. The stomach of the very poor is tough. I told him that if he would oblige me by keeping alive till morning we might save him yet.

We talked a little on the way. He was a Yezidi from the eastern end of the Jebel Sinjar, and he knew Ferjeyn. The Moslems hate the Yezidis even more than Christians, but have no fear of them. They are few, and do not put up any competition. Devil-worshippers they are called, because they think it tactful to be just as polite to the powers of evil as those of good. That seems to me very reasonable.

Times were hard in the Jebel Sinjar. The Iraqi end of the range is not so fertile as our little Syrian tip. So my Yezidi was going to live with his brother, who had a permit to cut and sell timber on the frontier. He had not wished to arrive empty-handed.

M. le Consul, I must apologise for all these details. You cannot be interested in the banal stories of criminals, which are not in essence very different whether they take place at the Porte de Vincennes or the head waters of the

Tigris. But I wish to show you the sort of people among whom I lived. They being what they are and I being an outlaw, my conduct becomes explicable.

There was a sort of doctor in Zakho, for the English had established a clinic there. The idea, I think, was public hygiene. But the people of Zakho are far more concerned with the cure of wounds. It's experience that counts. Me, if I had a hole in my belly, I'd rather be patched up at the regimental aid post than the finest hospital in Paris.

Well, whether it was the Iraqi doctor or a grateful devil, my Yezidi did not die. I remained in the neighbourhood. I had nothing to do, and to visit the sick-bed became an occupation. I met Merjan, the timber cutter. He was a man of magnificent moustaches, dressed in rags but well-armed. He told me that if his brother did not recover, he would send me to hell to be the dead man's servant; and if he lived, then all of his clan would be my friends for ever. It was hardly logical, but those chaps are composed of nothing but emotion.

When the man was up, with no more entrances to his stomach than the good Lord provided, I went to work with the brothers. As I had suspected from Merjan's heroics, timber-cutting was not his only occupation. It is incredible, the life between Lake Van and the frontiers. Into those remote hills the law penetrates so seldom that the tribesmen in their spare time are amateur cattle thieves and smugglers, and even professional criminals can sow and gather a crop before they have to move on. Merjan, under cover of his wood-cutting, was a sort of Thomas Cook for brigands. He was guide, intermediary and warehouseman.

I had little to do with all that. It was I who cut the wood, with two half-wit Turks to help me. I was allowed to make a living. I sold my horse to buy better tools, and often I had more cash in my belt than Merjan and his brother. The district is so poor and so wild that even by breaking the law there is little money to be gained.

M. le Consul, I am not naturally an outlaw. I cannot live away from my fellows; perhaps it is because my father was so long mayor of his town. I began to make the disastrous habit of going down to Zakho once or twice a week when the day's work was over. It was not so handsome a village as Ferjeyn, but more European, with shops of a sort and good paved streets. The landscape was not that of Syria and Iraq. There were willows and poplars everywhere, and meadows by the river that were green even in September. I dreamed of bringing Helena and my boys to Zakho, for I had begun to feel at ease across the Tigris. I had forgotten that to Arabs a line drawn on the map is of no importance. For us, to cross a frontier is to be safe; for them, a frontier is merely a god-sent convenience for making money.

I sat at the entrance to a wine-shop, talking with two friends. When business was over, Zakho was a silent little town. A footfall, the murmur of the streams, the low voices of women behind shutters and courtyard doors—those were all one heard. I did not expect the harsh voice of an Arab, calling me by the name of Nadim Nassar.

I looked up. It was a certain Zeid, a dealer in sheep and mangy camels—a wild-eyed barbarian who knew no law but what he misconceived to be his religion. I had seen him in the square of Ferjeyn, with foam on his villainous mouth and an old sword that had been used on women. I had unfortunately missed my shot at him. He was regarding Zakho with disgust, for it was a town of heretics: Yezidis, Shias, Kurds, Alaouites—let alone Christians and a few Jews.

'You do not appear very mad, Nadim Nassar,' he said.

'My mind has cleared, thanks be to God,' I answered, and my friends stared—for it was a pleasant bit of scandal that my name was Nassar and I had been mad.

'It has cleared very quickly. God is indeed Great,' Zeid replied.

M. le Consul, there was irony in his voice that would

have befitted a university professor — except that it lacked subtlety.

I hailed him as an old friend and took him by the hand and asked him where he meant to spend the night. The idiot was so full of contempt that he thought I was afraid. I left my friends and led him round the corner into a street where, I said, there was good coffee. He went with me, continuing to give thanks for my deliverance. His poor brain was pleased with the simple jest. He could not have told me more plainly what he meant to do on his return to his village. There was no one in the street, and it was nearly dark. I killed him quickly and mercifully, and laid his body behind a pile of dung and rubbish.

It was hardly the act of a respectable Frenchman. But what else could I do? Was Zeid to be allowed to return home and scream that Nadim Nassar had been pretending madness? He was just the type to conceal himself among Helena's olives with his rusty sword.

Beyond Zakho, it is true, there was a convenient lack of law and order, but in the town itself were more or less civilised police. I had to be far away before Zeid's body was discovered. Merjan, by good fortune, was at our timber camp. I told him what had happened. It was unnecessary to give details. I had only to sketch the character of Zeid, and explain that there was a blood feud between us.

The Yezidis meet with so few friends that they give absolute loyalty to those they have. Merjan on the instant took food, water and arms, and marched me off through the hills to seek a party of his clients from whom we could borrow ponies. Before dawn we had crossed into Syria. The next night we rode south parallel to the frontier — it was routine, that — and crossed back again into Iraq. By the third dawn we were among the rocks of the Jebel Sinjar, and exchanging shouts with Merjan's own people.

'Go where you will, freely,' Merjan said to me. 'And if you wish to visit Ferjeyn, you shall be passed from friend to friend as far as the last village of Yezidis, who will guide you across the frontier and receive you on your return.'

He left me with his parents, and rode back to Zakho with the ponies. I stayed at his father's house as long as politeness demanded, and then begged to be sent on to the western end of the Jebel. To my regret I saw none of the rites of their religion. The devil does no better or worse for them than for other mountain Arabs. They are hospitable, kindly and very poor. In the heat of their rocks there is a fine foretaste of hell — but if in the east one belongs to a sect that is hated it is as well to find an inaccessible home.

From village to village I was passed along the upper slopes of the range into Syria. There, in the no-man's land, I was still a long day's march from my home, but the plain below me to the north was the same that for eight years I had seen from the heights above Ferjeyn.

The Jebel between Ferjeyn and the frontier was worthless and eroded country, inhabited only by a few miserable goat-herds. I passed through it cautiously, seen only from a distance and, since I was armed, avoided. At dusk I arrived on the pastures above Ferjeyn. I was so excited that I could have embraced the nearest cow. But I contained myself. There were two horses grazing. They looked at me like gendarmerie horses. I was sure they belonged to no one in the commune.

When it was dark I dropped from terrrace to terrace and down the beds of streams. It was better not to take the path until I knew more about those horses. There was a light in my house behind the shutters, and I heard the voice of Helena singing to the children. I knelt in the shadows below the window and called softly to her. Her voice ceased. She thought it was only her singing which had summoned me. Then I called again, and she opened for me a window in a room that was dark.

M. le Consul, I do not know if you are happily married, with a family. If you are not, and I should describe my feelings, you would accuse me of exaggeration. If you are, I have no need to explain. In any case, imagine that for two months you have lived my life and have had no chance to send or receive a message. We were all wet with tears. I think I have made it clear that we were a singularly united family.

Helena told me that Ferjeyn was watched. It was said that Nadim Nassar had killed again in Zakho, and that he had taken refuge in the Jebel Sinjar. The Yezidis had sworn that they knew nothing of me, but Merjan had been seen returning north to the Tigris, and leading a saddled pony. Ferjeyn was terrified lest I should cross the Jebel and return. John Douaihy had not dared—in case some fool should talk—to tell them that I had only pretended to be mad.

I calmed Helena. I was not going to lose the joy of home-coming for the sake of worrying about what might never happen. A family is much like a squadron. The last man to show fear must be the sergeant-major. We closed down the shutters and made a feast. The harvest, thank God, had been good, and Helena was not in want. She had even set by a small store of money for me. And so the little family jokes were repeated, and we laughed at them as though I had never been away. At last the children slept where they sat, and we put them to bed.

In the morning it was a question where to hide. We did not live in luxury. There were four white-washed rooms in my house, all opening out of the little guest-hall. The furniture would not have concealed a frightened rabbit, and anyone passing could look in through the windows.

Helena went up to the flat roof, and reported that there were men of Ferjeyn on the terraces and the path, and that those who were working their fields were armed. It was idiotic that they should be afraid of me. But all the poor fools knew was that on my last appearance I had tried to kill my wife.

The children went to school. It was not necessary to tell them to say nothing; we warned them, however, not to show their excitement by a single look or word among themselves. Yes, M. le Consul, the priest has a sort of school at Ferjeyn. He teaches them to read and write Arabic, and such history as he knows; it is naturally somewhat specialised. They can read French, too, for I taught them myself. And I have always spoken French with them as much as Arabic. M. le Consul, I beg you — take them when the time comes. They are fine youngsters, and they will be valuable to France.

I had thought of going out to the barn, and making myself vanish among the fodder; but it was impossible to get there without being seen. Well, I am an old campaigner and I had need of sleep. What better than to take it, hiding under the bed? Sometimes I heard callers, and once Helena led a woman into the room and sat talking, being careful to wake me up lest I should snore. I did not care. I fell asleep again. The floor of my own home caressed my body.

Then John Douaihy arrived. Helena led him to our room so that I might know who had come and that he was unaccompanied. I assure you that he was telling Helena she should not remain alone in the house.

'God grant you more brains in your fat head, O my father!' I said to him from under the bed.

I could only see him from feet to knees. They trembled like those of a Syrian dancing girl. I poked out my head and told him not to be a fool.

'But you killed Zeid,' he stammered.

They are a feminine folk, the Arabs. After a while they are taken in by their own lies. By now John Douaihy himself had begun to believe I might be mad — it is possible that he had not forgiven me the salad — and if Helena had not laughed at him I think he would have backed out of the room. To be giggled over by a daughter — there's nothing like that for bringing a man back to common sense.

Yes, I had killed Zeid, and I told him why. He had only time to lean down — for I was still under the bed — and take my hand between his and promise to tell his people that it was shameful to hunt a citizen of Ferjeyn, whether mad or not, and that they must not shoot so long as my rifle was slung. And then the gendarmerie were at the door.

There were two of them. They came with the news that I must be lying up close to or on our mountain. The goat-herds of the Jebel Sinjar had seen a man with a rifle hiding among the rocks at dusk and looking down into the saddle between the main range and the hill of the Christians. It was true that for a few minutes I had been careless. But the first sight of Ferjeyn pastures was full of emotion.

All the doors from the guest-hall were open. In so fresh and empty and windswept a house the gendarmes could see at once I was not there. And both Helena and her father were calm. John Douaihy, from the moment of the knock on the door, had become the dignified headman of his commune. In spite of his appearance the old owl could surrender himself to his feelings like a child. During a mere five minutes he had been overcome by the demands of terror, of affection, and now of duty. He led the gendarmes away. As a father-in-law he was worth many more civilised. I should like to hold his hand again.

I was encircled, M. le Consul. And no means of breaking through. Two Syrian troopers were not much of a force against a sergeant-major, but what about my fellow-townsmen and, beyond them, the Moslems of the plain? I had no wish to start a battle with either. It looked as if I had only two alternatives: to give myself up or to remain in the house until the search for me slackened. But the latter was impossible. The oldest of my boys was only seven. At that age children can act a part for a few hours, but not day after day.

The tactical position was simple enough even for a

gendarme. There were a dozen routes by which I could leave my house, but if I went up I must somewhere cross the pastures on top of the hill; and if I went down I must go through Ferjeyn. So I knew more or less where the pickets would be. True, they were expecting my arrival, whereas I was trying to get away. But that made no difference.

I asked Helena to go out at dusk and try to report to me where the gendarmes were and what was the organisation of the people of Ferjeyn. All the same, I had not much confidence. She would be closely watched for her own safety, or because it might be thought that she was trying to find me.

'That is what I should do,' she cried. 'Nothing could keep me from going to find my husband.'

'But he is difficult to find,' I laughed. 'Since he ran away from you, he has learned too much from bad characters.'

'You would send me a message,' she said.

Well, there, out of our pleasantries, leaped the scheme. It was ready-made. It only needed details to be filled in by a woman's wit and a soldier's experience.

A basket of food to be left out for me. Excellent! Where to leave it? But the answer springs to the lips. Where there was a clear field of fire, so that the gendarmes could settle down on a rock overlooking the basket, and be confident. Then the men of Ferjeyn had to be considered. They must be decoyed away from the route I would take back to the Jebel Sinjar.

It was easy. There was a little glade on the south-western slope of the mountain, commanded by the necessary rock. It was a spot well-known to us, where we used to go in the heat of summer, before the babies could walk, and let them crawl on the grass. Now, if I were coming from the Jebel I should traverse the southern slopes of our mountain and reach that glade without ever crossing the pastures. And any man of Ferjeyn would be sure of it. So there was no need for any cordon across the top.

Helena made up a basket of food, and pretended to be taking it up the mountain to her uncle. Boulos was really there, hoping, I am sure, to warn me off if he could; it was not likely that John would have had a chance to speak with him yet. First, she had to find the gendarmes and act suspiciously and draw their attention. Then she must make them follow her, and pretend not to be aware of it. That was difficult—impossible if she had not been acting in character. But all Ferjeyn knew what she was. If a starving husband had managed to let her know he needed food, she would have blindly taken it to him, though he were armed and mad and had tried to kill her.

She returned at the beginning of the night. Meanwhile the children had come home and were keeping guard—all but the youngest who was under the bed with me. She had no doubt that she had been followed. The gendarme was clumsy when sneaking through the woods on foot.

I said my farewells, and plunged into a night that was also of the spirit. As I have said, I planned to go back to the Yezidis. The route, the people, the hiding-places, I had worked them all out. A lot of fuss about nothing. Such planning was against my principles. I should have known better.

On the track between my house and the pastures there should be a picket. Even if I were expected elsewhere, that was an elementary precaution to take for the safety of my wife and children. I was glad to find three of my fellow-townsmen alert and in the position I would have chosen for them myself. It gave me confidence that Helena was always in their thoughts. With all its faults, it was a gallant little town, my Ferjeyn. The three men were facing uphill, and I was able to leave the track and pass boldly round them. When they heard me, they challenged. I replied in the falsetto of an idiot that it was Nadim Nassar returning from his wife. They laughed.

It was impossible to guess the position of the rest. If the

men of Ferjeyn wished to capture me before I collected my basket of food, they would be under cover on the eastern slope; if they wanted the gendarmes to take all responsibility, they would be in the trees between the glade and my house, ready to pick up my body or intercept me if I escaped. In either case they would not be on the pastures.

As in all attempts to predict the behaviour of opponents, my reasoning was neither right nor wrong. There were, in fact, a few men on the top; but they kept to the east, well away from the gendarmes' preserves. The pasture was by no means an open alp. It was the rugged top of a mountain, sown with rocks and bushes, where the grass grew in hundreds of little patches rather than a continuous meadow. Well, with the half moon showing every bush as a movement and every shadow as inhabited, the men of Ferjeyn were nervous. They were smoking, and whispering to keep up their courage. They were not much use as soldiers. The cattle were in more danger than I.

Without difficulty I reached the little cliff which overlooked our glade. The basket was half concealed under a bush. Since I knew where to look for it, I could just distinguish the white cloth. The two gendarmes I could not see, but I knew exactly where they were — flat on their rumbling bellies under the overhang of the cliff with their carbines trained on the basket.

Their horses were tethered on the pasture, behind a rock. As soon as I found them I saw my opportunity. Good Lord, how right I had been to feel sceptical of my plans for returning to the Jebel Sinjar!

I inserted a prickly burr under the tail of one of those patient animals. He did not like that at all. You would have said, a charging elephant! One gendarme came up to see what was wrong. He was so much occupied with the horse that I was able to measure my blow. It was enough to leave him breathing quietly on the ground.

He could not answer enquiries himself and I did not

know him well enough to imitate his voice, so I only had time to change into half his uniform when the other gendarme, alarmed at the silence, advanced to see what had happened. He caught me at a disadvantage. I had his comrade's breeches round my ankles. I should have shot quickly. But, M. le Consul, I did not wish to become, like John Douaihy, frightened of myself. I pretended to be demoralised, to beg for mercy. And he, thinking of the boasting he could enjoy if he took Nadim Nassar single-handed, came too close to use his arms. Since he struck me twice across the face, I was not so gentle with him as with the other.

I left them well tied up with the spare reins and halter, confident that they would not be found till morning. And there! I had a horse to ride, another to lead, two carbines and two pistols as well as my own rifle. I trotted across the pasture and down the track, past the picket, past my house and through the streets of Ferjeyn. On my head I carried the spare saddle to conceal my face. I gave the impression of an extremely angry gendarme in a hurry, and answered questions only with muttered curses.

There were neither telephone nor telegraph in Ferjeyn. By riding hard due north across the Duck's Bill, I reckoned to be over the Turkish frontier before the alarm had gone out. They were two fresh horses and I did not spare them. In the morning, galloping through Moslem villages where they tried to stop me to hear why I was riding so fast, I may have aroused some suspicion. But once near the frontier I had no more trouble. It cannot have been an uncommon sight—a silent gendarme in a hurry, leading the horse of his dead comrade.

And then I made a circuit through the Turkish hills —not so easy, M. le Consul, that it can be dismissed in a sentence, but I am conscious that I may have kept you too long from more important work—and I descended cautiously upon the camp of Merjan.

It is a refuge, that country, and beautiful, but miserably poor. Three rifles, two pistols, their ammunition and two horses was a considerable capital. Merjan decided that he and his brother and I could live more freely than as timber-cutters and middlemen for smugglers. With a Russian deserter, a Turk and a Persian—of true officer material, but having felt it his duty to assassinate a political—we formed a band. I should not like you to think that we are criminals on a European scale. In the first place there is practically nothing here worth stealing. But we can go where we wish without interference, and we are on good terms with the tribes. In return for food, we give them protection from police and bandits. And if they do not wish for protection we make it desirable. Sometimes, too, we act as escort for smugglers. In fact one does what one can. But it is not a life for a man who loves to be in his own town.

M. le Consul, for myself I have no right to ask more than what I have. I live, and when I die there will be no fuss —unless Merjan and his brother devoutly say a prayer for me to the devil. But for my boys I beg your patronage and, through you, that of the Republic. I have no address, and Damascus is very far. Perhaps in the spring I shall be able to send another messenger to call on you. Perhaps he will bring back to me a word of comfort.

Awaiting your reply, I beg you to accept, M. le Consul, the assurance of my highest consideration.

Valentin Lecormier.

Annexe to the Statement of Sergeant-major Lecormier

Quai d'Orsay
20th April, 1952

Dear Consul and Old Comrade,

But what a document! It is not often in these days that we get anything from our representatives abroad to entertain us. You have the thanks of the whole department.

He's a type, your bandit! As I look at it, only once in his life has he made a wrong decision, and that upset him so badly that he denies we can ever make decisions at all. You really must do something for him. As a bureaucrat, one gets so bored with being inhuman.

Here is the minute I have received from the Ministry of War:

> *Lecormier, Valentin*
> *Three times mentioned. Croix de Guerre. Missing in Cyprus 1944. Believed killed in interallied brawl, or suffering from loss of memory. Character excellent. An outstanding leader of men, whether native or metropolitan.*

From discreet enquiries I learn that the major whom Lecormier crowned with a bottle — he now has his division — swore that they had both been attacked by drunken British. No one was more unhappy than he when Lecormier vanished, and it was he who suggested loss of memory.

Look, old man — that plea will be accepted. Lecormier, so far as France is concerned, has nothing whatever against his name. And we have urgent need of such old soldiers. We will find means of paying a passage to Marseille for his thirteenth-century Helena and the boys. As for him, you who are wise in the ways of the Orient can no doubt extract him, metamorphosed into a good French bourgeois, from his spider's web of frontiers. If he hesitates you may assure him that we know the taste of old warrant officers for garrison life, and that they are invariably stationed in a little town.

(Signature illegible)

236

9

Children's Crusade

HE found it hard to believe that Israel was as welcoming to every tourist. His host, Joseph Horsha, was a mere professor of history, internationally known but not so distinguished that he could lay down an invisible red carpet for any Englishman who happened to be staying in his house. Looking out over the glittering Mediterranean from the top of Carmel and green shade, Mayne's sense of wellbeing was near perfect, yet faintly disturbed by the suspicion that he was the subject of gossip, that everyone—Horsha, this Ben Aron woman and even the taxidriver who had brought her—knew something which he did not.

Aviva Ben Aron claimed mysteriously to have met him before, though he was quite certain she was wrong. A most exceptional woman. Calm—that had been his impression of her during lunch. Not a quality you would expect from an overworked Under-secretary of State in a new and sensitive country. It was as if she had had some experience—a superb love affair, perhaps—which gave her enough pity and self-confidence to last a lifetime.

'And all this time you have never been in Israel, when it was Palestine?' she asked.

'No. Only looked at it from afar like Moses. I was a soldier in Egypt then. It was 1919. So long ago and, Lord, how young!'

'Gloriously young!' she answered, smiling.

'Now, just what is this attractive mystery?' he demanded. 'Where did we meet?'

'I was one of the children, Mr Mayne—one of the twenty-six.'

It was like all his memories of the first war, vanished if he were alone, vivid the instant some sharer recalled them. At once he was back on the quays of Port Said, the dust blowing, the crowd of diseased and powerful Egyptian labourers laughing at a crane as it dumped on the wharf dead and dying horses from the holds of a cattle-ship which had met bad weather in the Indian Ocean. The sterile, vulgarian sun pointed the details of every dried and eddying patch of filth; and meanwhile the smart Italian freighter glided to her berth with twenty-six boys and girls leaning over the rails and staring with excited eyes at the hideous orient as if it were the gate of heaven.

He had not recognised the pattern of the future. At the end of that first and, to civilians, kindlier war there had been no need of any elaborate organisation to deal with refugees and displaced persons. The Middle East had few, and those belonging to obscure and persecuted Christian sects — simple souls whose problems could be solved by the loan of a donkey to carry their baggage. As for Zionists, nobody in 1919, outside political circles, had ever heard of them. In dealing with these astonishing Jewish children, who ought to have been in school and wanted to go to Palestine, Mayne had no precedent at all to follow.

The naval authorities and the Egyptian police had passed the muddle to him, for it was obvious that the children, if allowed to land, would become the responsibility of the Military Government. Mayne was the Port Control Officer. What he decided would be, for the time being, accepted. He had been well aware of his exact value to his superiors: a man who knew his own mind, saved everyone trouble and was sufficiently unimportant to be sacrificed if anything went wrong.

He went up to the captain's cabin under the bridge to see what the devil this Italian thought he was about. The fellow's enthusiasm annoyed him. It appeared that the children had made an overwhelming impression upon his emotional people; but twenty-six young lunatics from unknown depths of Central Europe, with the sketchiest of papers and very little money, couldn't just be dumped on the Port Said waterfront while a rapturous captain sailed back to Italy, rubbing his hands with easy satisfaction at a good deed done.

Under the circumstances a blaze of Latin oratory was impertinent. Mayne refused to allow the children to land, and posted a solid pair of sentries at the foot of the gangway.

'You had not the slightest idea of the difficulties,' he said, the memory of the day and the Italian captain adding a hardness to his voice.

'It never even occurred to us that there were any,' Joseph Horsha replied.

'Were you with them too, Jo? Why have you never told me?'

'Look—it was as if we had both assisted at some secret, sacred ceremony. Something to remember, not to talk of. And when we met again so many years later, I couldn't tell whether you recognised me or not. The silences of Englishmen are so effective. One has to respect them.'

Mayne searched his vague memory of the children whose eyes had followed him so gaily and confidently as he went ashore to put his sentries on the gangway. There had been five girls, more stern than attractive. Perhaps that was to be expected. A girl who preferred such a mad pilgrimage to the enthralling adventure of becoming a woman was bound to lack the charm of adolescence—or rather to have ripened her character before her emotions. That would account for the grey-haired, classical grace of Aviva Ben Aron. The foundation of her was indeed a love affair— though not in the generally accepted sense.

The boys—well, of course the quest itself had singled them out. It was impossible that any boy capable of starting and finishing such an adventure should not have the face of a dreamer. They looked like young Galahads, like any sentimental Victorian engraving of ardent youth. The oddness of some of the faces—to his Gentile eye—simply didn't count. If Joseph had been one of those boys, his whole warm character was still in keeping. The blade of youth, now sharpened down to a more serviceable flexibility, was set for ever into his lean, sensitive features and the eagerness of his mind.

'My name then was Joseph Wald. Horsha is the Hebrew translation.'

'Wald, of course! A fiery little scamp you were!'

'Not rude, I hope?'

'None of you was ever rude. You had no need to be. You knew you were irresistible.'

'That was really the impression we gave?' Aviva Ben Aron asked. 'I'm glad I didn't spoil it. I was just fifteen—and an imaginative little girl.'

'You weren't afraid?' Horsha asked incredulously.

'Wasn't I? To be put ashore in Port Said with no protection but you visionary male children—'

Perhaps those two round-faced Midland sentries at the foot of the brow had been justified after all, Mayne thought. To the girls, at any rate, rifle and bayonet couldn't have been half so frightening as all those evil Egyptian faces. After all the years he was still offended at the Italian lack of common sense in proposing to sling overboard, like so much cargo, twenty-six starry-eyed children.

'You leave the Italians alone,' Horsha told him. 'Responsibility is your forte. Emotional sympathy is theirs.'

'One does expect some sanity all the same.'

'No! Sanity would have been out of place in dealing with us. We had made our own world, where sanity didn't exist at all.'

The conspiracy, Horsha explained, had run through the high schools of Cracow like a childish epidemic. No one knew who started it; no one could tell who would resist it.

Those who went down with the highest fever had been the least Jewish of Jews. That wasn't surprising. The submerged and the religious had not yet assimilated the Balfour Declaration. To them it was just another prophecy, not an immediate invitation to act.

He told of his own romantic concept as precisely as if it had been read rather than lived. His family had been cultured Poles. The medieval courts of the legends had been as familiar to him as the court of King Solomon, and morally preferable. That had been true—though perhaps in a lesser degree—for most of his companions as well.

Their Zionism was the natural flower of Christian chivalry and Jewish tradition, owing nothing at all to propaganda. A last crusade had driven the Turks from Jerusalem. A statesman of the conquerors had declared that Palestine was open to the Jews. The facts did not belong to the modern world; they were gay and stirring as the summoning song of a minstrel. What gesture could one make in answer but to put up the Star of David upon an imaginary shield, and march?

At the first secret meeting there might have been a hundred boys and girls, aged from twelve to seventeen. When the cautious had weeded themselves out, thirty were left. They came from respectable, conventional families, but the ebb and flow of war had destroyed their natural fear of movement. Soldiers in thousands tramped over Europe, seeking their legitimate or spiritual homes. Therefore children could do the same, all the way to Palestine.

They even called themselves Crusaders, without any sense of incompatibility with their Jewish traditions. Who could refuse to let them pass provided that their voluntary dedication was plainly to be seen?

In the privacy of a ruined factory belonging to Horsha's parents they took their solemn vows—to be honourable in all their dealing, to protect the weak, to preserve chastity. That final promise, though at their age not hard to fulfil, seemed to them the most important. It was an echo not so much of saintliness as of the precepts of parents.

'It's unbelievable that we could have been so cruel to them,' Aviva said.

'Birds leave the nest.'

'Yes. You used that argument then. It sounded as if it meant something.'

'We did warn them,' Joseph protested, still with the guilty laugh of a boy.

Yes — and the parents had given parental and understanding replies. Of course the children, if they were sure, quite sure, they wanted it, could go to Palestine as soon as education was finished, as soon as the routes were open, as soon as arrangements could be made to receive them. Fathers and mothers could well afford to be sympathetic. Travel was manifestly impossible till the aftermath of war had been cleared.

But instinctively the children knew that only in a time of unrest could their crusade succeed. The world which they had imagined was close to reality. That casual, medieval society which endured for months before frontiers were formally re-established had little interest in stopping the determined traveller.

Horsha and Aviva Ben Aron, both talking at once as if they had eagerly returned to childhood, tumbled incident upon incident. The children had kept their secret profoundly well. They bought and hid packs and water-bottles, and put their money, collected by small economies and the naïve, ingenious tricks of the young, into a common store. They chose for their departure the early morning of a day when there was no school, and said — for they were determined not to start with a lie — that they were off on an expedition, that they didn't know when they would be back and that they promised all to keep together. The smallest, in much need of comfort, remembered the hundreds of boys who had enlisted well under military age without telling their parents.

So fathers and mothers, patient for a whole day and three-quarters of a night, discovered at last, like burghers of Hamelin, that their children had vanished and did not even guess, till a joint telegram arrived, what piper had summoned them. Meanwhile the thirty had pushed their way among peasants and demobilised soldiers from train to crowded train, and were beyond recall.

The two frontiers which they crossed were still hardly delineated, and officials easily allowed them to pass through to Vienna. They were subjects of the Austro-Hungarian Empire, and their identity cards were in order. It was nobody's business to hold them for enquiries.

But also it was nobody's business to send them back. The urgent requests of the Cracow police were presumably dropped into trays marked Pending. Austrians who were going to remain Austrians and Austrians who were going to be Czechs had no interest in the problems of Austrians who were going to be Poles. Children bursting with health and excitement on their way to Palestine? Good luck to them! It would be time enough to bother if the Italians refused to let them pass.

At Vienna they bought several days' supply of bread and sausage, and used the last of their money to travel clear of the too curious city and its suburbs. When they got off the train they were as destitute as all the sanitly beggars of history. That, indeed, was high adventure for the sake of their quest. They felt at last free. Confident and singing, they began their march over the mountain roads towards the Italian frontier two hundred miles away.

Aviva laughed like a girl at the memory.

'I've never been so sure in my life that what I was doing was right — unsurpassably right!' she said. 'And ever since, when I think my conscience is happy, I have been able to test it by that day.'

'We were giving joy, too,' Joseph added. 'I don't think

any of us realised it then. We just assumed that the world was as good as the first day God made it. But to the villagers we were the return of joy and innocence after four years of war. It was enough for them to see our faces. They gave us barns and sometimes their beds to sleep in. They showered us with milk and food.'

'And wine,' said Aviva. 'How inhuman little male saints can be!'

'No, no! You never understood. It was essential that our spirit should not be lost — that nothing should be dissipated.'

'I don't know what you're taking about,' Mayne reminded them.

'One of our sixteen-year-olds got drunk,' Aviva explained. 'The other boys court-martialled him and sent him home — or rather back to Vienna, where he fortunately had an uncle. The mayor of the village lent him money for his fare.'

The mayor had done his best for the offender, too. Drunkenness wasn't such a crime, he told the children. Why, before the war the dear *Wandervögel* were often merry in the evening! Yes, he understood that they had set themselves a religious standard, but didn't the boy's shame count with them?

It did not. The young faces regarded advocate and criminal with blank severity. They knew they were right. Horsha still declared that they were right. They were following, quite blindly, a European tradition. Only that tradition, reflected in their joy and their purity of manners and living, could carry the pilgrims through the Holy Land.

As they drew nearer to the frontier, they were told again and again that the Italians would never let them through. The Italians, said the sentimental Austrians, were not in the least like themselves. The children would meet the victors in full flush of insolence. And what of girls of fifteen and sixteen unprotected among Latins?

The whole countryside was fascinated by their march, and in committee for their welfare. It was considered that they would appear to have some official backing if they crossed the Julian Alps by rail; so friendly railwaymen gave them a lift in a goods train over the pass, and unloaded the twenty-nine on the frontier station.

'You must have felt pretty forlorn then,' said Mayne.

No, Joseph insisted, they had not. But possibly their faces showed enough anxiety to make them appear as suppliants—enough to prevent the feeling in any sensitive official that his beloved frontier was about to be ravished against its will.

The children's unity of purpose was such that it had never occurred to them to elect or appoint a leader. But the Latin mind demanded a leader. One couldn't talk with twenty-nine children at the same time—that was reasonable, wasn't it? It was indeed, though to the children the problem was how to explain themselves at all when eight Italians were talking at once. At last there was no sound in the mountain silence but the hissing of the locomotive. The utter improbability of the situation had imposed itself.

Those kindly Italians! A sergeant of Bersaglieri laid his hand upon the shoulder of the youngest, choosing him as spokesman. He was twelve and looked, after the hardships of the journey, no more then ten. The sergeant questioned him in bad German, while the frontier officials, instantly appreciating this paternal gesture, gathered round them.

The boy spoke up boldly. Money? No, they hadn't any. Was it then so important? They had reached Italy without it, and so they could reach Palestine.

But the sea? Hadn't one to cross the sea to go to the Palestine?

Yes, certainly, said the twelve-year-old spokesman,

surer of his geography than the sergeant. The English who had promised them the land and who had so many ships would provide.

Italian imagination, swift to identify itself with generosity, assumed its part in promise and victory alike. Had not Italy ships? Had not Italy, too, been engaged against the Turks? And was it not a historic occasion, this arrival of pilgrim children on their frontier?

'It was you, I remember, who put that point to them, Aviva.'

'Yes. I felt it so strongly that I found myself stammering it all out in spite of shyness. I was sure that we were the first of many—the first, that is, to go in a body to a Palestine that was ours again. How right children are and how absurd! A little big-eyed prophet telling the commander of an Italian frontier post that the eyes of history were on him!'

It had been enough, at any rate, for the commander to spread his wings and send a wire to Venice. Meanwhile the children, no longer laughing but still confident that these excitable strangers could not refuse them, were herded into the barracks by the friendly sergeant and given two empty rooms—a large one for the boys, a smaller for the girls.

That was their worst night. They made their first acquaintance with hungry bugs. They remembered the warnings of the Austrian peasants. Crusading gallantry rose to the occasion. Horsha and his bosom friend slept on the bare boards of the passage outside the girls' door, and awoke to find the licentious Italian soldiery tenderly tiptoeing about their military business with bare feet in order not to disturb them.

The following afternoon came a reply, permitting the Polish children who claimed to be Jews to be sent down to Venice.

'Our frontier friends couldn't have put it better,' said

Horsha ironically. 'Polish children who claim to be Jews sound much more sympathetic than Jewish children who claim to be Poles.'

'And all that is over for us!' Aviva exclaimed. 'All finished by the name Israeli!'

They caught the imagination of a people. The newspapers christened their march a new Children's Crusade. The great, grave Jewish-Italian families took them to their bosoms.

'You can't imagine how we were fêted—and how it seemed somehow to spoil all the beautiful simplicity!'

Even the Church was fascinated, and held up the children as examples of the conduct to be expected of Christians as well. But Christian children, who had no comparable objective, only felt that self-discipline when presented as adventure was a fraud. What it was really worth while to imitate they understood. Parties, armed with axes and their fathers' carving knives, set out in stolen boats to conquer Fiume or Africa, and were brought home weeping. The Church quietly and decisively moved the pilgrims on to Rome.

At Rome it was harder still to preserve their common flame. By letters they were in touch at last with parents, and their proud sense of isolation was disturbed by remittances of money and loving reproaches. Then the Roman matrons put out as well the light of chivalry by separating girls from boys. To march singing across the foothills of the Alps had been easy. The journey through Vanity Fair was a more searching test.

The boys insisted on remaining together. Their dormitory was the vast empty salon of a palace, where the neat beds were lined against marble walls like insignificant white mice. Only their impatience saved them from being extinguished. To go on. That was all they wanted—to go on. Their hosts, though ravished by their innocent courage, found them obstinate and insensitive.

One of the girls fell in love and became engaged to be married — as young as Juliet and just as ecstatic. They thought this an indecency, plain evidence of the approaching moral rot. And then the eldest of them, a few months over seventeen, was led astray by the daughter of a Jewish family which was great but not so grave.

If he had confessed, he might have been expelled with dignity. But he boasted.

'We flung him out,' said Horsha savagely, 'flung him out with everything that belonged to him!'

'They had to keep their illusions,' Aviva explained in half apology. 'Illusion was the driving force.'

'I had no idea that the girls were not in full sympathy,' Joseph Horsha remarked, still with the remains of disquiet from thirty-five years before.

'We were. But it was such a relief in Rome, for a little while, not to have to play your game. Attachments had grown, you see — all very innocent and romantic.'

'Not with any of us!'

She did not answer. But even if a few of the little warriors were being civilised in secret by their ladies, there was no deflecting either from their purpose. The Roman matrons found their pets untamable, and dismissed them with the magnificent gesture of a free passage to Egypt.

Presumably some diplomat, general or influential prince was ordered to approach the British authorities. He may indeed have written; but, if he did, his letter was slipped into some file reserved for the improbable and impossible. Palestine did not yet exist, only a Syria about to be divided between French and British. There was no government but the staff of Allenby's army, sorting out, with brusque military common sense, the unfamiliar complexities of Turkish administration.

At Genoa twenty-six children, overjoyed to be again together and in movement, went on board the freighter and down to a baggage room which had been roughly partitioned for the boys and girls, and furnished with camp beds. Of the original thirty, one was to be married, two had been guilty of unknightly behaviour, and a fourth had died in Italy of influenza. They couldn't have said what on earth they expected to find on arrival: turbaned Turks, perhaps, or even some modern remnant of Pharaoh's linen-kilted courtiers—certainly not an impersonal military organisation, with its Captain Maynes and its sentries blandly unaffected by any crusade but their own.

After the first hours of looking down from the deck upon Port Said, excitement lost its edge. Not even imagination was justified. True, there were palms and sand. But Egyptians did not ride camels; they unloaded dead horses and loaded coal. Where were the glittering caravans of the orient, and the British cavalry which had ridden to Jerusalem? Where the curiosity or enmity that their arrival should have occasioned? The heroes of Balfour and Allenby were red-faced, red-kneed soldiers, wearing ridiculous shorts like very little boys. They entered things in note-books and bawled at the Egyptians instead of clinking their sabres magnificently up and down the quay. This busy world had nothing in common with kindly Europe, continuous, in spite of varying scenery and manners, from Cracow to Rome.

During the morning all action was inhibited. Outside the refuge of the ship's awnings the sun smote dishearteningly upon stone and iron. The strange inhabitants of the quay continued to work. The Italian captain was fuming and unapproachable. British naval and military officers came and went, passing the eager group with non-committal smiles.

Then the spirit of the crusade reasserted itself. There was a moment's talk, and the children picked up their packs, without any order given or any formal agreement between them, and marched together down the gangway. They ignored the casual request to hop it and the subsequent sharp command to halt. Nor was the sentry's bayonet in itself decisive.

The bayonet belonged in their world—which, after all, contained the possibility of martyrdom though no chance of it had yet appeared. But while the boys hesitated before that unwavering point at the foot of the gangway the sentry's companion gave them a broad grin and a wink, and with a jerk of the thumb dismissed them. His confidence was unshakeable as their own, and his friendly gesture intelligible; it pointed out that the bayonet was not really sharp steel but merely a wall, an unclimbable wall, around the stately park of empire. The irresistible force had met the immovable object.

'And in the end there is no way out of that,' Aviva said, 'but to learn to hate.'

'No, you can't find parallels,' Horsha went on. 'There aren't any. The British, as they were in 1919—yes, and later—had the art of making the rest of the world feel ashamed of impatience. That sentry—with his tiny private share of it—was quite enough for twenty-six crusaders.'

Thereafter the slow mass of bureaucracy crept over and engulfed them. Up and down that gangway, to them forbidden, passed the Egyptian police, the port authorities, the Italian consul and the agent of the line. From the conferences in the saloon the Italians emerged profane and glowering, the English unyielding and self-satisfied; and all of them combined to make the children appear in their own eyes young nuisances rather than young heroes. But never did it occur to them that they were unreasonable, or that their knightliness could be defeated. Hardest of all to bear was the young army captain, Mayne, who spoke in courtly French quite intelligible to the high school students, and merely seemed to be amused.

'You didn't mind the general,' Mayne protested. 'He was just as amused as I.'

'We were good Polish citizens,' Joseph answered. 'We

treated generals with respect. And he understood us. A man who isn't a boy at heart can never become a general. Half his job is to persuade men that they are really having the marvellously exciting time they dreamed of when they were twelve.'

'It wasn't till much later,' explained Aviva, 'that we realised you had brought the general yourself.'

Well, of course, he had. And it was true that he had been amused — delighted was a better word — by the glorious folly of the pilgrimage. He was surprised to find himself most reluctant to have the children's fire put out by a great wad of paper, or to return them to Italy. His sentries, as a precaution, were correct; as a solution, they were intolerable.

He persuaded the general to take the children off the ship and, pending a decision, to send them down the Suez Canal to a camp at Kantara. The old professional had been impressed by their quality — by their tremendous button-polishing capacity if they had any buttons. All the same, he insisted, some inexpensive method of returning them to Poland would have to be found. It was impossible to allow them into Palestine, utterly impossible.

'He didn't really mean us to go on then?' Joseph asked.

'He dithered. We both did. So you were always in command of your own destiny.'

It hadn't felt like it. There the children were, just as on the Italian frontier, under the benevolent control of military; but this time nobody's enthusiasm suggested that something was bound to happen. They were merely well looked after, and visited occasionally by the smiling Captain Mayne who told them to be patient as if he had never realised that a divine impatience was their inspiring force. The only contact with the world of their imagination was that they were living in tents on the edge of the desert.

And that hard, lion-coloured surface was all which separated them from Palestine? Couldn't they walk there?

Hadn't all the conquerors of ancient history crossed the Sinai desert? In the grey of dawn, stealthily, an advance party set out with their water and the unexpended portion of the day's rations. Their tents were outside the military cantonments. No one saw them leave but the prowling Egyptian children; sleepers and scavengers who rose from the dust and accompanied them, mocking, capering and gesticulating obscenely. The little column marched on unconcerned, following a straight course across packed sand and gravel never disturbed by the wheel-tracks of any of the armies which had cautiously hastened from Egypt into Syria. The palms of the Canal vanished over the horizon. The native children scuttled back to the safety of mud walls.

'I am always surprised that you found us,' Horsha said.

'Oh, it wasn't difficult! The trouble was that I had been away. So you had two days' start, and the little wretches you left behind wouldn't say a word. But I knew exactly what you would do. Didn't I tell you that I, too, was very young then? You would march on Jerusalem by your compass.'

That was their route when Mayne and his hastily borrowed cavalrymen discovered them marching east-north-east through the midday heat, stumbling, their water gone, but still in good close order. They reckoned to cover another five miles of deadly emptiness before they collapsed.

No more resistance was possible for the general. There were two good reasons for that. One was the children's determination. They could not be guarded night and day to prevent some further lunacy. The other was their chivalry. The beauty of the relationship between girls and boys was so obvious that it had never occurred to Mayne or his general that anyone could object to the proximity of their various tents. But there was no keeping out the chaplains and the welfare workers, and it was their business to protest.

The plaguing of the general increased and, like Pharaoh, he had no reasonable solution. He might have invented an excuse for putting one or two children on the new military railway to Haifa, but not twenty-six—for he was only the commander of a base. He would have had the politicians down on him, let alone Allenby's Chief of Staff.

'Did he put the blame on you?' Aviva asked.

'Only damned my eyes in a general way. There were no real reproaches. We were both emotionally affected by your spirit, you see. You had to go to Palestine. Had to go. That was why at last I gave you my promise that you should.'

It had been a knightly gathering, though the banners and shields were only there in the eye of imagination. The children were drawn up in the space between the tents and took oath, eager-eyed and solemn-faced, that they would not leave the camp without permission. And in his turn Mayne gave his word of honour that he would lead them to Palestine.

'You were tremendously impressive,' Horsha assured him. 'You, the young Count of the Empire who had galloped up to our rescue!'

'Then it was my turn to radiate a confidence I hadn't got,' Mayne answered. 'I remember wondering how on earth I was going to keep my word.'

But the fact that he had given it was a third good reason for the general, who provided all that was in his power to provide—two lorries and rations, a week's leave for the importunate Captain Mayne and a pass which would take the whole party to Palestine so long as no one questioned it. And he wrote privately to the Chief Rabbi of Jerusalem, for he could not think of anyone else to arrange the children's reception.

'We addressed him as Your Grace,' said Mayne with a chuckle. 'His rank, we reckoned, must be equivalent to an archbishop. And we told the general's pet runner, who carried the letter, to be extra polite and mind his saluting.'

The still Canal had just ceased to reflect the stars when the two lorries drove down it towards the desert track. The children were the first band of illegal immigrants, although, as in all their journey, they had no thought of breaking any law. Where there was none, their spirit supplied it.

Mayne, the drivers and their mates caught the infection of romance. They felt themselves explorers, and would have deliberately supplied adventure if there had not been enough in reality. The crossing of deserts by motor vehicles was then too new to be taken for granted. The lorries on their solid tyres ponderously ground and bumped over irregularities of surface. Halts were frequent, and the running repairs of heavy complexity and doubtful value. The children were battered and bruised by the journey; but at night, wrapped in blankets on the sand, they abandoned themselves utterly to sleep—sleep which all their lives, said Joseph and Aviva, they remembered for its quality of peace. The next day they would have conquered.

Of this they were so sure that Mayne, against his better judgement, resumed the journey with a single lorry; the other had to be abandoned to await a tow to workshops. But even springs and axles obeyed the children. The remaining truck crept stolidly north until, instead of lonely shepherds, they saw huts with men and women sitting idle after harvest at the doors. Patches of sparse stubble began to appear among the scrub and dry thorn.

Was it at last Palestine? Well, no one could say for certain. But it was decidedly not Egypt. Two hours later the lorry limped into an Arab village and approached a group of European colonists, deep-eyed and sunburned, who waited patiently and could not yet see what precious freight was packed on blankets under the canvas hood.

Again the children asked if they had come to Palestine, and this time, though maps and politicians might be unwilling to commit themselves, history had no doubt. Mayne could not remember what he answered. He was very anxious to hand over his charge and retreat into the desert before civilians and military could overwhelm him with embarrassing questions. Nor could he trust himself to speak, for long war and sacrifice and promise, children and place and the ancient sanctities of Jew and Christian were of profound emotional power.

'You said,' Aviva reminded him: 'this is Beersheba. I must leave you now.'